The
Confessions
of
Owen Keane

TERENCE FAHERTY

TERENCE FAHERTY

The
Confessions
of
Owen Keane

Terence Faherty

For a Mystery Lover!

Crippen & Landru Publishers
Norfolk, Virginia
2005

Cover painting by Carol Heyer

Cover design by Deborah Miller

Crippen & Landru logo by Eric D. Greene

ISBN (signed limited cloth edition): 1-932009-32-9

ISBN (trade softcover edition): 1-932009-33-7

FIRST EDITION

Printed in the United States of America on acid-free paper

Crippen & Landru, Publishers
P. O. Box 9315
Norfolk, VA 23505-9315
USA

E-Mail: info@crippenlandru.com
Web: www.crippenlandru.com

To my nieces and nephews, God bless them.

"A detective is only human. The less of a detective,
the more human he is."

– P.G. Wodehouse

TABLE OF CONTENTS

INTRODUCTION

Owen Keane, my failed seminarian turned amateur sleuth, first appeared in print in *Deadstick*, a novel published in 1991 and nominated for the Edgar Allan Poe Award. As of the writing of this introduction, Keane has returned six times in book-length adventures for a total of seven novels, the most recent being *Orion Rising*, published in 1999.[1]

The Confessions of Owen Keane brings together seven additional cases, six short stories and a novella. Four of the short stories, "The Triple Score," "The Third Manny," "Main Line Lazarus," and "A Sunday In Ordinary Time" were first published by *Ellery Queen Mystery Magazine*. The novella, "The Headless Magi," was commissioned by Keane's paperback publisher, Worldwide, for its Christmas collection, *Murder, Mayhem and Mistletoe* (2001). The stories making their print debuts in this volume are "St. Jimmy" and "On Pilgrimage."[2]

Keane was dubbed a metaphysical detective by an early reviewer, and the label stuck, though he tends to be a pretty down-to-earth investigator. His obsession over his failure in the seminary is useful to me as a way of explaining his continuing career. I think amateur sleuth is the hardest of the mystery subgenres to write realistically in series form. How do you involve an amateur in a succession of dangerous cases without eventually losing credibility? With Keane, the answer is that he is compulsively drawn to mysteries. He has the odd idea—born of too much childhood mystery reading—that he can find clues to the spiritual questions that haunt him by investigating crimes.

Keane gets his mystery reading background from me. After Franklin W. Dixon, God rest his pseudonymous soul, the first mystery writer I devoured was Sir Arthur Conan Doyle. An aircraft designer once complained that the Wright Brothers had "used up ninety percent of the magic." I think that the mystery writer, especially the writer of short stories, must concede the same thing about Doyle. (I'm consciously overlooking Doyle's borrowings from Poe. Overlooking borrowings is the least one writer can do for another.) One of Sir Arthur's tricks was to have Watson refer to cases he would never go on to describe, in order to create the illusion of a life for Holmes and Watson beyond the fifty-six stories and the four longer works.

I've used the same trick myself more than once. Unfortunately, I can no sooner mention an unexplained case from Keane's past than I feel an urge to come up with a story to go with it. Two of the titles in this collection, "Main Line Lazarus" and "The Headless Magi," resulted from that impulse.

Revealing that would be enough to start my readers searching the novels for the references that inspired these stories, if I had the kind of readers Sir Arthur had and has. But few mystery writers are blessed with quite that kind of reader, Sherlockians who pour over the stories like Biblical scholars, producing an endless stream of talks and papers on the Holmes and Watson universe. (They even attempt to explain away Doyle's careless errors, an invaluable service.)

A Keanesean scholar, were such a being to exist, would observe that while Keane the first-person narrator carefully dates each novel, he doesn't bother with the shorter stories. The scholar would go on to point out, however, that these tales are dateable using internal evidence. For example, "Main Line Lazarus" takes up a few days after the first novel, *Deadstick*, leaves off, placing it in the fall of 1981. "The Triple Score" follows another of the novels, *Die Dreaming*, but by weeks rather than days. Keane tells us that the story begins on New Year's Day, which would make the year 1989. There's a holiday tie-in to the novella "The Headless Magi," too, of course: Christmas. It takes place during a December sometime in the early eighties, according to Keane's asides. He also mentions that a couple of years have passed since he worked for Harry Ohlman in New York (in *Deadstick*), so it's probably December 1983. "The Third Manny," has no such tie to a holiday or book, but from the clues Keane drops (I'll let you work this one out for yourself) it must occur sometime between *The Ordained*, set in 1993, and *Orion Rising*, set in 1995. Dating "A Sunday In Ordinary Time" doesn't require any familiarity with the series. Keane tells us that it is the Sunday following the attack on the World Trade Center. More on that story later.

While it lacks a definite tie to a particular novel, "The Third Manny" does feature a major character from the books, Keane's reluctant girlfriend

Marilyn Tucci. In addition to Marilyn, several characters from the novels make appearances in these shorter pieces, including Harry and Mary Ohlman and their daughter Amanda, Jim Skiles, hermit storyteller of the Pine Barrens, and Keane's faithful 1965 Volkswagen Karmann-Ghia.

"The Third Manny" is one of my favorite titles, and it reflects the story's origin. I mentioned earlier the careless mistakes Doyle made in the Sherlock Holmes stories (Watson's mobile wound, for instance, and his mysterious second wife). "The Third Manny" started out as my attempt to correct a small mistake of my own. While proofing the manuscript for the sixth novel, *The Ordained*, I stopped to look up something in *Deadstick*. I came across a one-page character I'd completely forgotten named Manny. I knew there was an entirely different Manny, also a very minor character, in the fourth novel, *Die Dreaming*, and it bothered me that I'd used that unusual name twice without realizing it. I decided to make a virtue of this slip by writing a story in which Keane meets yet a third Manny and remarks on how odd it is that he should have known three. I'm not sure whether my earlier carelessness now looks like careful planning, but I'm very fond of the resulting tale, which opens this collection.

In a way, the two previously unpublished stories bookend the five published cases. "St. Jimmy" is the oldest Owen Keane story and "On Pilgrimage," written especially for this volume, is the newest. I wrote "St. Jimmy" in 1979 for a night-school fiction class. When I later began work on *Deadstick*, I turned to "St. Jimmy" for my protagonist and even incorporated the frame of the short story into the structure of the novel. Its basic incident is mentioned in passing by Keane in at least three of the early books and is described by him as the time he met his Moriarty. Several rewrites have failed to remove all the story's early awkwardness, but I'm including it because it is Keane's origin story. And because it contains what I still consider to be Keane's finest moment and maybe his defining one: when he stands his ground on the dark beach awaiting the approach of the unknown, terrifying thing.

In "St. Jimmy," Keane tells us that he is about to enter his senior year in high school, which would place the story in the summer of 1967. The other unpublished piece, "On Pilgrimage," takes place much later in Keane's career, in 1995. (The giveaway is Amanda Ohlman's age.)

"On Pilgrimage" may be the quintessential Keane story because it illustrates how big a part storytelling plays in Keane's detective work. While participating in a fundraising walk, Keane and Amanda stumble across a crime in the making. The clues to the mystery are in the stories the walkers tell one another to pass the time, in imitation of the pilgrims in Chaucer's *Canterbury Tales.* In "On Pilgrimage," the stories come to Keane. In most of his other cases, he must go about collecting stories. When he's gathered enough of them and worked them together into a single story he can tell someone else, he's solved the mystery.

Finally, a word about "A Sunday in Ordinary Time." At a mystery conference held in the fall of 2001, I spoke with other authors and learned that many of them had been unable to write for a time after September 11. I had a completely different reaction. I think I wrote almost every day of that long week, if only for an hour or two. It was a relief for me to spend that time in the Keane novel I was working on. When I sat down to write "A Sunday in Ordinary Time" a few months later, I knew Keane would seek the same kind of relief, that he'd spend those hard days doing what he'd always done, looking for big answers in little mysteries.

Terence Faherty
Indianapolis, June 5, 2004

Notes

[1] The titles between *Deadstick* and *Orion Rising* are *Live to Regret, The Lost Keats, Die Dreaming, Prove the Nameless,* and *The Ordained.* All were published by St. Martin's Press.

[2] Though "St. Jimmy" has never before appeared in print, a version of it was serialized on my website (www.terencefaherty.com).

THE THIRD MANNY

One

Manny is an unusual name, but I've known three bearers of it. The first was a Brooklyn garage owner who once stored a car for me. The second was the supervisor of a sweatshop bar I'd briefly tended in Atlantic City. The third Manny, Manny Vu, very nearly killed me.

My name, incidentally, is Owen Keane. Manny Vu and I came together on Route 9 in the southernmost tip of New Jersey one rainy afternoon. The rain was light but steady, just enough to disappoint the summer renters on the barrier islands to the east, the "shoobies," as the year-round residents derisively dubbed the tourists. I was no shoobie, having lived for years on the northern edge of Great Egg Bay. But as I headed south to visit an old friend who was renting a house in West Cape May, I was entering unfamiliar territory. Even so, I felt safe enough leaving the Garden State Parkway when I encountered a traffic backup near the Burleigh exit. I knew that wherever the Parkway went, the older Route 9 eventually followed.

I was no sooner settled onto the two-lane than I came to a long break in the oncoming traffic. The gap let me see the car from some distance, the little blue Japanese coupe that was passing three slower cars in a single bound. The coupe never recovered from that pass; it was already skidding when it reentered the northbound lane. I thought for a heartbeat that the car would hit a pole on its side of the road. But the driver corrected, then overcorrected, then came at me across the center line.

There was a picket fence to my right. I would have taken it in preference to the oncoming car if I'd had time to think. But I didn't have time. I hit the breaks hard, not remembering to pump them until I began to hydroplane. By then the oncoming car was pirouetting, its front end turning away from me and toward the fence. I saw the coupe's left rear fender perpendicular to my Chevy's snub nose and a foot away. Then I closed my eyes.

13

When I opened them again, I was sitting at an angle in my seat. That is, the seat was at an angle, the Chevy having come to rest in a shallow ditch. Smoke was pouring from its sprung hood. Even after my brain had correctly reclassified it as steam coming from the smashed radiator, I stayed panicked. I fumbled with my seat belt, forced open my door against the resistance of the ditch bank, and tumbled out.

The blue coupe had gone through the fence and into the yard beyond. It was still upright, but it had skidded around to face the street. I could see the crumpled passenger side and the front end, which was wearing broken pickets like an obscene garland.

I stumbled to the wreck. The little car's windshield was starred. I couldn't see the driver until I reached his open window. Then I didn't see him clearly for the warm rain in my eyes. I could just make out a slight, dark-haired figure slumped over a bloody steering wheel. Before I could reach out to touch it, someone touched me. She moved me aside without really looking at me, a young woman with clipped hair and sun glasses as narrow as swimmer's goggles.

"Let me," she said. "I'm a nurse."

I tried to watch through the ruined windshield, but I was distracted by a slip of paper tucked behind the visor. It was a computer printed receipt for the Cape May-Lewes Ferry with a banner headline: "THIS IS NOT A BOARDING PASS."

There was more to read—something about the number of axles and a time and a date—but the rain was in my eyes again. I brushed at them with my hand. It came away bright red.

I tapped the nurse on the shoulder and showed her my hand. She looked past it to my face and then addressed someone behind me.

"Sit him down before he falls down."

Two

Two ambulances responded to calls placed on cell phones by New Age Good Samaritans. Before the driver of the coupe had been removed from his car, I was in the first ambulance, on my way to Cape May Memorial, strapped to a board as a precaution against neck injuries. I'd already decided that I'd live, having eavesdropped on an exchange between the rescue technician and the nurse with the narrow sunglasses. I'd heard "Superficial scalp wound, the kind that bleeds like a son of a bitch." The second opinion had been a reassuring "Yep."

At the hospital, they took a more circumspect approach. It was one of the rare times when I had health insurance, and the emergency-room doctors made the most of it. After my wound had been sewn up and covered with a nearly invisible dressing, I was x-rayed from a number of angles, with and without my board. Then I was placed in a room whose only reading material was a chart of the human endocrine system. That was just as well, as my head was aching seriously by then. Also my chest, where the shoulder harness had caught me, and my left knee. I slumped in my chair, held a cold pack to my head, and thought of the motionless driver of the coupe.

Other than the receipt from the ferry, I'd noted only the car's New Jersey plates and its make and model: Nissan Sentra. I ran over this scant information again and again in between replays of the crash itself. Whenever a nurse came by to promise me the prompt attention of a radiologist, I asked about the Sentra's driver. Each time I was told he hadn't been admitted.

That mystery was finally explained to me by a Cape May County sheriff's deputy who arrived to take my statement. She was a blond of no great height named Nelson whose belt—as crowded with equipment as Batman's—made her hips look incredibly wide.

I regretted that unkind observation when I got to know Deputy Nelson, a process that happened almost as fast as the accident had. Before she'd gotten my brief statement down, I'd seen pictures of her kids and heard her opinion of Route 9—dangerous—and the hospital—first-rate.

"Don't worry about your dancing partner not showing up, Mr. Keane," she said, referring to the driver of the coupe. "He might have been taken to County General. That's the older hospital down south. They get the county business, by which I mean the people without health insurance. Could be the other driver—" She consulted her clipboard. "Could be Mr. Vu didn't have health insurance. A lot of people don't these days. I can call down there for you if you want. But it wasn't your fault, the accident. You did everything you could do."

She'd already assured me of that several times. I wondered if she considered all accident survivors to be sensitive on the point or if I was projecting a particularly guilty aura. "I could have turned into the fence," I said.

"Then he would have hit the car behind you. That was the nurse who stopped to help you. She had two kids in her car. If you'd crossed the center line, you would have hit the car behind Mr. Vu, a subcompact with two retired teachers in the front seat. So you see, it worked out about as well as it could have. God was directing things out there today."

Including the initial skid, I thought. It was a theological perspective that led a person to dwell on minor details, something I was inclined to do by nature. At the moment I was interested in the information the deputy had on her clipboard. I was straining my sore neck for a better view when Nelson surprised me by handing the board over.

"I wasn't able to interview him," she said. "He was still unconscious when they took him away. But I got some basic information from his driver's license."

I was reading it. Name: Manny Vu. Address: 52 McClelland Street, Jersey City. Age: eighteen.

"Feel free to make a note of that for your insurance company," Nelson said. "Or you can wait for your copy of my report. I'm not sure about Mr. Vu's auto insurance," she added, preparing me for the blow. "I called the number information had for that Jersey City address, but the girl I spoke to was too upset to tell me much."

A doctor arrived then with a packet of X rays. The deputy greeted him like a candidate for office and then took back her clipboard.

"I'll call County General," she told me. "I'll know something before you're through here."

She was back before the radiologist had even unpacked. "Something's wrong down there, Mr. Keane. I'm going to drive down and check it out. I'll call you at home."

"Did he die?" I asked.

"No," she said. "He walked away."

Three

My old friend, the temporary resident of West Cape May, came by the hospital about four-thirty to pick me up. Her name was Marilyn Tucci. She was a New York City office worker two weeks into a three-week vacation. A shoobie, therefore, although I'd never have actually called her that. She'd been my girlfriend, once upon a time, but I'd never dared to call her that, either.

When she arrived at the hospital, Marilyn hid her concern for me under a mask of irritation. She hid it so well that only someone as familiar with her as I was could even glimpse it.

"It took you a week to talk me into an afternoon visit," Marilyn said as she walked me to her car, a tiny station wagon. "Now I suppose you're expecting to stay over tonight."

"The doctors did suggest that I be kept under observation," I said.

"I've been suggesting that for years," Marilyn replied.

As she drove us south on Route 9, I did a little discreet observing of my own, noting Marilyn's biohazard tan and her hair, a symphony of sun lightened kinks and curls barely held in place by a deceptively girlish headband. And I wondered whether, sore bones and all, there might be a possibility of progressing beyond observation to an actual physical exam.

Marilyn settled the matter a mile or so later. "You can stay. I've a second bedroom I'm not using."

I returned to a consideration of the outside world just in time to see the site of the accident coming up. I pointed it out to my driver. She slowed, but didn't stop.

"You're lucky to still be walking around, Keane. Come to think of it, I've been saying that for years, too."

I thought about using the crack as a segue to the subject of Manny Vu, the man who had walked away from County General. Before I could, I spotted a sign for Rio Grande. I asked Marilyn to take the next right.

"Why exactly?"

"My car was towed to a lot in Rio Grande. I want to check it out."

"Okay, but if there's an overnight bag in the trunk, you're walking home."

Rio Grande wasn't a big place, and I had the lot's address, given me by Deputy Nelson. But it still took us a while to home in. J & S Towing was well outside of town, on a road that had almost petered out by the time it reached the salvage yard's sandy drive. The whole establishment consisted of a tin-roofed building and a quarter acre of rusting cars surrounded by a chain link fence.

The entrance to the little building was guarded only by a screen door, unlatched. I could hear a phone ringing just inside. I'd been hearing it ever since Marilyn parked her car. I went in, calling "hello" but not expecting an answer.

The customer area was a room with discount store paneling and shag carpet that had enough sand in it to grow tomatoes. I tracked in a little more on my walk to a chest-high counter. It held the ringing phone and two business card stands. Both displays contained J&S Towing cards. Those on the left belonged to someone named John Pardee, those on the right to a Stu Hunter.

Beyond the counter was a desk that supported a citizens band radio and an obsolete computer. Behind the desk was the obligatory calendar featuring the more than obligatory woman. She was wearing only her underwear and carrying an assault rifle. The combination seemed incongruous to me, but she looked comfortable with it. While I was meditating on that, the radio came to life.

"Crabber to Clammer, come back. John, you there? Come back. Where the hell are you? Come back."

"Please do," I said.

I found Marilyn waiting next to her car. "Nobody home?" she asked.

"Looks that way. I'm going to find the Chevy."

"Be careful, Keane. Meaner than a junkyard dog is more than just a snappy lyric."

Despite that reservation, Marilyn walked with me around the shack to the fenced lot. The fence had a gate and the gate had a chain and a padlock. But the lock was open and the chain was hanging loose.

"They're a little slack on security," Marilyn observed. "Then again, who'd want to steal these beauties?"

The inventory consisted of a dozen wrecks in various stages of decay. The one I'd come to see was front and center, a red Chevrolet Cavalier, a foot or so shorter than it had been when it left the factory in 1986.

"Totaled," Marilyn said, peaking under the tented hood.

The Chevy was only the second car I'd ever owned. I'd never felt any real love for it, but we'd been through a lot together. I hated to see it squatting in the weeds.

Marilyn had circled around behind the car. "Someone's been in your trunk," she said.

"It must have popped open during the wreck."

"Your spare tire's been thrown out. And your jack."

It was true. Even the old blanket I kept on hand for emergency picnics was on the ground.

"You don't have a flat. Somebody's been searching for goodies. I don't suppose you had a CD changer in there."

"Never heard of such a thing," I said. I opened the passenger door and then the glove compartment. Its contents were untouched, as near as I could tell. I took the registration and the insurance papers and left the rest of the clutter.

Marilyn was calling to me. "This one's been rifled, too."

She was standing next to Manny Vu's Nissan Sentra. Its hatchback had been popped open and its spare tire and jack removed.

I looked inside the Sentra, avoiding the bloody steering wheel. The backseat had been pulled apart. The bottom section now rested against the backs of the front buckets. The coupe's glove box had been opened and emptied. Forgetting my fear of dried blood, I checked the visor for the receipt from the ferry. It was gone.

"Think we scared away one of Rio Grande's notorious spare tire thieves?" Marilyn asked.

"I hope so," I said.

Four

Marilyn's rental was a toy Cape Cod a long way from any beach. "You can save a lot of money if you're willing to drive a little," she said as we parked.

She needn't have troubled to explain. I knew Marilyn. She wanted the ocean and the beach and even the restaurants and shops in moderation. But what she really prized after forty-nine weeks in New York City was privacy. She'd found it in West Cape May. Her little house had a deck that looked out on a flat yard bordered by crab trees. Neither the yard nor the trees seemed even to have noticed the afternoon's rain. Beyond the tree border was an even browner field.

We sat considering the view, Marilyn drinking Chablis and me iced tea. Instant iced tea, which my hostess had whipped up herself. She talked about her vacation-to-date and her job. I thought about Manny Vu.

After a time, Marilyn said, "What about dinner? I can make something or we can order a pizza."

I stole a glance at my glass. The ice cubes were brown with the residue of undissolved iced tea mix. "Hold the anchovies," I said.

Before Marilyn could stir from her seat, her phone rang. She went to answer it and came back quickly and displeased.

"It's for you. A Deputy Nelson. You told her you'd be here?"

"I called it a remote possibility," I said and moved inside as fast as my sore knee would let me.

The deputy's friendly voice was comforting, but the feeling didn't last. "We've got a real mystery here, Mr. Keane. I don't know much more than I did the last time I saw you. They're telling me that Mr. Vu just got up and walked out of here."

"He was okay?"

"No, he was badly hurt. His condition was described to me as serious but not life-threatening. They had him stabilized and they were going to do more tests. When they went to check on him, he was gone."

"When was this?"

"Around three-thirty is when they think he left. He was last checked about twenty after three."

"He wasn't hooked up to any medical monitors?"

"One. It was switched off. The nurse's station was busy and nobody noticed. He removed his own IV, too. And get this. He made his bed."

That interesting detail didn't jibe with the vision I'd been having of a bandaged Manny Vu trashing his wrecked car and my trunk.

"We're searching the area," Nelson was saying. "No one saw him walking around. None of the local cab companies called for him. We haven't gotten any reports of stolen cars. Like I said, I can't tell you much."

I wasn't sure why she was telling me anything. I decided that she needed to tell somebody and I was handy. I felt a similar temptation regarding what we'd found in Rio Grande, but I overcame it.

When the deputy finished with me, I dug out the two towing company business cards. I noted that the office numbers were the same on both but the emergency numbers were different. I decided that each was the home number of the partner whose name appeared on the card.

I dialed the office number. It was picked up on the first ring by a man who said, "John?"

"Mr. Hunter?" I asked back, shuffling my two cards. "My name is Keane. My car was towed to your lot this afternoon. A red Cavalier."

"Right. Sorry. Things are a little messed up here. I don't have your paperwork in front of me. Let us know if you want the car moved someplace else. If your claims adjuster wants to inspect the car here, he should call first so someone can be here to unlock the gate."

"I was there an hour ago," I said. "The gate was wide open."

"Shit. Sorry. Didn't know you'd been here. My partner was supposed to be watching the store. He went off somewhere and left everything open. He's the one who towed your car, so he'll have to get your ticket ready. Your bill, I mean. You're probably not in a hurry for that."

"Somebody broke into my car after it got to your lot."

"Shit. I didn't go in there to look. I locked things up again though."

"I'd like to talk to your partner about it."

"So would I," Hunter said with some feeling. "But I don't know where he's gotten off to."

"Is there any chance he'd be at his home number?"

"Not unless he just got there. I drove past his place on my way here and there was no sign of John or his truck. He does this every once in a while when the weather's nice. Takes off, I mean. One of us will call you tomorrow and straighten all this out."

He asked me for a phone number. I looked up at the number on Marilyn's rented wall phone but decided not to risk it. I gave him my number in Mystic Island and hung up.

Five

Before rejoining Marilyn on the porch, I checked the cabinet nearest the phone. The phone book was tucked inside it, a combination white and yellow pages rolled up like a sleeping bag. In it, I found a John Pardee with a Rio Grande address. The phone number was the same one given as the emergency number on his business card. The clincher, if I needed one, was that the address was on the same road as J&S Towing. Stu Hunter had just told me he'd passed by his partner's place on his way to the lot. I tried Pardee's number and got no answer.

Outside Marilyn was mellower than I had any right to expect. I discreetly checked the level of the wine in her bottle and decided it was safe to proceed with the plan I'd hatched in her kitchen.

"I'd like to borrow your car for an hour or so," I said. "I can stop while I'm out and pick up dinner."

"Where do you think you're going?"

"Back to Rio Grande. I want to talk to the man who towed my car."

"About what? The trunk being opened?"

"That and other things."

"Let's have it, Keane. Don't stop until you're sure I won't say, 'Go on.'"

I told her the little I knew about Manny Vu's disappearance.

"What makes you think this Pardee knows anything about that?"

I shrugged.

"Call him."

"I tried. He's not at home or he's not answering his phone. He might be in for visitors."

"And if he's not, you can nose around," Marilyn said, reading me like the top line of an eye chart. She knew me that well. Well enough to know that I'd never been able to resist a mystery, despite having decades of good reasons for resisting them.

I could no longer surprise Marilyn, but she could still surprise me. "I'll go with you," she said.

It was still light and would be for a while. The drive back to Rio Grande felt shorter, as return trips always do. It helped that we stopped short of a full round trip to J&S Towing. About a mile short. I was driving, due to Marilyn's high Chablis content. Driving and navigating both, since I was the one who spotted the mailbox marked "Pardee" in faded script.

The box belonged to an old farmhouse, not recently painted, and a barn, never painted. I parked next to the open barn door, which made it a logical first stop on the walking tour. There were no vehicles inside, no tow trucks, no cars, no motorcycles. Just a pile of old junk ready for a trip to a garbage dump or a flea market. The walls were hung with hoses and ladders and a pair of rakes that were unlike any I'd ever seen, long-handled with light tines that curled up from a basket-like base.

I found Marilyn outside next to a tomato patch that lay between the barn and the house. A former patch, I should say, as it had been harvested in a very complete but unorthodox way. The dozen or so plants, heavy with green and red tomatoes, had been pulled out of the ground, stakes and all. The victims lay in neat rows on either side of the rectangular bed.

"What the hell?" Marilyn asked, summing up the situation.

By then I was stepping up onto the farmhouse's listing front porch. A bumper sticker had been pasted to the little gable above the porch. "Second Amendment Spoken Here." Beneath it, the front door was standing open, its job being done by a patched screen door. I had a flashback to the deserted office at J&S Towing. Nevertheless, I knocked before trying the screen door. It wasn't latched.

"You don't believe in signs?" Marilyn asked from down on the drive. "This Pardee is a gun nut. You go in there, you're giving him a free shot."

"Mr. Pardee?" I called out. Like my earlier knocking, the words seemed to live on for a long time inside the house. "Stay there," I told Marilyn. "If you see anyone, whistle."

The front room smelled of old cigarette smoke and sweat. The whole house probably did, but I stopped noticing fairly quickly. I was too busy trying to decide whether the house had been searched. Like the barn, it was a mess, things scattered everywhere, junk mail and back issues of hunting magazines mostly. But that might just have been Pardee's way of keeping house.

The question got black-and-white as soon as I entered the bedroom. There I found a full-size bed completely disassembled. The footboard and headboard leaned against facing walls to my right and left. The mattress slumped against the wall facing me, blocking most of the light from the room's only window. The box spring stood next to my doorway, not leaning at all. I stepped into the gloom, tripping on the bed rails and slats, and confirmed what I'd glimpsed from the doorway: The mattress had been slit open from corner to corner.

Marilyn's whistle interrupted what might have been a very long reverie on the subject of the bed. I went out through a back door and found her standing near her station wagon, looking out toward the road. A man was looking back from the road's far side. He was big and dressed in a T-shirt as long as a nightshirt. He had shoulder-length hair that looked silvery in the last of the sunlight.

"Can we go, Keane?" Marilyn asked. "The greenheads are starting to bite."

"Where did he come from?"

"The last house we passed on the right. I saw him step out just as we were turning in here. He must watch the place for Pardee."

Watching was all he seemed interested in doing at the moment. "It's time for dinner, I think," I said.

A spigot poked through the brick foundation of the house on the driveway side. I turned it on and let it run for a moment, Marilyn and the man with the silver hair both watching me. Then I turned it off and scraped up two handfuls of sandy mud. I smeared one handful across the station wagon's front license plate and the other across the rear plate.

"What's going on?" Marilyn demanded, her earlier mellowness already halfway to a hangover.

"Whatever it is," I said. "I don't like it."

We drove out past the watching man. At the last second, I thought to put my hand over my bandage.

Six

Marilyn's displeasure lasted through dinner at a roadside hamburger stand named Doc's, through the uneventful night, and well into breakfast the next morning. She brightened somewhat toward the end of that meal, the thaw coinciding with my request that she drop me at the nearest rental car agency.

Marilyn was so happy about the plan that she generously offered to drive me up to Atlantic City, much closer to my home. That would make dropping the car back off easier, she argued. And keep me from coming anywhere near Cape May again while she was there, I thought, but I took her up on the offer. Half an hour later, Marilyn deposited me at a Budget Car Rental on Route Thirty. She was gone before the clerk had finished explaining the damage waiver.

For once, I was happy to be deserted, as I was feeling distinctly like a lightning rod. I rented the cheapest car on the lot—a Dodge Neon described by the clerk as green but actually chartreuse—and drove to my little house in Mystic Island.

After I'd showered, I felt a little less stiff and sore but no easier. I paced through my few rooms until my knee started to ache, then went out to sit on the edge of the marina where my neighbors docked their boats. I left the sliding door on the back of the house open in case Deputy Nelson or John Pardee or my insurance agent called. No one did, not even Marilyn to see if I'd gotten home all right.

When the sun got too warm for sitting, I fished in my wallet for Nelson's phone number. I came up instead with Manny Vu's address in Jersey City. Before I could talk myself out of it, I was headed north on the Garden State Parkway, trying to hear the Neon's tinny radio over the whine of its transmission.

I hadn't thought to rescue my well-worn state map from the Cavalier, so I was navigating by a complementary Budget map, which was far from detailed. In fact, it seemed to suggest that there were large parts of New Jersey that hadn't been explored, a feeling I'd sometimes had myself. Luckily, I'd thought to consult an old atlas before leaving my house. It had told me that Jersey City was situated on the Hudson at the western end of the Holland Tunnel, that it was a shipping and manufacturing center founded in 1630 by the Dutch, traces of whom could still be found, notably a statue of Peter Stuyvesant. More helpful had been a street map that had shown Manny Vu's street, McClelland Street. It was very near the river.

So I took the Parkway to the New Jersey Turnpike and the Turnpike north to the last exit before the Hudson. I'd seen the exit many times, the sign for the New York ferry always catching my eye. The ferry operation turned out to be bigger than I'd imagined. According to its signage, it catered to theater and museum goers as well as humble commuters. I passed a row of modern blue and white boats and block after block of fenced parking lots, occupying ground that must once have held warehouses.

At a private lot just outside the ferry company's chain link fence, I asked for McClelland Street. The old man at the lot's gate—a rope between two oil drums—told me it was one block up the street I was on, Pike.

"But you'll never squeeze a car in there," he added. "Not even a mouse car like that."

I took the hint and left the Neon with him, paying the daily rate, the only rate he offered. The climb to McClelland Street was short but steep. Halfway there, Pike's asphalt paving ended in an irregular line that looked like a wave of spilled crude. From there up, the pavement was brick so old Peter Stuyvesant might once have trod it.

McClelland Street seemed to be paved with people. Asian people. The street was an open-air produce market, crowded with shoppers at what my stomach told me was half past lunchtime. In addition to fruits and vegetables, some of which I actually recognized, stands sold smoked and fresh fish,

cooked and uncooked chickens—the cooked ones hanging by their feet—
and dry goods, no can or box of which had a label I could read.

For that matter, I couldn't understand most of what was being said by
the busy people around me. Even at the stand where I bought some grilled
meat on a stick, the only two words of English I recognized were "three"
and "dollars."

Number 52 McClelland Street was on the far edge of the market block,
a narrow brick building whose first floor was a jewelry shop. I asked there
for Manny Vu. The proprietor directed me to a stairway in an alley between
the shop and its neighbor.

When I was halfway up the metal stairs, a door opened off the landing at
the top and a young Asian woman stepped out. She was barefoot, dressed
in jeans and a Knicks T-shirt, her black hair lying loose across her shoulders.
When she saw me, her face fell. It was beautiful nonetheless.

"Yes?" she asked.

"Sorry for bothering you. I'm looking for Manny Vu."

"He's not here," she said, her only accent a north Jersey one. She'd held
the door open behind her. Now she backed toward it.

"He and I were in an accident yesterday," I said speaking quickly. "Down
near Cape May. I was wondering if he was okay."

I was also wondering whether this was the girl Deputy Nelson had spoken
to on the phone. I decided she was. She'd frozen in place the moment I'd
mentioned the accident.

"Come in, please," she said.

Seven

The doorway off the iron landing opened directly onto a living room, dark
and warm and crowded with furniture. In one corner, a television played
softly. I recognized the movie, the original *Ghostbusters*, but not the dialogue,
which had been redubbed. Hunched next to the television on the end of a
sofa was a hairless old man wrapped in a heavy robe. He was watching the
screen with rapt, unsmiling attention.

The old man didn't notice me until the young woman switched off the
VCR beneath the color set. Then he smiled, almost toothlessly. The woman
spoke to him in something that sounded to me like Chinese, her words so

fast and flat that I could barely spot the breaks between them. He replied briefly. Then she turned to me.

"I told my grandfather that you were in the accident with my brother. He said he he'd noticed that you'd been hurt. I'm sorry I didn't myself."

"It's nothing," I said.

"Can you tell us what happened? The deputy who calls is too busy consoling us to give us much information. She frightens me."

I told them about the accident, laying the blame on the wet roads. The woman translated softly as I went. The old man nodded once, after I'd mentioned the Cape May ferry. I ended by repeating the question about Manny's condition. His sister hesitated for a long time, as though expecting the old man to answer. "We haven't heard," she finally said.

"But you know he walked away from the hospital," I said.

Her stricken look told me that she did. To relieve that look, I asked what I thought was an innocuous follow-up. "Was Manny down south on business?"

Now the sister looked stricken and frightened. This time, the old man did break the silence. The translation was: "Would you like some tea?"

She left to make it without switching back on the VCR. I was tempted to do it myself, to distract Manny's grandfather from his examination of me. Instead, I glanced around the room. I was looking for Manny. I found him on a small table that held only a group photo and a votive candle in a green metal holder. The group was a small one: the old man, a younger man who might have represented the missing generation, and two teenagers. They were Manny and his sister, I guessed. Judging by her age in the photo, it had been taken three or four years earlier. In it, Manny Vu was a smiling kid with a broad face and bushy hair. I decided that the middle-aged man was Manny's father. The background of the shot was the Hudson River and a section of the New York skyline.

New York figured in the tea service the young woman carried from the kitchen. In my mug specifically, which bore the ubiquitous "I love New York" slogan.

The old man used his mug as a hand warmer and began to speak. The young woman translated, sitting beside him on the couch.

"You noticed the picture of Manny and his father. We four escaped from Vietnam together in 1985. We were three weeks in an open boat and six months in a refugee camp in Thailand."

Listening to the sad-eyed woman, I got the sense that she knew the story so well and had heard her grandfather's version so often that she was summarizing as much as translating.

"Then we were allowed to come to this country. Manny's father, our father, still had American friends from the army. They helped him get a job here. Working on the ferry boats."

I looked at the group portrait again, noting for the first time the metal railing against which the four stood and the invisible breeze that blew strands of hair across the girl's face and stood Manny's up in front. The photograph had been taken on the deck of one of the ferries.

"My grandfather says that's why Manny took the ferry ride down south. He was visiting in a way with his father who died two years ago in an accident on the river. Manny was reconciling with his father yesterday, grandfather thinks. Reconciling with his death. Manny hasn't been the same since our father died. He couldn't accept it. He wouldn't go near the Hudson ferry boats. He wouldn't accept a job from the ferry company when they offered him one."

The old man talked on for a long time, but the woman was silent and, I thought, alarmed. When he finished, she said, "My brother was a good man. He was raised to be good always. Our father's death hurt him, opened him up to the many dark temptations of this country. Now my grandfather knows that Manny is safe. When he stepped onto that ferry, he turned his back on the darkness. My grandfather thanks you for bringing him word of this."

She looked considerably less grateful herself as she stood up expectantly. I set down my mug and stood, too. Manny's grandfather and I exchanged nods, then I was out on the iron landing, suspended between the sounds of the street market and the noise of the river traffic.

I turned to the girl, startling her. "I forgot to tell you my name. And I want to give you my phone number."

She held up her hand. "It's better we don't know," she said.

Eight

I got back to Mystic Island just in time to take a long, unpleasant call from my insurance agent. I'd run in from the carport to catch the ringing phone, certain it was Marilyn. When my doorbell rang later that evening, I jumped to the same hopeless conclusion.

The person I found on my doorstep was a woman. And she was about Marilyn's age: late thirty-something. She may even have been a New Yorker. She held herself like one: erect, blond head back, her slightly beaked nose sniffing the Mystic air critically. But she wasn't on vacation. I deduced that from her attire—tailored tan slacks and a sleeveless white blouse of some soft matte material—and from the badge she flashed me.

"Mr. Keane? My name is Nancy Wildridge. I work for the ATF. The Bureau of Alcohol, Tobacco, and Firearms."

"I hope you're here about alcohol," I said. "I don't stock the other two."

Wildridge passed up the opportunity to display her smile. "Actually, I'm not. May I come in?"

She gave my living room a once-over and said, "This was built as a weekend getaway, right? The whole street was. How did you ever find this hole-in-the-wall?"

I wasn't sure whether she meant the house or Mystic Island. "It's my uncle's place. I'm watching it for him."

"What else do you do, Mr. Keane?"

"At the moment, I seem to be answering questions. I'm not sure why."

Wildridge gave off checking a dusty bookcase for fingerprints and considered me. "That alcohol you mentioned, what form does it take?"

"Beer."

"Sounds good."

By the time I'd collected two bottles, Wildridge had exited via the rear sliding door. I found her staring down into the lagoon. I handed her her beer and steeled myself for more byplay. But that part of the scene was over.

"I understand you were involved in a traffic accident with a man named Manny Vu."

"Yes," I said. "Do you know what happened to him?"

"Only in general terms." She picked up a pebble from my pebbled backyard and tossed it into the lagoon. "That happened to him."

"I don't understand."

"He disappeared, Mr. Keane. More precisely, he was made to disappear. Given all the water you folks have around here, I wouldn't be surprised if he's in some right now. Way over his head."

"You think he's dead?"

The agent was watching the ripples she'd caused on the glassy lagoon. "What do you know about John Pardee?" she finally asked.

"He towed my car to Rio Grande, where it was broken into. I tried to talk to him about it, but he'd ..."

"Disappeared, too?" Wildridge suggested. "So did his truck." She picked up two more pebbles but must have decided the business was too theatrical, because she dropped them at her feet.

"Neither one has turned up. We're trying to trace two people who stopped by Pardee's house last night. Man and a woman. Man looked something like you, although our witness, a nosy neighbor, didn't mention anything like that patch on your forehead. He didn't get their license plate number, either. The man smeared the plates with mud. That's an odd thing to do, don't you think? An innocent man might stop by to discuss something— to complain about his car being broken into, for instance—but why the mud? Only a man who was up to something would do that."

"Or a man who had stumbled into something, who had found something disturbing."

"Like a slashed mattress and a dozen disinterred tomato plants?"

"And a nosy neighbor."

Wildridge took a long drink from her sweating bottle. "Whatever spooked this guy, his instincts were sound. This is definitely something you don't want to be involved in."

"Seems like I already am."

"I don't know. You're still here, aren't you? I was half expecting to find your house open and empty tonight. Maybe it will be tomorrow night."

"You're wasting it," I said. "I'm as scared as I get right now. Why don't you just tell me why the ATF is interested in Manny Vu?"

"Because it's better that you don't know."

That reminded me of Manny's sister's parting remark. "Tell his family what happened to him, then. They're desperate to find out."

"You've talked with them?"

"I was up there this afternoon."

Up until that moment, I'd felt as though I'd been dealing with a salesperson who was sure I couldn't afford anything in her shop. Now I'd suddenly produced a gold card.

"Buy me another beer," Wildridge said.

Nine

We went inside for the second beer, since the mosquitoes had begun siphoning it off as fast as we could drink it. Wildridge chose the kitchen table for our talk. Under the table's dangling light fixture, her blond hair looked overdue for root work and her blue eyes dry and tired.

"What did you think of the Vus?" she asked.

"They seemed like nice people."

She wrinkled her beaky nose. "You were especially taken with the sister, I'll bet. Sam."

"Sam?"

"Short for Samantha. Her American name. Her late father thought his kids needed them to fit in. I don't know where he got Manny. Maybe from a Pep Boys ad."

"What happened to the mother?"

"Died before they left Vietnam. That's the story. For all I know, they ate her during the boat trip."

"You don't think much of the family," I observed after we'd stared at each other for a time.

"What did they tell you about Manny?"

"That he was a good kid. A little shaken up over his father's death."

Wildridge was nodding and smirking at the same time. "A boy scout was Manny. A choir boy. Except you couldn't trust his singing. Did they happen to mention Shadow Street?"

"No, where's that?"

"How about a gang Manny might have belonged to?"

"No," I said again, but I was thinking of the old man's cryptic reference to dark temptations. "Is Shadow Street where this gang is located?"

"Originally. The real street is spelled *S-H-A-D-O-E*. Shadoe was a Civil War general, like McClelland. Jersey City liked to name streets for them, way back when. The gang members use the more conventional spelling to better reflect their method of operation, which is stealth itself. Know much about Vietnamese gangs?"

I shook my head.

"They haven't gotten the press they deserve. But they're a real problem. In New York's Chinatown, they're *the* problem. Their members are mostly young ex-refugees born into the mess we left over there after the war.

They're extremely violent, ostentatiously violent, since a good bit of their income comes from protection rackets, which means it comes from fear.

"Shadow Street goes exactly the opposite way. No publicity. No public beatings or executions of uncooperative merchants. The unlucky party just disappears. It's ingenious in a way, since the gang gets the credit for any unexplained happening, whether they're involved or not. I'd congratulate their *Ank kai*, their leader, if I knew who he was. But the only gang members we know by name are the small fry."

"Like Manny Vu?"

"He was well on his way to becoming a member. Someone interrupted his initiation. Owen Keane. When Manny smacked into you yesterday, he was making his first trip as an official Shadow Street mule."

Wildridge paused to let me guess what Manny had been carrying for the gang. I considered the three options offered by the name of her bureau. "Guns?"

"Exactly. Twelve machine pistols purchased by legitimate buyers down in easygoing Virginia and passed to our boy Manny, part of a steady stream of guns headed north to New York City. Uzis or Tech-9s; Manny wasn't sure which they would be."

"Manny told you about them?" Now her earlier quip about a choir boy made sense. A choir boy whose singing couldn't be trusted. "Manny was an informant?"

"I thought so. I bought into his whole doe-eyed-refugee, American-dream act. He was supposed to drive north yesterday on I-95 and stop to have coffee with me outside Philly."

"So you could take the guns?"

"We hadn't made a decision on that. Manny's potential as an informant was golden. A source inside Shadow Street would be worth a lot more than a dozen guns. But Manny took the decision away from us when he drove east out of Baltimore, crossed Delaware, and took that ferry."

"What happened after the accident?"

Wildridge had been doing most of the talking, but she'd somehow also finished her beer. She rolled the empty bottle back and forth between her palms. On each roll, it clinked against a diamond engagement ring.

"I doubt we'll ever know for sure," she said. "We do know that Deputy Nelson, one of Cape May's finest, called Sammy Vu around two-thirty, half an hour after your accident. I think little Sammy called someone connected with Shadow Street."

"I find that hard to believe."

"Most men would," Wildridge said dryly. "Nevertheless, at three-thirty Manny was spirited out of the hospital."

"No one could have gotten down from Jersey City in an hour."

"I know. But the gang has branches, notably in Philadelphia. We've also heard rumors of an operation in Atlantic City, which would be close enough. Somehow the gang did it. The way Manny's bed was made up was as good as a Shadow Street calling card."

"Why would they kill him?"

"To keep him from talking to us."

"Are you sure it wasn't because he'd already talked to you?"

Wildridge shrugged. "Meanwhile, back in Rio Grande, a tow truck driver named Pardee was finding the guns hidden in Manny's car. Being a public spirited citizen, he decided to keep them. I figure he had maybe an hour to stash them somewhere. Then the gang picked him up."

"And he told them where the guns were hidden?"

"That's the rub. Pardee had to know his life was at stake. So he had to have told them. Unless he pulled a gun of his own and forced the issue. But there were no reports of a gun battle around Rio Grande, and people would notice something like that down there. So I'm thinking Pardee told them but they somehow misunderstood him. Either he tried to be cute with them or there was some kind of language barrier or cultural barrier. None of these kids are English majors. They felt confident enough that they'd find the guns to kill Pardee. Then they didn't find them."

"How do you know that?"

Wildridge looked at her watch and stood up. "I don't know, Mr. Keane. I'm guessing. You do a lot of that with Shadow Street. Pardee's nosy neighbor is a Vietnam vet. Yesterday evening around six he heard something that froze his blood: someone cursing in Vietnamese. He snuck up on Pardee's house and saw men in black arguing. The old guy was half convinced they were Vietcong. You're lucky he didn't shoot at you when you rolled in an hour later.

"The way they were yelling at each other and the way they left Pardee's place, it wasn't Shadow Street at its best. Discipline had broken down. That's what makes me think they didn't find the guns."

She led me to the front door. On the threshold, she turned and handed me two bits of paper. One was her business card. The other was the slip of hospital notepaper on which I'd written Marilyn's number for Deputy Nelson. "You might suggest to your lady friend that she cut her vacation short. I don't think the gang can trace her, but it's better to be safe."

"What do I cut short?" I asked.

"Good question. Since you've introduced yourself to Sammy Vu, I don't know what advice to give you."

"She wouldn't let me tell her my name."

Wildridge pondered that for a time in the darkness of the carport. Then she asked, "What were you looking for at Pardee's?"

"Answers, not guns."

"I'd settle for the guns. I'd take one up to Jersey City and wave it at the Vus to show them what a scumbag their darling Manny really was."

Ten

After Wildridge left me, I drove to a convenience mart and called Marilyn, afraid to use my own phone in case some all-powerful gang had tapped the line. I blurted out a not very coherent warning. Marilyn laughed at me and hung up. When I fell asleep hours later, I was still wondering how I would convince her, how I would convince myself that what Wildridge had told me was true. When I woke late the next morning, the answer was my first thought: Find the guns.

If the ATF agent was right, there'd been some miscommunication between Pardee and his captors. She'd offered two explanations. Either Pardee had given a false answer or the gang members had misinterpreted what he'd said. If Pardee had lied, the guns could be anywhere. If he hadn't, the places Shadow Street searched were clues to where the guns were hidden. To find them, I only had to identify Pardee's answer and interpret it correctly.

That and risk my life. I spent the morning trying to whittle the risk down mentally. The gang had already written off the guns, I told myself. Probably they'd already replaced them. And they hadn't connected me with their disappearance. If they had, I'd have disappeared myself.

Then I thought of something that made all my rationalizing obsolete. I figured out what Pardee's slashed mattress, ruined garden, and missing truck had in common. Ten minutes after that, I was headed south in my chartreuse Neon, clashing with every tree I passed.

I stopped at a Parkway phone to try Marilyn again. This time she hung up between the initial and terminal syllables of my first name. With the last of my change, I called Stu Hunter of J&S Towing. My insurance agent had promised me that he'd deal with Hunter, but I was hoping he hadn't called him yet. He evidently hadn't, because Hunter didn't seemed surprised to be hearing from me. I asked him to wait in his office until I got there.

As I drove through little Rio Grande, I wondered about Hunter's frame of mind, which I hadn't been able to gauge over the phone. If Agent Wildridge had told him about Shadow Street, he might greet me with a shotgun. He'd certainly be leery of any questions from me.

As it turned out, Hunter, a short man with a backwoodsman's beard, was friendly and relaxed. I decided that Wildridge had questioned him but not briefed him. He seemed genuinely confident that his partner, "old John," would turn up soon, probably hung over.

I went through the pretense of scheduling a showing of the wrecked Chevy for my claims adjuster. Then I steered the conversation back to Pardee. "I was here in the waiting room when you tried to radio him the afternoon of the accident," I said. "You called him something odd. Was it Clammer?"

"Right," Hunter said. "His CB handle. John's Clammer and I'm Crabber on account of he clams all the time and I prefer to catch crabs. There's at least a little art to netting a crab off a piling or trapping one. Doesn't take any brains to rake up a clam. Edible rock collecting, that's what I call it."

That confirmed the guess I'd made about the strange basket rakes I'd found in Pardee's barn. "Where do you clam around here?"

"More places all the time, since the water's gotten cleaner. Almost any water that's shallow enough to walk around in or work from a skiff at low tide. For old John, though, there's only one place. His ancestral clam bed, he calls it. Claims it's belonged to his family since the Revolution, which is bullshit. It's a swampy little inlet off Jarvis Sound."

I looked blank and pointed west. Hunter patiently pointed east. "It's out at the end of Sanderling Road, past the bird sanctuary."

"Can you catch crabs there?" I asked, having learned all I'd hoped to learn.

"Hell no," Hunter said, and launched into an exhaustive description of blue shell crabs. I listened for half an hour, until I was certain my clam questions had been safely buried. As I left, I casually mentioned that my insurance agent would be calling to finalize the details.

At a Route 9 filling station I asked for Sanderling Road and was told to follow the signs for the famous bird sanctuary. I passed this landmark a few minutes later, after a lonely drive through weedy mud flats on a narrow two-lane. The road continued past the sanctuary entrance but seemed uncertain about the decision. As was I.

Half a mile later the road ended at a metal barricade. I got out, kicking beer cans left by local romantics. Their tire tracks marked the sandy berm. I looked for and found a set of heavier, broader tracks, the kind a tow truck might leave. So far, so good.

I stood between the tracks and stared out at Jarvis Sound, a quiet expanse of dark blue water bordered by reeds so uniform in height they might have been regularly mowed. Running up to a muddy little beach before me was a narrow finger of the sound. John Pardee's ancestral clam bed, I hoped.

Bed was the key word, the answer to riddle posed by Shadow Street's quixotic search. Pardee's bed was the epicenter of their work in his house. A garden plot might be called a bed. A truck has a bed. Whatever Pardee had told his captors, it had had something to do with a bed. "The guns are under my bed," maybe. They'd killed him, thinking his information too simple to misconstrue. And they'd been wrong.

If my nose was any judge, it was low water. I took off my sneakers and socks, rolled up my the legs of my shorts, and wadded in, armed with a driftwood branch. The bottom was a sandy muck. I moved forward slowly, probing on every side with the branch and doubting furiously. How would Pardee have waterproofed the guns? He'd only had an hour to work with, less driving time. What kind of container would both keep the guns dry and not float?

I couldn't think of one. I found that I couldn't think of anything except an image Wildridge had left with me, a picture of Manny Vu's body, lying weighted down in some lonely body of water. Perhaps this water. In no time I had myself convinced that I was as likely to find Vu and Pardee as the guns. More likely.

Just as I had that thought, I scared up a snowy egret that had been crouching on a reedy bar near the mouth of the inlet. When my heart stopped racing, I found I was staring at the little island. As far as I could tell, it was dry even at high tide. I waded toward it, forgetting to prod with my stick, imagining new last words for Pardee: "The guns are behind my bed."

The bar was half the size of a tennis court. To search it, all I had to do was climb the bank and stare. Near the center of the driest land was a pile of driftwood and uprooted reeds, some of them still green. At the bottom of the pile I found a nylon duffel bag.

Eleven

At two the following afternoon I stood on the observation deck of the car ferry *Cape Haloran* as it droned across a placid Delaware Bay. I stood at the forward railing, which overlooked the lines of parked cars and the open bow with its webbing gate. Out on the horizon Cape May was only a flat line of blue gray, its lighthouse still a speck.

I was staring toward the cape, but I was seeing a different horizon, an island so crowded with buildings that it looked like a mountain range pushed up from the seabed. Manhattan. That was the view Manny Vu's father had had on every outbound trip of his ferry. A prospect that had symbolized opportunity for generations. And on every return trip, he'd seen what? Jersey City, with its Saigon market and its streets named for forgotten heroes of a civil war. The past.

I wondered how often Mr. Vu had thought of his voyage from Vietnam to Thailand as he'd worked on his ferry. Every day? Every trip? Never? Had he seen his round trips on the Hudson as an ironic commentary on his voyage of escape or a constant celebration of it?

And how had Manny seen them? Did he turn down a job on the Hudson ferry because the link to his father's life and death was too strong or because the job was too smalltime for him? And what had he seen on the last day of his life when he'd stood where I was now standing? The promised land or the first stop in an endless series of round trips?

The answer depended on which view of Manny was correct. Was he the good but troubled kid or the refugee on the make? Had he ridden the ferry on that last afternoon to reestablish some link to his past or to outsmart the law?

Or both. The more I thought about Manny, the more I saw him as somewhere between the two extremes. Not a bad kid or a good one, just a kid in a bad spot. A stranger in a very strange land, despite his American name, all of whose choices were hard ones. The hardest was the deal Wildridge had offered him: Trade your friends for a pat on the back from your new country. Trade your past for your future. That was a deal I'd never been able to go through with myself.

I hadn't believed Wildridge when she'd said the ATF hadn't made a decision regarding Manny's guns. I doubted Manny had believed her either. Had he still been trying to make his own decision as he'd crossed on this ferry? I opened my mind to the moment—to the sun on the water, to the fishing boats bobbing on the horizon, to the gulls keeping station on the stiff breeze—and waited for an answer, as Manny Vu might have done.

My answer came in the form of a woman in huge sunglasses, a jogging bra, and biker's shorts who poked my shoulder. Marilyn Tucci.

I'd shown up on her doorstep the evening before disguised as a pizza deliveryman, one of the Uzis hidden in my white cardboard box. Being Marilyn, she'd had to reach out and touch the thing before she'd finally believed me. Then I'd made the mistake of telling her what I intended to do with the guns, and she'd insisted on coming along. We'd taken a morning ferry to Delaware and killed an hour in colonial Lewes. Now we were on our way back.

"This is it," Marilyn said. "The water isn't going to get any deeper. There are a couple of smokers out back, but I think I can distract them."

I hadn't explained the symbolism of the ferry ride to Marilyn, so there was no point in telling her I needed more time to work on my composite picture of Manny. "Lead the way," I said.

We walked around to the rear of the ship, where Marilyn prepared to sunbathe for the enjoyment of the fantail smokers. I descended a steep metal stairway to the car deck. The deck was open to the sky on the rear of the ferry, just as it was on the front. And the stern was as unprotected, the gap through which the cars had been driven closed only by a net woven of broad straps.

The Neon was parked three cars from the end of the leftmost row. I walked to it casually, on the lookout for jaded commuters napping in their cars. I took a very heavy nylon duffel bag from the backseat of the compact and walked to the open stern. Once there I removed a camera from the bag and pretended to photograph the Lewes breakwater as it faded in the distance. Then I looked up at the observation deck. No one was watching me. I wondered if Marilyn was sunbathing topless. However she'd done it, she'd given me my chance.

I crouched behind a van and unzipped the bag completely. The guns were all there, boxy and ugly, wrapped in some oily toweling. They would never be used by any gang members. But they'd never be turned over to the ATF, either. I was afraid Wildridge would make good on her threat and wave one of the guns under the nose of the old man on the sofa. I'd unwittingly brought him the message that his grandson was safe. I wanted him to go on believing that. For some reason, I wanted to believe it myself.

Beyond the crash net, the ferry's wake boiled white. I tossed the guns into the wake, one by one.

MAIN LINE LAZARUS

One

You claim not to have any knowledge of Jim Skiles's disappearance, Mr. Keane, and yet you showed up at his cabin this morning with your lawyer in tow. That's a little suspicious, don't you think?"

The man with the pointed question was a sheriff named Chadwick, whose paternal facade was spoiled by a bull neck that was getting redder by the minute. There were four of us seated in Chadwick's sunny office in the Ocean County Courthouse in Tom's River, New Jersey: the sheriff, my friend Harry Ohlman, who happened to be a lawyer, Harry's wife Mary, and me.

"We've explained our presence at the cabin, Sheriff," Harry said in a tone so close to condescension I wanted to kick him. "Owen needed a ride down here to retrieve his car, which he left with Mr. Skiles. My wife and I were happy to help. In addition to having been Owen's employer until very recently, I'm an old friend of his. My wife and I are old friends of his. If necessary, we can prove a relationship of long standing with Owen. I was his college roommate, for example, which is documented."

And Mary was my college love, I thought, which was totally undocumented. I wondered if she was thinking the same thing, but there was no way to tell. Harry, big featured and darkly handsome, was showing the same signs of high blood pressure as the sheriff, but his wife was sitting with perfect relaxation in her Saturday sweater and tweedy slacks, her sky blue eyes open and guileless, her face, beneath the Dorothy Hamill wedge of honey hair, pale but unconcerned. Was she confident in my innocence or in her husband's ability to argue? I couldn't tell that either.

I forced my mind from Mary and back to the matter at hand as Chadwick addressed me.

"You said you first met Skiles last Wednesday, Mr. Keane?"

"Yes," Harry said before I could open my mouth. "Owen was down here doing some research for my firm, Ohlman, Ohlman, and Pulsifer." He gave the firm's Manhattan address, which the sheriff failed to jot down. "The subject of that research is, I'm afraid, confidential."

He had good reason to be afraid. My investigation of an old plane crash in the New Jersey Pine Barrens, a huge tract of sand and scrub pines on whose edge we currently sat, had come close to destroying the Ohlman family firm, because I'd uncovered two murders and attracted the enmity of a powerful corporation. That case was now safely closed, but it might open again in a hurry if Chadwick started poking around.

"Confidential," the sheriff repeated, getting close to condescension himself. "I've got a ransacked cabin and a missing old man, Mr. Ohlman. And I've got the suspicious circumstance of Mr. Keane here leaving his car in the middle of a forest and taking off. How do you explain that?"

"Owen and Skiles had a falling out," Harry said. "Owen came to see him in the first place because of Skiles's reputation as an authority on local history. Owen had been led to believe that Skiles was a native of the Pine Barrens and illiterate, but in the course of his visit to Skiles's cabin, Owen found a volume of essays with Skiles's name and a Philadelphia address written on its flyleaf. Skiles reacted badly to being found out. He contrived to strand Owen in the forest with night coming on."

My skin crawled as I remembered standing in the little fern-covered clearing and realizing that Skiles had slipped away. Then the nightmare march, fighting an endless tangle of pine branches and my own rising panic.

Harry failed to do the moment justice. "Owen made his way to State Road 539, where he found Skiles waiting for him. Owen was able to flag down a ride and escape, leaving his car back at Skiles's cabin. We three drove down from New York City this morning to retrieve it. We found the front door of Skiles's cabin kicked in and the interior in total disarray."

"And you found Mr. Keane's car, which he'd left unlocked, totally untouched," Chadwick interrupted. I'd wondered about that myself, but Harry wouldn't be sidetracked so close to the end of his summation.

"While we were searching the cabin, the patrolmen you posted on the highway to keep an eye on Skiles's road arrived and took Owen into custody."

Harry's recounting was perfectly accurate. We'd driven down that morning without the slightest idea that we'd be facing anything more threatening than Skiles's bad temper. Even the sight of the patrol car parked opposite

Skiles's sand road hadn't broken through our blissful ignorance. That happy mood had taken us as far as Skiles's shattered front door. We'd found the three rooms beyond the door thoroughly tumbled about. They didn't have the look of rooms that had been searched; the result was more chaotic, like a tornado had blown through. On the other hand, except for the front door, there hadn't been much real damage either. None of the windows were broken out, for example.

Of the cabin's owner, there'd been no sign, dead or alive. And though there'd been a number of books in the wreckage, ripped from Skiles's secret library, we'd failed to find the collection of essays that had gotten me into trouble on my first visit, the little leather-bound volume of Montaigne. I'd located the old metal bread box in which Skiles had hidden the book, but inside that I'd found only a yellowed index card on which was written a name, Eva Lisk, and four Philadelphia addresses, all but the last one crossed off.

I'd been in the process of pocketing the card when Chadwick's men had shown up. Now, before I could stop myself, I reached up to touch the shirt pocket where the card currently resided, a move that might have been fatal if Chadwick had been paying attention. But he was smiling over his own memories of the ransacked cabin.

"Gleason got the shock of his life when he found all those books scattered around," the sheriff said happily. "Skiles took him in but good with that illiterate act."

"Tim Gleason," I said by way of reentering the conversation. Editor of a local paper, the *Sunbeam*, and the man who had suggested I visit Skiles in the first place.

"The same," the sheriff said. "He's the one who found the cabin all upside down. He drove back in there yesterday to apologize to Skiles for sending you in uninvited, so to speak. When he found what he found, he rushed to Bargersville—to the nearest phone—and called me."

"And you did what?" Harry asked.

"Started to check Skiles's background, which is what Gleason should have done when he first heard of the guy, instead of accepting him as a born-and-bred Piney and writing stories about him. Still, Skiles has been living in those woods longer than Gleason's been alive, so I guess I can't fault him too much. We'd only just gotten started on our background work when you three showed up and disturbed what may be a crime scene."

"We did what any conscientious citizens would do," Harry said, inspiring me to sit up straighter. "Which was to ascertain whether Skiles was lying hurt inside. While we're on the subject, why wasn't the cabin clearly marked as a crime scene?"

"Like I said, we've only just started looking into this. We didn't even know if we had one missing man or two. We couldn't contact Mr. Keane here at the address he gave when he registered his car. He'd moved to …" He let the statement trail into a question.

"Brooklyn," I said, hoping for the laugh the name always seemed to rate on television. I didn't get it.

"Are you sure you didn't leave the cabin unsecured and post a patrol car nearby hoping to entrap Owen when he came back for his car?" Harry demanded.

"How was I to know he'd even left the area?" Chadwick replied a little warmly. "In fact, how can I be sure he did leave the area? What proof do I have that he didn't arrange a rendezvous with you and your wife somewhere in the county just before you drove up to the cabin? Aside, of course, from the testimony of two old and dear friends."

"The Thompsons," Mary said from behind her hand. She'd listened to the whole story of my run-in with Skiles on the drive down. And taken notes, evidently.

"Right," Harry said, without missing a beat. "If necessary, we can produce the testimony of the couple who picked Owen up Wednesday night when he hitchhiked out. The Thompsons of …"

"Allentown," I said, not hiding behind my hand.

"Of Allentown. They saw Skiles alive and well by the side of 539. My office can trace them in less than an hour."

"You must run a very efficient operation," the sheriff said evenly. He settled back in his chair, his uniform shirt wrinkling as though he were leaking air. "Well, I must own that I'm disappointed. I'd hoped you could shed some light on this, Mr. Keane. I suppose there's no point in spoiling more of your Saturday. Or of holding on to your car. You brought it along when you agreed to accompany my deputies, I hear. Just leave your current address so we can come see you if the Thompsons thing doesn't pan out."

Harry and Mary began to stir, but I settled in, a la Chadwick. I was curious about something, a not uncommon condition with me. "You said you'd started to check into Skiles's background, Sheriff. What have you found?"

If Chadwick heard Harry's sigh, he ignored it. "No offense, Mr. Keane, but why should I give you my information when you have nothing to give me?"

"A trade?" I asked and thought about it. "What's the name of the place in Bargersville where Tim Gleason placed his panic call to you?"

"Nash's. It's what they used to call a general store. Now I guess you'd call it a convenience store."

"Ask them if Skiles made a long-distance call from their phone the day before Gleason was in. On Thursday, the day after I talked to Skiles. That will give you something to trace."

Chadwick stared at me for a moment. Then he pushed a button on his phone and told the voice that answered to place the call. After another minute's staring, he was speaking to someone at Nash's and nodding his head.

"How'd you know?" he asked when he'd hung up.

"I guessed," I said.

"That so? Well, even a guess is worth something. So I'll tell you this much. Once upon a time, our Mr. Skiles was a lawyer, like Mr. Ohlman here. Must not have been quite as good as Mr. Ohlman or not quite as lucky, because he ended up serving a nice little prison term."

Two

"Did you hear that guy?" Harry was actually stomping his feet as we stepped from the courthouse into the October sunshine. "That Chadwick made it sound like all lawyers belong in jail. The only ones not locked up are just lucky."

"Or good," Mary reminded him, patting his arm.

"Skiles a lawyer," I said, amazed. "He hates lawyers." He'd managed to work that into our brief conversation more than once.

"Who doesn't?" the still-wounded Harry demanded.

"Maybe that's the way his prison time left him," Mary said. "Or maybe it's a reaction to whatever sent him to prison."

We reached our cars, which were parked side by side. My 1965 Volkswagen Karmann-Ghia looked tiny next to the Ohlman's shiny new 1981 Lincoln. In fact, it looked depressingly like the circus car all the clowns climb out of. Those two cars were apt symbols for the very different paths our lives had taken since college. The Ohlmans were successful up-and-comers who'd even found time to have a baby, Amanda, currently in the care of Mary's parents. I'd held a number of dead-end jobs, most recently the research position with Harry's firm. But I'd always only been one thing: a compulsive pursuer of mysteries, large and small.

"So are you going to tell us?" Mary asked me. And then, as I blinked at her, "How you knew Skiles had made that phone call. Did he ask for spare change as you were hitchhiking by the road that night?"

I tried to reconstruct my chain of logic, or rather construct one to impress Mary, since my admission to Chadwick that I'd simply guessed pretty much described my standard procedure. "It can't be a coincidence that Skiles disappeared just after I spoke with him. My visit has to be the cause of his disappearance."

"Because of the Carteret business?" Harry asked, nervously naming the case that had almost scuttled his firm.

"No. Because I got Skiles thinking back on his past by stumbling across his old Philadelphia address. And then running off without hearing his story. He tried to get me to listen to it right at the end. But I was too busy escaping. So I left him stirred up on the subject."

"I'm with you so far," Mary said.

"The rest is easy. It can't be that Skiles's past just happened to catch up with him the moment I left him. Too big a coincidence again. So Skiles must have gotten in touch with someone from that past. By phone, given how fast things happened after that."

Harry shouldered in then. "You asked about that phone in Bargersville because it's the one the Gleason guy used. The nearest phone to the cabin, the sheriff said. Whomever Skiles called arranged for him to be snatched or mentioned the call to the wrong person and that someone made the arrangements. How long did the old guy live in the woods?"

"I don't know. Decades."

We were sitting on our cars, Harry on mine and me, in retaliation, on his. Mary stood between us.

"I wonder what they were searching for in his cabin," she said.

Harry shared my impression of the damage. "Didn't look like a search to me. Looked like somebody just wrecked the place. Maybe using Skiles as a wrecking ball."

"What could he have done to have earned a grudge like that?" Mary asked. "Run off with tong money?"

"Mafia money around here," Harry said. "But Skiles wouldn't have gone to prison for that. He'd have gone into heavy construction. Literally." When I failed to laugh, Harry finally noticed that I hadn't joined in the guessing game. "What's the matter, Owen?"

"Skiles didn't change his name."

"That's right," Mary said. "If he was hiding from someone, he would have. And he didn't move very far from Philadelphia. Only about what, fifty miles?"

"That cabin of his is farther from Philly than the moon," her husband said.

"And he let that editor interview him for the local paper," Mary continued without noting the interruption. "A man hiding out wouldn't do that. Not unless he wanted to be caught."

"Maybe he did want to be caught," Harry said. "Maybe he's been wanting his past to catch up with him for years. Maybe he was sick of using an outhouse. Owen blundering in just made his mind up for him."

"What could he have done?" Mary's rhetorical question brought us full circle, which Harry and I acknowledged by standing. Mary took my hand. "Where are you off to now, Owen?"

Earlier that morning I couldn't have answered the question. Not truthfully. Now I said, "The City of Brotherly Love."

"To trace Skiles?"

"To help him. I owe him that. For blundering in. I just wish I knew everything Chadwick knows."

"I can do better than that," Harry said. "If Skiles was a Philadelphia lawyer and he went to prison, the fraternity will remember him. We have pretty close ties to one of the older firms down there. In fact, we recently did them a favor. They'd be happy to repay it with a little gossip."

"Do they gossip on Saturdays?"

"You want me to call them today?"

"Yesterday might not be soon enough, not from Skiles's point of view."

Harry nodded. "How will I get in touch with you?"

"I'll get in touch with you. In an hour?"

"Be a sport. Give me two."

He was already getting his reward: Mary was hugging him. She hugged me next. "Be careful, Owen."

"You know me."

That must have been the wrong thing to say, because her hug stiffened until we were standing together as uncomfortably as junior-high dance partners. I kissed her as I wiggled free, shook her husband's hand, and headed west.

Three

I took my time crossing New Jersey, allowing the Ghia to be passed by every dump truck and farm implement on the Atlantic City Expressway. I told myself that I was giving Harry time to reach home and track down his informants by phone, but my wandering thoughts returned again and again to the condition of Skiles's cabin and to Harry's mob hypothesis.

I was aided in my dawdling by the traffic. Philly traffic, I mentally called it, though it began in Jersey as little roads and big roads came together to form the approach to the Walt Whitman Bridge. Several lanes of the bridge had been closed for some Saturday maintenance. We crossed the Delaware at a crawl, which made it safe for me to gawk at passing container ships and—down toward the bay—a giant tanker. On the western side I traded expressways for normal streets as soon as I could, making my way into the heart of the old city circumspectly.

As I drove from one red light to the next, I had the odd feeling that I was recreating my expedition into the Pine Barrens, the one that had taken me to Skiles in the first place. The landscape couldn't have been more different, more urban, both sides of the street lined with buildings—first warehouses, then office buildings, then row houses—all packed as tightly together as the Pines' namesake trees. Still, the déjà vu was there, prompted by the feeling that I was once again moving into Skiles's domain, a place where I was a stranger and he was right at home.

Or maybe not. Fairmount Park, when I finally found it, looked very little like the old engraving of it I'd seen on the wall of Skiles's cabin during my unhappy first visit. I hit the park near its southernmost tip, a thin strip on the banks of the Schuykill River. Pickup basketball games were the first signs of life on this mild fall day. As I drove north through the park, the ground became hillier and the trees thicker, some of them already shed of their leaves and some barely turned, and the ball players gave way to joggers and walkers of large, dangerous-looking dogs.

Near the reservoir, I turned east and found the street I was after, Thirtieth

Street, only a block or two from the edge of the green space. The houses were older than I'd expected, nineteenth century banker specials, most of them stone or brick and a few rundown to the point of collapse. Here and there a house had been brought back to nearly new condition and stood out like a gold tooth in a skull.

Skiles's old home, if the address in his secret books had in fact been his home, hadn't been restored. Nor would it ever be, for the simple reason that it was gone, replaced by a rubble-strewn lot. I spoke with those neighbors I could find and learned that the house had been torn down four or five years earlier, following a space heater fire. None of the neighbors could remember the names of the home's last residents, and no one had heard of the Skiles family.

By then it was past my lunchtime. At one end of the block, an old mansard-roofed building had been turned into a neighborhood store. Some-one had hand-lettered a menu of its principal offerings on one outside wall, and the fifth item from the bottom of the list caught my eye: hoagies. I knew hoagie to be Philadelphian for submarine sandwich, so I moved the Ghia to the nearest parking space and went inside.

The man who made my Italian sub—working in an island counter around which the store's shelves were arranged—was a neighborhood veteran who had survived the hard years and now saw sunny days ahead.

"You seen them houses they're fixing up. You mark my words, ten years from now this whole street will be turned around. When them whatcha call 'em—yuppies—get done, we'll have brick sidewalks and them fancy gas street lights. You come back in 1991 and see."

"I hope I can," I said.

"Young guy like you? What's your problem?"

I thought of my immediate one. I inquired after a public phone and then, remembering Nash's general store and my earlier lucky guess, I described Skiles and asked if he'd stopped by to make a call.

"Little old white guy needs a shave?" the store owner repeated. "Dressed in a flannel shirt and rolled up pants? Give him a bottle in a paper bag, and he'd be our old clientele. That's all behind us now."

Four

The phone hung on the front wall of the store, next to a display of anti-freeze. I called Harry collect just for the fun of listening to him accept the charges.

"You okay, Owen?" Harry asked when the operator had left us.

"So far. But Skiles's old address near Fairmount Park is just a gap in the street. I hope you've done better."

"I think I may have," he said, his false modesty coming across louder than his words. "I was able to reach a senior member of that firm I mentioned. So senior I was sure he'd be at home. I just wasn't sure his nurse would pass him the phone."

I noted that Harry hadn't mentioned the senior member's name. For fear I'd show up on his doorstep probably. I was too busy eavesdropping to take offense. In the background I could make out a baby crying—Amanda, rescued from her grandparents. I heard Mary next, first speaking and then, faintly, crooning.

"Anyway," Harry was saying, "this guy remembered Skiles right away. And the old scandal. Got some paper to write on?"

"Yes," I said. I had the waxed stuff still wrapped around my hoagie. That paper wouldn't have been a very discreet choice, as it had been rendered transparent by leaking Italian dressing. Not that it mattered. I didn't have anything to write with, but Harry hadn't asked me about that.

"Around 1950 Skiles was a junior associate in the law firm of Gimbel and Bellaby. They specialized in estate planning and trust management for Main Line families."

"Main Line families?"

"Philly's social register set. You must have heard of the Main Line. You grew up right across the river."

"Not right across," I said in my defense. "It does sound familiar. Did they take the name from a rail line?"

"Exactly. The old main line of the Pennsylvania Railroad. It ran through a series of villages where Philadelphia's rich and famous resettled when they outgrew places like Skiles's Fairmount Park neighborhood. You've heard of Ardmore, right? And Bryn Mawr?"

"Right," I said.

"Gimbel and Bellaby catered to that fox hunting crowd. Henry Gimbel was old money himself, Alexander Bellaby less so."

"What about James Skiles?"

"His family was around the day the Liberty Bell cracked," Harry said, trying to be colorful. "Just the kind of man Gimbel and Bellaby would want on board. Lots of connections and no risk. Or so they must have thought. You getting all this down?"

"Spell Gimbel."

As he did, I traced the letters with my finger in the dust on an antifreeze container.

"The scandal involved the misappropriation of funds from a trust set up for a severely disabled boy by his parents. There was a lot more money in it than was needed for the kid's care, and Skiles helped himself to the surplus. He must have felt safe doing it because the parents were dead and the boy was in no shape to ask for an accounting."

"What was his name?"

"My contact couldn't remember, which I'm not sure I believe, since he did recall that the poor kid died sometime in the early sixties, years after Skiles went to prison."

"How did Skiles get caught? Some kind of internal audit?"

"No. An internal audit at a place like Gimbel and Bellaby would have stayed internal. Skiles was turned in—fingered, you detective types would say—by a disgruntled former employee. The story I was told had a Gimbel and Bellaby secretary being let go for some infraction unrelated to the embezzlement. She knew about it though and called the police as her way of getting back at the firm. At least that's how my contact reconstructed things at the time, after he'd done a little poking around. A friendly policeman told him that their tips had come in the form of phone calls from an anonymous woman.

"You're going to ask me next what the secretary's name was. My gossip hound couldn't remember her name either. I believed him on that count because he made a genuine effort. He said it was something like that old soap brand, Lux."

"It wasn't Lux," I said. I dug in my pocket for the clue I'd forgotten I had, the index card I'd been examining in Skiles's cabin when the patrol car pulled up. "Her name was Lisk. Eva Lisk."

Five

For a long time after I'd finished with Harry, I stood staring at the little yellowed card. The four addresses, three crossed out, and the deteriorating handwriting suggested that Skiles had kept track of Eva Lisk for years, perhaps ever since he'd been released from prison. But why?

Had Lisk been the recipient of Skiles's mystery phone call? No phone numbers were listed on the card, but a number was easy to get if you had a name and an address. I was tempted to call information myself right then, to phone Lisk and warn her. But trying to phrase that warning stopped me. Beware of a man you wronged thirty years ago. It didn't make sense, not in the context of Skiles's wrecked cabin. He was the victim, not the danger.

Still, for lack of a better move, I decided to visit Eva Lisk. I asked the man who had made my uneaten lunch for directions to her last address, 811 Linden Avenue. He sold me a map with a close-up of the downtown on one side and Philly and its suburbs on the other. I needed the larger scale map to find Linden Avenue, which was in the northeast part of the city, just shy of the Bucks County line.

Unfortunately for the property values, Lisk's neighborhood was also very close to I-95 and a parallel corridor of railroad tracks as wide as the interstate and overhung with power lines for electric locomotives. Not Fairmount Park for atmosphere, but the neighborhood I found beyond the tracks was a living one, with Halloween pumpkins on the front steps and kids playing around the parked cars while their parents raked up leaves and memories in tiny yards.

No such seasonal activity was on display at 811 Linden, the better-kept half of a well-kept double. Things were so quiet in fact that I thought I'd reached another dead end. Then, after my third go-round with the doorbell, I heard a chain rattling and a bolt snapping back.

Eva Lisk was fifty something, which meant she'd been in her twenties when she and Skiles had interacted so unhappily. She was small and iron-haired, with big, almost black eyes that seemed to have bled outward, forming dark rings on her otherwise pale face.

"My name is Owen Keane," I said. "I'm looking into the disappearance of James Skiles."

A name from her distant past, but it didn't take her a full second to place him. "Him," she said, almost sneering it.

"May I come in?"

"No." She looked toward her nearest raking neighbor. Her protection from me, I realized. But she made no move to call to him or to close her door, so I reconciled myself to the porch.

"Have you heard from Skiles recently?" I asked.

"Recently? Not recently. Not since he fired me. Not since he sent me out to starve, with a baby on the way."

"You were pregnant?" I hadn't raised my voice, but Lisk reacted as though I'd shouted, stepping backward into the house. I followed her, blocking the doorway.

"Skiles disappeared from … from where he's been living since he got out of prison," I said before she could order me out. "He may have been abducted. I think it could have something to do with Gimbel and Bellaby."

"Gimbel and Bellaby," she said, really sneering this time. "Those old hypocrites. I waited years to read their obituaries—decades for Bellaby's—and they were all lies. Nothing about their shady deals. Nothing about how they kicked a girl out in the street for being pregnant with no husband. Or had their hatchet man, James Skiles, do it."

"You were fired for being pregnant?"

"What did I just tell you?"

"Was Skiles the father?" I asked, revealing that I'd spent too much time with paperback mysteries and not enough with Montaigne.

"Are you crazy? Do you think I would have let him get away with what he did if he'd been the one who knocked me up?"

"Did you let him get away with it?" I used my best accusatory voice, but Lisk ignored the question, returning to the cheery subject of obituaries.

"When the *Inquirer* ran Bellaby's notice last year, I almost wrote them a letter. I wanted to tell the whole city the truth about him. I would have, too, if it hadn't been for Joan, his wife, the angel. I wouldn't have been able to raise my baby, my Vera, without her, never would have been able to send her to college without those checks every month. She had a conscience. She knew what her husband and her brother had done to me."

"Her brother? Henry Gimbel?"

"No, James Skiles, that no-good son of a bitch. Probably wouldn't have gotten his job in the first place if his sister hadn't been married to a senior partner. How she picked a man like Alexander Bellaby to marry, I'll never understand. But for her sake, I held my peace about him. I wouldn't do anything to hurt her."

"You sent her brother to prison."

Lisk's smile chilled me. "He sent himself," she said.

Six

Eva Lisk had given me a lot to think about, but instead I wasted time wondering why Harry's contact hadn't mentioned Skiles's angelic sister. Before I was settled again in the Ghia's worn driver's seat, I'd decided that I had to talk to Joan Bellaby.

That left the problem of finding her. Luckily, my late, unlamented days with Harry's firm had been largely spent doing library research. I considered various options, including obtaining a copy of her husband's obituary in the hope it would mention a church or a lodge. But I began where I always began, with my personal oracle and the amateur detective's best friend, the phone book. I didn't expect to find someone of Bellaby's social standing in the "Philadelphia and Suburban Areas" white pages—especially not in the grease-stained copy I borrowed at an Amoco station near the interstate—and I didn't. I did find the next listing I looked for, the one for Philly's Free Public Library.

I punched the number into the gas station's phone and asked for the social sciences department. Harry had called Philadelphia's wealthy the "social register set." I'd heard the expression before, of course, but I wasn't sure if the register referred to was a physical document or a state of mind. Still, it couldn't hurt to ask.

The social services phone was answered by a gentleman with an Indian accent. I asked him my basic question: Was there such a thing as a social register?

"Yes," he said, "but you're not in it."

I begged his pardon.

He laughed. "I always say, 'If you have to ask, you're not in it.' "

"Ah," I said, laughing myself, or trying to. "But there is such a book."

"Certainly. Published annually by the Social Register Association. Contains names, addresses, phone numbers, and social organization memberships."

I asked him to look up Joan Bellaby. Before the first negative thought could enter my head, he was back on the line with Bellaby's address, which was in a suburb called Ashcroft.

According to my trusty map, it was closer to Independence Hall than Eva Lisk's neighborhood, though outside the formal boundary of the city, being due west and therefore farther from the Delaware, the river along which Philly sprawled. Ashcroft was nestled between two of the towns Harry had mentioned, Ardmore and Bryn Mawr. In other words, it was on the Main Line, Gimbel and Bellaby's old hunting grounds. I drove south briefly on I-95, picked up I-76, and followed it north and west to the old Lincoln Highway, which shadowed the rail line that had given the area its name. I shadowed it, too.

There was a village feel to Ashcroft. It had a central square, a little green space bordered by a drug store, a one-room train station, and a restaurant named, in what I assumed was a burst of candor, the Snooty Fox. The neighborhoods arranged around this center were less forthcoming, thanks to some very mature landscaping and impressive walls, complete with gates. Luckily, the drawbridge was down at Joan Bellaby's Ashcroft Terrace, which is to say, the front gate stood open. No one was out raking leaves in the yards I passed on her curving tree-lined street, and no children were dodging cars.

The Bellaby place was genuinely impressive: large enough to be a mansion and not just a house with pretensions. It was built of gray stone and had the soaring roofline of a French chateau. The drive had its own gate, but like the main one, this backup was open. An open door or gate usually suggested a trap to me, and this wrought iron number was no exception. I took the precaution of turning my Volkswagen around and pointing it toward the street before I left it on the apron of paving stones that led to the front walk.

By the time I'd rung the bell, my paranoia had given way to self-criticism, my other standby. I was asking myself what visiting mansions had to do with helping Skiles, who was probably lying hurt or dead within a hundred yards of his cabin. I'd no sooner had the thought than I was picturing the scene, with Skiles's body a little bump in the forest floor covered over with pine needles. Then the door opened, and I stood face-to-face with the corpse himself.

Seven

I might not have recognized Skiles if he hadn't been in every other thought I'd had that day. He'd shaved his tight beard from his leathery face and slicked back his gray hair. In place of the flannel shirt and army surplus pants in which I'd previously seen him, he wore a dark blue suit, a crisp white shirt, and a paisley tie.

Then he smiled, and the holes in that smile left by Pine Barrens dentistry increased his resemblance to my storytelling hermit wonderfully. "Owen Keane," he said, "the ghost chaser himself. What in the world are you doing here?"

"Looking for my car," I managed to say.

The non sequitur didn't even slow Skiles down. "However did you find me?"

"That's a long story. The Ocean County police picked me up at your cabin this morning. The place had been ransacked, and you were missing."

For a moment, Skiles's little eyes lost their twinkle. "Missing? I was right here. Do I look missing?"

"Guess you forgot to leave a forwarding address."

"Guess I did. Didn't think anybody would care. Come on in, long as you're here. Let's make ourselves comfortable."

My distrust of the old man was still such that I hesitated on the threshold. He pretended not to notice, walking away slowly and talking to me over his shoulder as though I were once again following him along a woodland path.

"My cabin ransacked you say? Sounds like the work of my neighbors down the road, the Perkins brothers. Always up to no good when they're up at all."

By then I'd caught up with him, unwilling to miss a word of his explanation. We crossed a foyer of white marble, passing beneath a chandelier suspended from a domed ceiling several floors above us. Skiles led me through double doors and into a study, massively furnished but cold, the walls showing the naked gray stone of the exterior.

"My late brother-in-law's cozy little getaway," Skiles said. "His suit, too. What do you think of the fit?"

"Not much," I said, though it was no baggier than the last outfit I'd seen him in.

Skiles showed his laugh lines again. "Maybe I'll grow into it. The food's good around here. Have a seat."

He chose one of a pair of leather armchairs placed midway between a Spanish Inquisition desk and a dead fireplace. I sat in the facing chair.

"Coffee, Mr. Keane? Something stronger? No? Well then, why don't you tell me how you tracked me down."

I started with Sheriff Chadwick's teasing reference to Skiles's past.

"The sheriff called here just about an hour ago," Skiles said. "He'd traced that reverse charges call I'd made from Nash's."

"He didn't tell you about your cabin?"

"I never gave him the chance. Never had any use for policemen. And he started off with that nonsense about me being missing. Guess I should have heard him out."

"Why did you call your sister?"

"Never tell two stories at once, son. Finish yours first."

I picked up with the gossip Harry had collected. Again Skiles interrupted. "Forgot you worked for a lawyer. If there's anything a lawyer can dig up in a hurry, it's dirt on another lawyer."

That left me with Eva Lisk. Skiles shook his head steadily as I recounted my interview with the ex-secretary. When I absentmindedly produced the index card that had led me to her, he leaned forward suddenly and snatched it from my hand.

"Where'd you get that? Helped yourself to it in my cabin, didn't you? Maybe you're the one who did the ransacking after all."

"Why did you keep track of her all these years?"

"That's my personal business."

We stared at each other for a time, as we'd once done deep in a pine forest. I'd broken first then, and I broke first now.

"You were going to tell me how you came to be here."

Skiles stood up. "First there's someone I'd like you to meet."

Eight

He led me far into the house, so far we came out the other side. Or almost out. We ended up in a large greenhouse tacked onto the rear of the mansion, a hot humid greenhouse, thanks to the still potent sun. I immediately thought of Philip Marlowe's interview with General Sternwood at the start of *The Big Sleep*, and not just because of the steamy setting. Skiles had brought me to meet his sister, and like Sternwood, she was confined to a wheelchair.

That was as far as her resemblance to the frail general went, for Joan Bellaby, though an invalid, was anything but delicate. As we approached, she was supervising the trimming of a large rubbery-looking plant in drill-sergeant tones. She took it down a notch when she spotted her brother and ceased fire entirely when she saw me.

"Jimmy," she said. "Why didn't you tell me we had company?"

Her mildly reproachful tone was more than canceled out by the grateful looks the two assistant gardeners laid on Skiles as they gathered up their tools. He lost that good will by telling them we'd only be staying a minute.

"Just a friend who was worried about me," Skiles said after the formal introductions. "Owen here is in our old business, the law."

Bellaby was dubious. She was as tiny as Eva Lisk, but not as spare, and she wore a paisley dress that came remarkably close to matching her brother's tie. She also had his small keen eyes and very gray hair. Absent was his easy smile. "A lawyer?" she asked.

"A hanger-on," I said, though even that was no longer true.

"Well, any friend of Jimmy's is welcome here. Although I must say, the way he described his recent life, I expected all his acquaintances to be wearing coonskin caps."

"Mine's grazing out front," I said, surprising even myself. I'd decided this conversation was one of Skiles's famous stalls, and that had spoiled my manners.

Bellaby didn't hold the lapse against me. "I'm glad there was someone looking out for Jimmy. I know what it's like not to have anyone." As there were two servants hovering within ten feet of her, I figured she was referring to some long past life. She wasn't. "It's made the biggest difference for me to have my brother here. You can't imagine."

At that point, Skiles announced that I had to be going and led me away. Before we'd gotten out of earshot of the conservatory, the defoliation project was on again.

Nine

We went back through the house the way we'd come. This time I was able to spot two more servants, young women in formal black and white, taken unawares by Skiles the woodsman and his habitually stealthy movements. Then we were back in the study, and it was story time. My host was in the mood to pace—back and forth across the cold hearth—so I stood, too, with my wing chair between us.

"Promised I'd tell you how I came to be here, Mr. Keane. I have to start with a little correcting. You see, most of the old gossip you dug up—the official history of James Skiles—is just plain wrong. I did work for Gimbel and Bellaby, of course, and I was disbarred and sent to prison. But I never took any money. Don't know why I should care what you, a relative stranger, thinks of me, but there it is: I do."

"There was no embezzlement?"

"Oh, there was plenty of that. It was the work of my employers and benefactors, Henry Gimbel and Alexander Bellaby. They'd gotten into some short-term financial difficulties and dipped into that trust. They didn't think anyone knew about it—I surely didn't—but someone else did."

"Eva Lisk."

"The very one. As luck would have it, Miss Lisk got herself in the family way right about that time. We couldn't have an unwed mother besmirching the holy name of Gimbel and Bellaby, so those two sanctimonious crooks decided she had to go. I was given the unpleasant task of firing her."

"So when she called the police anonymously to report the embezzlement, she named you."

"I was fresh in her mind, so to speak. That left me with a dilemma. I could have cleared myself, but only at the expense of my brother-in-law, which is the same as saying, at the expense of my sister. I couldn't do that to her, so I took the blame and went to prison.

"That's a lot of what I wanted to tell you last Wednesday night out beside 539. Not that it would have made much sense to you then. But your finding that book with my old address in it had gotten me wanting to talk about my past in the worst way. I'd avoided that temptation for twenty years, a real accomplishment for a gregarious soul like me. I sometimes think that's why I became a storyteller in the first place—one of the reasons—to relieve the pressure of not being able to tell the one story I really owned, my miserable life's story.

"Anyway, once you'd gone I was in a quandary. I couldn't talk to anyone in the Pines without exposing myself as a phony. And an ex-con to boot. It came to me to call someone who already knew my history. Joan, my sister. To be honest, I'd had it in my mind to do that for some time. We'd been out of touch so long.

"I caught me a ride to Bargersville the very next day and did the deed. Ended up being quite a phone call, with me so wrought up to start with and Joan telling me about Alex passing on and her being forced into a wheelchair by her arthritis. She begged me to come see her, and I said I would."

That memory stopped him in his tracks, but only for a moment. "I went home long enough to pack a few things I really didn't need, like a certain book of essays. Then I set out, using your method." He pantomimed a hitchhiker. "That's how I came to be here. No big mystery, you see. Guess I should have left a note on my cabin door, but, more than likely, the Perkins boys would have just torn it up."

"More than likely," I said. "Why are you wearing the lawyer outfit?"

Skiles resumed his pacing. "I could call it camouflage—make a joke of it—but the truth's a little more complicated than that. You see, Joan wants me to move in here with her. She's pretty well fixed—very well fixed—but she's lonely. Her idea is, we should take care of one another. Keep each other company, now that we're old."

"How do you feel about that?"

"Ambivalent. There's a word I couldn't use as Jim Skiles the illiterate storyteller. Ambivalent. I mean to say, Joan's my sister. She looked out for me in the old days. Got me my start at Gimbel and Bellaby. Talked me into the profession of law in the first place. All I really wanted to do back in college was study American folklore. There was quite a flowering in that field just before the war."

"Sounds like what I found you doing," I said.

"Exactly. My name was mud around these parts after the scandal. And I knew about the Pine Barrens from my college studies. So, when I got out of prison, I disappeared into that great woodland, just as outcasts and outlaws have done since colonial times. Made a new life for myself. Not the most comfortable life, but one I've enjoyed. One I'd miss.

"But that decision is my problem, not yours. You've got questions you want to ask, I know. You're a man who wears his questions like a lover wears his heart, right on your sleeve. But I have to ask for a slight recess. I promised Joan I'd have a little chat with the cook. Been putting it off all day. It won't take but few minutes. Make yourself at home."

Ten

I sat down in the wing chair after Skiles left me, but less than a minute later I was up again, pacing as he had done on the hearth. It didn't help. Things just weren't coming together the way I'd expected them to when my only goal had been to find Skiles and hear his story.

That story had been far from his best work. It hadn't explained anything convincingly, not his wrecked cabin, not his long surveillance of Eva Lisk, not his sacrificial jail term. The story hadn't even explained my presence in the Bellaby mansion in a way I could accept. I couldn't believe I'd come to Ashcroft in response to a false alarm. In fact, I was beginning to suspect that I hadn't even come there of my own free will.

An ordinary black telephone occupied a very modest place on the Spanish desk. I dialed Harry's number, not bothering to reverse the charges. He and Amanda answered. I could hear the baby's cooing so clearly that I knew her head had to be resting on Harry's shoulder, inches from the phone.

"Owen. What is it now?"

"Something you told me earlier that I didn't pick up on right away. You said the police had received anonymous calls—plural—regarding the embezzlement. Is that what you meant to say? Was there more than one call?"

Amanda murmured something I couldn't quite catch while Harry pondered. Then he said, "Yes. I'm pretty sure I was told that. I'm positive. The first call exposed the graft. The second named Skiles. Why is that important?"

"Just updating my notes," I said and hung up.

I made my way back through the house, wishing I'd left a trail of bread crumbs on my previous trip. Eventually, I found the conservatory. Joan Bellaby and her crew were still there, though they'd moved on to a new bed. A little black plaque on its edge said that it contained philodendrons, though the stalky plants were many times the size of the vine of that name dying back in my Brooklyn apartment.

"Mr. Keane," Bellaby said. "I understood that you had gone. Where's Jimmy?"

"Talking with the cook. I thought we might chat, too." I looked toward her two assistants as I added, "I'd like to ask you about Eva Lisk."

"Time for a break, Luis," Bellaby said without taking her eyes from mine.

The gardeners hurried off toward the back of the greenhouse. I watched them go, listening to the sounds of the place, the hum of the exhaust fans and the steady cascade of water into some unseen pond. I said, "So you recognize the name."

"I'm not likely to forget the name of the viper who sent my brother to prison."

"Happen to know where she is now?"

"In hell, I hope."

Where I was welcome to join her. There was some movement in the foliage behind Bellaby, near a stunted palm with bark textured like a pine cone and fronds like a common fern's. Luis, back in search of something, I thought, but he never appeared.

"You haven't kept in touch with her?"

"Why on earth would I, Mr. Keane?" She was struck—almost literally—by an idea. "You're not that awful woman's child?"

It was a leap worthy of an amateur detective. I was about the right age, by an odd coincidence. But I never seriously considered donning the disguise. I was satisfied to have learned that Bellaby didn't even know the sex of Lisk's love child.

"I'm a friend of your brother's, remember? But I did speak to Eva Lisk earlier today. She lives about twenty miles from here as the crow flies. She told me your brother sent himself to prison."

"Ridiculous," Bellaby said. "She turned him in. Everybody knew that."

"Everybody thought that. But there were two calls to the police. One tipping them to the embezzlement, one naming Skiles. Each one anonymous. Each one from a woman. The same woman, everyone assumed. I think it was two different women. Lisk made the first call, but she didn't name any names. When she heard later that your brother had taken the fall, she assumed he'd done it voluntarily. But he'd been pushed.

"You made the second call, Mrs. Bellaby. You knew your husband was looking at ruin—you were looking at ruin. So you handed over your brother to save yourself."

Again a movement in the little rain forest beyond Bellaby's silver head drew my eye. And there was Skiles, standing silently behind the squat palm, watching us. I looked away quickly, but I needn't have hurried. Bellaby was staring off into space.

"You intend to tell my brother that malicious lie?" she asked, still far away.

I decided to gamble. "I already have. He laughed at the idea."

"Of course he did," Bellaby said, back with me again. "He loves me. I could tell him the truth myself, and it wouldn't make a bit of difference to him. He'd stay with me."

"What is the truth?"

The old woman must have decided that I posed no threat. "I couldn't give this up," she said, gesturing to the world around her with a single raised finger. "Not the smallest part of it."

I looked to Skiles for some sign that he'd heard her, but he was gone.

Eleven

I didn't see Skiles during my return trip to the study or in the room itself when I looked in briefly on my way to the front door. I wasn't too concerned by that. We'd established a pattern, he and I. He left me places, I found my way out, and he got there first. Sure enough, when I'd followed the front walk to the little cobblestoned parking area, Skiles was waiting for me.

He was resting against the side of my car, head bowed. "What made you ask her that?"

He'd already heard what passed for my evidence. I decided we would discuss something else. "I just tried to figure out what you'd brought me here to ask her."

Skiles looked up from the pavement. "Brought you here?"

"Maybe I should say lured me here. You knew I'd be back for my car, so you set a trap for me. You tossed your own cabin. That's why my unlocked car wasn't touched and why no really substantial damage was done. It was all just for show, with one vivid exception: the kicked-in front door. That made the rest work. But the real bait was the index card you left in the old bread box where I'd found the Montaigne. You knew I'd open that again if I did nothing else. You weren't counting on Tim Gleason calling in the cops and the cops nabbing me. You thought I'd get your background from my law firm contacts or Lisk. Either way, I'd be calling on your sister sooner or later."

Skiles had gone back to counting the cobbles. "Why would I do such a crazy thing?"

"Because you knew your sister wanted you back here and you weren't sure you wanted to stay with her. You've always secretly suspected that she was the one who turned you in to the police. You wanted to know for sure. You wanted an out."

"You think I have one now?"

I noticed that he'd lost his paisley tie. "You know you do," I said. "You don't owe your sister any more sacrifices."

"I'm not sure I agree with you, Owen. I think I may have hurt Joan worse than she ever hurt me. Ruined her life, maybe."

"How?"

"By taking the blame for her husband's sins and leaving her to live out her empty days. Who knows how she might have responded, how she might have changed if all this had been yanked from under her.

"That was the turning point for me: the day I lost everything. That's when I really started to live. Sure I saw prison as a noble sacrifice, but I knew even then—down deep knew—that it was also my escape. Eva Lisk had given me a way out of a life I hated, or so I thought. It was really Joan who did it. I owe her for that."

"So send her a check every month like you've been doing for Lisk."

"Figured that out, too, have you?"

"Why did you use your sister's name?"

"So Eva would take the money. She hated Jim Skiles. Joan Bellaby was just a name to her. Eva was in a bad spot, a woman raising a kid alone back in the fifties. Alex gave me some money when I was paroled. Conscience money. I didn't need it myself, so I put it to good use. Had a friend here in Philly keep tabs on her and her baby. Did you happen to see a picture of Eva's daughter when you were by there? Vera?"

"No," I said.

He stood up and brushed at the fender of the Ghia, though his suit pants had gotten the worst of the exchange. "Too bad. I've always wanted to know what she looked like, whether she was happy. Thought you might have noticed a picture. You're a noticing kind of man."

"Is that why you picked me for this?"

He laughed his old cackly laugh. "You were more or less born for the job, Owen. Remember what I said about you back at the cabin? You'd disbelieve nine stories out of ten. That's what I needed, a doubter, a questioner.

"Besides, you'd gotten me into this mess in the first place, by inspiring me to call Joan. Only right you should get me out again. Be honest. You crossed the Delaware to rescue me, didn't you? Well, you did it. You saved me, and I thank you for it."

"So you're going back to the Pines?"

"If the Pineys will have me. The truth about me will have gotten around pretty generally by now. I can thank the sheriff and Tim Gleason for that."

"And me," I said.

"Still, that could be for the best. I was Gimbel and Bellaby's man once. After that I was the property of the state of Pennsylvania. Then for a long time I was a story I'd made up. Now maybe I can just be me. Maybe. 'The greatest thing in the world is to know how to belong to oneself.' Our old friend Montaigne said that. Something for you to remember, Owen." He held out his hand.

"I'll try," I said.

THE TRIPLE SCORE

One

I was seven hours into an eight-hour shift. My back hurt from standing. My eyes burned from cigarette smoke. The vibration from the blenders I was using to grind ice had loosened the fillings in my teeth. Or maybe having to grind so much ice was causing me to grind my teeth as well. I'd made so many margaritas that morning I was developing an accent. The salt was raising my blood pressure. I was in danger of contracting lime disease. Take your pick.

When the lady in the ancient, fur-collared coat sat down and ordered a sweet Manhattan, I was grateful for the change of pace. And for having a real, live customer for once. Most of my customers were out on the casino floor, starting the new year off the way they'd ended the old year, by giving their money away. They sent their orders in to me via waitresses who all seemed to be pushing tequila and fruit juice, frozen.

I'd seen the Manhattan lady before, but I couldn't place her, which piqued my curiosity. Not that it ever needed much piquing. The lady herself provided more than enough. She was past sixty, but how far past was anybody's guess. Her thin hair was dyed a reddish brown, almost the same color as the spots on the backs of her large hands. Her friendly eyes—also large—had blue irises that were clouded slightly. She had a broad, flat nose, and there were spaces between her very white teeth.

She was alone, particularly alone, which wasn't that unusual in a casino on New Year's Day. It didn't seem right for her, though, and that impression helped me place her about the time I was delivering her second drink.

She was a former customer of mine, someone who'd been in the bar the previous Thanksgiving Day, when I'd been working another holiday shift as a favor to the bartenders who had families. The woman had sat on the same stool, wearing the same coat and the same expression: wistful sadness.

When I said, "Hello again," to show that I remembered her, she took up our previous conversation as though we'd last spoken the day before.

"I've found a new one," she said.

"A new what?" I asked.

"Family," she said. "You remember. I told you I'd lost my family the last time we spoke."

I did remember. She'd been looking around the casino expectantly that day, searching the crowd. I'd asked her if she'd lost something. It had been a silly question, even for me, a casino being a place where most people lose things. She'd answered me patiently and politely, telling me she'd lost her family. Just that. No explanation. No tears, either, which the holidays and sweet Manhattans often produce. She'd just said it and left.

Now she was back. "A family is very important, you know," she said. "Do you mind if I ask your name?"

"It's Owen," I said. "Owen Keane."

"How nice. My name is Ethel Peters. Mrs. Frank Peters. My late husband never went by Francis, only Frank.

"As I was saying, Owen, a family is important. It keeps you looking outwardly. Do you know what I mean? The great danger is looking inwardly too much. If you're alone, that is. Are you married, Owen?"

"No," I said.

"You have a girlfriend, though. I thought so. Then you know what I'm trying to say. I'm sure she keeps you looking outwardly."

Actually, she kept me looking dazed, but we weren't there to discuss my problems.

Ethel checked her watch and then pushed her empty glass across to me. "Perhaps one more," she said.

I brought her another drink, a double if you went by maraschino syrup. She sipped it and nodded her head appreciatively. "If you look inwardly too much, you can get swallowed up by your problems and fears. There's no future in that."

I agreed that there wasn't.

"When Frank was alive and the kids were at home, I never had two minutes back to back for sinking into my own problems. Everyone was drawing me out of myself all the time. 'Look over here! Watch this! Help me! Listen to me!' "

Ethel gave every command a different voice, which made me smile. Her own smile dimmed a little with each impersonation. She looked at the empty stools on either side of her and blinked.

"Tell me about your new family," I said.

"It's not a real family," she said, smiling again. "Not a traditional one, I mean. It's the kind you see on television nowadays, where people band together with friends and coworkers and organize their own families because they don't have the old-fashioned kind. You know the shows I mean, like the one that's set in the bar where everybody knows everyone else. Being in your bar makes me think of that show."

I was lucky if I knew the waitresses in my bar on any given shift, but I nodded encouragingly.

"My new family is like that," Ethel said. "People of all backgrounds and ages. From all faiths, too, although we've put those differences behind us. We meet in a church, but we're not a religion. We're more of a spiritual community, but we don't discuss beliefs. We find that tolerance is so much easier if no one actually mentions their beliefs. We talk instead about the things that worry us and frighten us. Listening to other people's problems gets you looking outwardly in a hurry."

I'd found that to be true enough, at least at first. It had been my experience, though, that other people's troubles had a way of becoming my own.

I wanted to hear more about Ethel's spiritual community, but when she checked her watch for a third time, she reached for her shoulder bag. From it she took a purse and from that a hundred dollar bill. She handed the bill to me, but kept on searching.

"I thought I had something smaller," she said.

The C-note was new, but it had already been disfigured. To the right of Franklin's portrait, someone had written "Happy Birthday" in lavender ink.

"Here we go," Ethel said, pulling a twenty from the bottom of the purse. "Trade you."

I gave her back the hundred and took the twenty to the register to get her change. She was applying a fresh coat of red lipstick when I got back and didn't glance up from her mirror.

When I passed her spot at the bar again, she was gone. She'd left a single dollar behind. It was also a new bill, but it didn't say "Happy Birthday" or "Happy New Year" or anything else.

Two

When my shift ended, I made my way out through the casino itself, using it as a shortcut to the boardwalk. I disguised myself by buttoning up my trench coat and cinching it at the waist. Only my black pants and shoes, the white collar of my uniform shirt, and my black bow tie showed, which made it possible for me to pass as a New Year's Eve reveler still wearing his tuxedo. Or so I hoped, as I had no desire to field drink orders. It would certainly have helped the disguise if all the buttons on my trench coat had matched.

The main casino wasn't as crowded as I'd expected. The gamblers were changing shifts, too, I decided. The all-nighters were starting to filter out, and the day crew was just coming in. I passed row after glittering row of slot machines, at least half of them idle. By noon there wouldn't be a vacant seat. A high roller had drawn a crowd at one of the crap tables. He drew me, too, for as long as it took him to miss his point. Then I wandered on, past roulette wheels and blackjack tables, most of them doing modest business.

One blackjack table was doing a little better. The dealer was someone I knew, a young woman named Theresa Rendeja. She'd been a member of my employee orientation class when I'd hired on at the casino. Theresa was a dark-haired, pretty girl, but what had stuck with me most about her was her extreme shyness. I'd wondered how she would do at a job that required so much human and very nearly human interaction.

When I paused to watch her table, it wasn't to evaluate how Theresa was handling her shyness. It was because the last empty spot at the table had been taken by a woman in an ancient cloth coat with a fur collar. I circled around behind Theresa to make sure that the newcomer was really Ethel Peters. I ended up in a knot of people who were gathered around a big six wheel that stood behind the blackjack table. Beyond the wheel and just to the left of Theresa's slender back was the woman who had been drinking in my bar an hour earlier. Everything about her was the same except her expression. Her wistful sadness had been replaced by icy concentration.

The other players at the table, one other woman and three men, watched with the same intensity as Theresa prepared to "wash the cards." In striking contrast were the attitudes of two men who flanked the table. Both ignored Theresa as she spread five blue-backed card decks out face down for the initial shuffle, the "chemmy shuffle," the process of scattering and then gathering up the cards.

I followed the gaze of the man standing to the left of the table, a short, heavyset guy with a toupee that had surely come from the Graceland souvenir shop. He was looking in the direction of one of the security teams that patrolled the casino floor. I checked the man on the right, a taller guy in a cowboy hat. He seemed to be watching the pit boss of the blackjack area, a woman standing a few tables a way. The cowboy was doing more than watching the pit boss, I realized. He was keeping himself between the woman and Theresa, blocking the boss's view of the dealer.

Something was going to happen at Theresa's table. The flanking men were lookouts, working with one of the players. I wanted to step forward and warn Theresa, but I knew if I did, nothing would happen. The lookouts would just walk away. The confederate would never reveal himself, and I would never get to see his play. So I hesitated, fatally.

Theresa finished the chemmy shuffle and divided the cards into five piles of roughly equal height. She performed an expert riffle shuffle on each pile and then stacked them all together. Then she produced a single yellow card, which she pushed across the table to Ethel. It was the cut card, the card a player inserted into the giant deck to indicate to the dealer where the stacked cards should be cut. Once they were cut and in the shoe, the game could begin.

Ethel's hands were at her sides, out of sight. She raised her right hand and extended it across the table. She didn't pick up the cut card. She couldn't have. Her large hand already held a stack of cards equal in height to the ones Theresa had shuffled. Ethel placed the blue stack next to Theresa's waiting shoe. Then she took the shuffled deck and dropped it into her shoulder bag. Her movements were quick and sure, so quick that she'd finished before I'd made sense of what I'd seen.

I'd identified the confederate at the table. It was the sweet old lady who had rattled on to me about her families, old and new. But that wasn't the news flash that froze me in place. Theresa had stood there and watched while the decks were switched. Theresa was in on it, too. She was slipping the loaded deck into the shoe as I stared on.

Before she finished, Ethel turned and left the table. One of the lookouts, the short, fat Elvis, was also melting into the crowd. The cowboy had already gone. As I stood fixed to the floor, Ethel's place was taken by a man in aviator's sunglasses and a matching leather jacket. His arrival seemed to signal the start of play. I watched Theresa deal the first card to prove to myself that she'd really go through with it. Then I took off after Ethel.

I'd given her a healthy head start, but I didn't think I'd have any problem catching her. I'd forgotten that little old ladies make up a significant percentage of the traffic in a Jersey casino. I spotted false Ethels all the way to the boardwalk but never the real one. On my way back to Theresa's table, I checked the bars and scanned the rows of slot machines and never saw the right fur-collared coat.

At the table I joined a small group of gawkers who were whispering about the play of the man in the aviator glasses. The flyer's pile of chips had more than doubled in the time I'd been gone. As I watched, he doubled it again, standing pat with hands of seventeen, sixteen, and eighteen and forcing Theresa to break three times in succession.

Theresa was playing strictly according to her dealer training. There was no reason for her to cheat now. The stacked deck insured that her bad luck would be as odds defying as the flyer's good luck. The blackjack pit boss came up beside me to watch the play. Watching was all she could do as the house lost hand after hand. One word from me, though, and the game would be over. I watched Theresa, her dark eyes almost black against her pale skin, and said nothing.

Three

I had the next day off, my reward for working the holiday, but I drove down to the casino just the same. When I got there, I rode the employee elevator up into the casino offices and called on a friend in the security department.

Robert Guineri wasn't really a friend. He was a customer, like Ethel Peters, a dry Martini drinker who admired the way I could wave a vermouth bottle over a shaker of gin without actually pouring any in. We'd discovered a shared interest—crime—and he'd invited me more than once to visit his office to watch his collection of casino surveillance tapes.

Guineri was a generously laid out man who liked to dress in comfortable clothes woven in man-made fibers, materials that would outlast his arteries by a generation, as he liked to joke. I found him seated in his small cubicle with a green-barred computer printout spread on the desk before him. He was leaning over it, one hand supporting his head and the other shielding his eyes from the glare of the fluorescent lights in the ceiling.

I tapped on the frame of his open door, and the way he started told me he'd been asleep.

"Lay off that banging, damn you," he said when he'd settled himself. He peered at me through his thick glasses, whose black plastic frames were as fashionable as his suit.

"Oh, it's you," he said. "Owen Keane, student of crime. This is a coincidence. I was just thinking of stepping down to your office to get a little pick-me-up. You don't happen to have something medicinal on you by any chance?"

"You're thinking of a St. Bernard," I said. "I'm just a bartender. Enjoy the holiday?"

"I blew past enjoyment the night before last. Kept on going, too, right through exhilaration, higher consciousness, and, finally, unconsciousness. What can I do for you?"

I told him I'd come to see the tapes he'd mentioned, the ones that showed con artists at work.

"There's an idea. I've been trying to think of something painless I could do that would pass for work. Pull up a chair while I find a tape. If my boss should stop by, you're a visiting auditor from the Cayman Islands, come to study at the feet of the master. Lucky for us, you dress like an auditor."

"Thanks," I said, although "ouch" would also have worked.

There was a small television on the credenza behind Guineri's desk. It had an even smaller VCR built into its base. The auditor selected a tape from a shelf full of tapes and popped it into the machine. The title "Casino Fraud" appeared on the screen.

Guineri settled back in his chair. "I use this in a lecture I give at our conventions. Legalized gambling is spreading so quickly, there's a real training gap in the security field. These clips are from casinos here in Atlantic City and in Vegas. We start off with slot machine tampering."

We started with slots and stayed with them for a long time. I watched what seemed like an hour of fuzzy, black-and-white video of slot machines being drilled, poked, and even dismantled. The video was enlivened by Guineri's running commentary.

"See that? He stuck a magnet on the side of the machine. His partner was supposed to be blocking the view, but the camera picked it up. These guys often work with partners who do double duty as lookouts and screens."

I sat and watched and asked a question once in a while. The next segment of the tape featured dealers and croupiers palming chips.

"Their hands are never supposed to be out of sight," Guineri said. A dealer isn't supposed to reach for a Kleenex or scratch himself without first flashing his open hands to the camera to show that they're empty. Watch this guy. He's palmed a chip. Now he's going to hitch up his pants. Did you see it? He stuck the chip in his waistband."

Guineri patted his stomach. "If I were to turn this waist of mine to crime, what a career I could have."

Several of the clips ended with security teams showing up to lead crooked employees away. "Got you," Guineri said after one of these mini dramas. "Go directly to jail, baby. I love to see these goombahs go down."

I didn't feel like celebrating. I'd just about given up hope that I'd learn something useful. Then the picture switched to an overhead view of a blackjack table. None of the foreshortened figures around the table was recognizable, but their arrangement was very familiar. I'd seen the same grouping at Theresa's table the day before.

"Here's something special," Guineri said. "Everyone you see in this shot is in on it, dealer, players, and the two screens. They're going to substitute a shoeload of cards. The lookouts have a signal for all clear. I think it's when they have their arms crossed. Yeah. See? Here comes the switch. The bald guy's going to do it. The new deck—we call it a 'cooler'—comes out of his pocket; the old deck goes into his pocket. Bang. Now chrome dome hustles the legit deck out of the casino. That's one of the beauty parts of this scam. By the time play starts, all the evidence is gone. The lookouts step away. New players—also bad guys—step in, and the casino gets reamed."

"What about the camera?" I asked. "They didn't even try to block the view of the camera."

"They couldn't. So they took their chances. The real pros know it isn't much of a risk. It's impossible for the people monitoring the cameras to see everything at once. Hell, the cameras don't even see everything. We try to convince our employees that they do, but it's a bluff."

"How is it the camera caught those guys? Luck?"

"No, a tip. The security people got word that a scam was going to go down. They knew the dealer involved, so they had a camera zeroed in on his table. None of those grifters made it out of the casino."

"Who were they?"

Guineri shrugged. "Small-timers. A group of no names who came together for this one play. 'Gypsies,' some of them, which is our slang for bad guys who travel around from casino to casino. A couple were probably local talent. That tape was shot in Vegas, where there's no shortage of indigenous grifters. A local connection is important. You've got to convince a dealer to go along, which generally takes some time and some smoozing. Sometimes all it takes is a wad of money. Human nature sucks, Owen."

"Where do they get the cards?"

"That's the real challenge. As you may know, our security department keeps logs of the number of new decks distributed to each table and the used decks turned back in. The numbers have to match. And the number of used decks has to match the number of decks destroyed. We drill holes through our old decks. Sometimes a security guy will go bad and finagle with the logs so he can slip out enough decks to sell. The other potential source is the company out in Nevada that prints the cards. They're supposed to have their own controls, but from what I hear, their system is looser than a goose's bowels.

"It's an evil world, Owen. Take it from a professional. Our work is founded on the premise that the average person is a crime waiting to happen. I wish I could say it's a false assumption."

"So do I," I said.

Four

Theresa was that rare thing, a casino worker who actually lived in Atlantic City. Most weren't making enough money to live there, or they were making too much. Atlantic City's housing fell into two categories, the luxurious and the leaning. Theresa's apartment building, the Bell Street Arms, was leaning, but only slightly. It stood across the street from a public housing project, buildings that were much newer but in no better shape. The project was alive, though, with human sound: music, babies, voices, laughter. The Bell Street Arms was dead in comparison.

I'd actually been to Theresa's apartment before, for the going-away party of a mutual friend, another casino bartender named Donna. The lost Donna was the basis of my approach to Theresa. When she answered my call on the tinny front-door intercom, I gave my name and told her I'd come to ask for news of our friend.

Theresa said, "Sure," and buzzed me in.

Her apartment was on the second floor. By the time I'd climbed the flight of stairs, I'd amended my master plan. I'd offer to buy Theresa a cup of coffee at a diner I'd spotted when I'd parked my car. That might sound better to her than letting a man she barely knew into her apartment.

When Theresa opened the door—without first setting the security chain—I made the suggestion.

She looked backward over her shoulder. "That would be nice, Owen. The thing is, I'm waiting for a phone call. You come in, and I'll make you a cup of coffee."

The little apartment was as neat as I remembered, and as light on furniture. The living room—a sofa, throw pillows, and a standing lamp—opened directly onto a dining area that opened directly onto the kitchen. The dining room was furnished with a card table and four chairs. There was a game board set up on the table, a Scrabble board. On opposing sides of the board stood two little, wooden racks holding lettered tiles. Several words had been laid out, crossword style, on the board.

"The game break up early last night?" I asked.

Theresa looked over from the sink where she was filling a kettle. "No. I was just practicing this morning to pass the time."

"I've never heard of anyone practicing Scrabble," I said.

Theresa smiled. It might have been her first of the day. "You've probably never heard of Scrabble tournaments, either," she said. "Or Scrabble clubs."

I had to own up.

"I've never played in a real tournament," Theresa said, "but I belong to a club here in town. We play our own little tournament every week. It's fun."

"A little slower than blackjack," I said.

"Yes," Theresa said, and her smile faded away.

She changed the subject on me, telling me all the news about Donna, which was that she'd abandoned bartending for barber college. Stylist school, Theresa called it.

"She says she already has the hard part down, which is being a good listener. Do you ever get tired of listening to other people's troubles, Owen?"

I said I didn't, but I must not have sounded sincere, because Theresa didn't take advantage of the implicit offer.

She'd finished making the coffee by then. We sat down at the card table, using the chairs that had the racks of Scrabble pieces in front of them. Theresa had run out of Donna stories and didn't have much else to say. I had plenty to say, but I couldn't bring myself to blurt it out. I spotted a framed portrait on a shelf behind Theresa's head. Given their proximity, the resemblance between the woman and the young man in the photograph was impossible to miss.

"Your brother?" I asked.

"Yes," Theresa said, looking not at the portrait, but at the kitchen phone. "He lives in Pleasantville, across the bay. He goes to college. He's studying to be an artist."

"I have a friend who paints," I said to keep the conversation going.

"It's very hard work," Theresa said. "But it's very important work, too."

"Yes," I said.

"Not like what I do. I'm very proud of Raul."

She drained the hot liquid from her cup in a series of determined gulps. It was the signal for me to drink up and go.

To extend my stay, I asked, "How do you play two racks of tiles at once? Doesn't knowing what's in the second rack influence your play?"

"I don't know all the tiles in the other rack," Theresa said, relaxing a little. "In a normal game, you draw new tiles as soon as you've made a play. When you're practicing, you wait to draw the tiles until after you've played from the other rack."

When she'd finished explaining, she pretended to drink from her empty cup by way of handing me my hat. I took a long, slow drink of coffee and said, "Is anything worrying you, Theresa?"

"No," she said, as pale now as yesterday. "What makes you ask that?"

"I was in the casino yesterday after my shift. I saw you at your table." The dark eyes nailed me, and I faltered. "You looked ... wrung out."

"It's the holidays, Owen. Everybody looks tired after the holidays."

"So there's nothing wrong? Nothing I can help you with?"

Theresa stared at me for a long time. "You can help me finish this game," she finally said. "I'm tired of playing alone."

I said okay. I had visions of laying out some word on the board that would unlock her secret. "Bunko," maybe, or "confess." But coming up with the right word at the right time had never been a talent of mine. I couldn't even make small talk with Theresa while the game was on. She played with the concentration of a chess master, answering my questions with a single word when she answered at all.

The last word she played cleared all seven tiles from her rack. "Bingo," she said. "I made bingo, Owen. That's what we call it when you use seven tiles on your last play. I've never done it before. And it's a triple word score. Wow. I'm so glad there was someone here to see it."

I was glad, too, her joy making me forget my errand for a moment. Then I looked down at the word she'd grafted onto "hare," my previous play. She'd used my *H* and her seven letters to spell out "hopeless."

Five

When I left Theresa's apartment, I thought I'd finished with her mystery. As anxious as I was to help her, I wouldn't force a confession out of her; there'd be no point in that. And I'd never turn her in. The casino owners' loss meant even less to me than it did to their bottom line.

I went to work at my normal time the next day, driving down from Mystic Island in a steady rain that was just on the friendly side of sleet. The rain had made a ghost town of the boardwalk and its shops and brought the gulls up from the beach. I scattered noisy groups of them as I made my solitary passage.

The crowd inside the casino was small, which I understood, given the weather. The employees I passed on my way in were unsmiling and distracted, which I didn't understand. In the lounge next to the employee locker room, two women were crying, one of them uncontrollably. The other, a waitress I knew named Chastine, sobbed at a more measured pace. It occurred to me that she was only crying to keep the first woman company.

"Keane," Chastine said. "Have you heard? Theresa Rendeja was killed. Murdered."

I sat down in a red plush chair, wet trench coat and all.

Chastine nodded as though I'd spoken. "I know," she said. "None of us can believe it either. Everybody liked Theresa. She was quiet but sweet. Real sweet."

That sketch was vivid enough to provoke renewed crying from the other woman. I asked, "When?"

"Last night sometime. One of her neighbors heard the noise and called the cops. That's all we know."

I pictured Theresa as I'd last seen her, distracted even during our good-byes by the possibility the phone would ring. "I wonder if her brother knows," I said.

"Raul," Chastine said and put a hand to her mouth. "He'll be totaled. They were really close. Theresa was putting him through school. Did you know that?"

I shook my head.

"She was so proud of him. He's a writer. Gonna be a writer."

"A writer?" I asked.

"A book writer," Chastine said.

"An author," the other woman corrected between sobs.

"Marla in personnel will know Raul's phone number," Chastine said. "I'll go ask her."

"Me, too," the crying woman said.

As they left, Chastine handed me a copy of the morning *Post*, folded down to the size of a paperback. The story on Theresa was smaller still. It was little more than a bulletin rushed into the early edition, and it didn't tell me any more than the sobbing waitresses had, not even how Theresa had been killed. I was grateful for that omission.

Six

I hung my coat in my locker and went out to my station. The bar was already busy, but not busy enough to keep Theresa out of my mind. If there was a connection between what I'd seen her do at the blackjack table and her murder, then what I'd done about what I'd seen—nothing— was also connected to her death. I'd had the chance to step between the cause and effect of Theresa's end, and I hadn't taken it. No amount of measuring and mixing could pull my mind from that.

I was so busy working myself over that I didn't notice Robert Guineri until he was settling himself on his stool. The security man was wearing the same gray polyester suit he'd been sleeping in the day before, but he'd dressed it up with a hot pink shirt and tie.

"A Martini, Owen," he said. "Rocks. Extra, extra, dry."

"Should you be drinking during business hours?"

"I've got that all worked out," Guineri said. "If anybody pimps me about it, I'm going to say that I bought the drink as a cover, that I was really down in the bar quizzing a suspect."

"Who?" I asked, filling the empty spaces in a glass of ice with gin.

"You."

I checked the filling a little past the rim of the glass. "Of what am I suspected?"

Guineri grunted. "Tight-assed grammar. You're also suspected of being involved in a murder. And don't ask by whom. By me."

I managed to skewer two olives with a single thrust of a plastic rapier. I dropped the victims into the glass and blotted up the displaced gin with my bar towel. "Sounds like you've already interviewed several bartenders this morning."

Guineri grabbed the drink and grunted again. "Don't I wish. I've been on the phone with a policeman friend of mine. He's on the county's Major Crimes Unit. Knew all about the Rendeja killing."

"Why did he call you?"

"I called him. It was after I did a little checking up on Rendeja, which was after I read the *Post* story about her. That story made me want to know if there was anything unusual about her from a humble security man's point of view. Turns out her table got burned big on New Year's Day."

"That happens," I said.

"Yes, it does. But the dealer involved doesn't often end up beaten to death."

Beaten to death, I repeated to myself. I said, "Coincidence?"

"I hate coincidences. Here's one that really bugs me. The morning after Rendeja's big loss, you showed up in my office to watch the tape on casino fraud I offered to show you months ago. You were only politely interested until we got to the section on blackjack fraud. Then you sat up and took notice."

"It was the camera work," I said.

Guineri studied me. His thick glasses, behind which his eyes were pale blurs, should have made it a painless procedure. Instead, I felt I was being magnified, that every hair on my guilty head was standing out like a tree trunk.

"My friend the cop told me something interesting," Guineri said. "The murder was reported by Rendeja's downstairs neighbor. The neighbor is a busybody. He saw a man enter the building yesterday evening, a man in leather with a shaved head. He took special notice of this stranger because he couldn't remember hearing anybody buzz him in.

"A little while later, the busybody saw Rendeja enter the building. That got his attention, too, because Rendeja usually stayed out late on Tuesday evenings. Then he heard the sounds of a fight and called the police. They got there too late."

Guineri tried to lean his bulk over the bar. "Now for the interesting part. The nosy neighbor remembered another visitor from earlier in the day, a guy he was pretty sure ended up in Rendeja's apartment. He was a thin guy in an old trench coat. Had a hangdog expression on his face, the neighbor said, like a pallbearer at his own funeral. Sound like anybody we know?"

I was spared the job of lying by my supervisor, Manny. He yelled my name from the other side of the bar, where unhappy waitresses were stacking up like planes over a foggy airport.

Guineri hauled himself off his stool. "I'm going up to study the surveillance tapes from New Year's Day," he said. "If I see any interesting camera work, I'll send for you."

Seven

As soon as the bar traffic thinned, I told Manny I was going home sick. He didn't like it, and I didn't care. I didn't think much of my chances of collecting a casino pension. Not if Guineri spotted me standing near Theresa's table in the surveillance video. Just staying out of jail might be a challenge then.

On my way out of the casino, I tracked down Chastine, the waitress friend of Theresa's. I asked her if she'd managed to get Raul Rendeja's phone number.

"No," she said. "Personnel didn't have it. They didn't have a number for any of Theresa's family. That's so sad."

"I just heard something else," I said. "Theresa wasn't supposed to be home last night. Was she scheduled to work?"

"Not that I know of," Chastine said. "If she left work early, the gossips around here would know about it."

I tried to remember the rest of the gossip Guineri had passed on. "What I heard was, she was usually out on Tuesday nights."

"Oh," Chastine said. "I bet it was that club she belonged to."

"The Scrabble club?"

"Yeah. I couldn't remember the name of the game they play, Scrabble. Theresa was really into that club. I think it was the people she liked the most, being around the people. Her not having much family, you can understand that. Something like a club gets to be family."

I almost said "bingo," but that echo of Theresa caught in my throat. Chastine had given me the connection I should have made in Theresa's apartment. "Do you know where the club meets?" I asked.

"No. Except that it was a place you wouldn't expect. What was it now?"

I thought back to what Ethel Peters had told me about her substitute family, the spiritual community that never discussed beliefs. "A church?"

"Yeah, a church. That's right. But I don't know which church, except that it's somewhere here on the island."

Eight

I traded some bills for quarters at one of the change stations near the slot machines. Then I went out onto the rain-swept boardwalk to a phone booth that had had an intact directory the last time I checked.

The book was still here. First I looked for a name I'd been given in the bar on New Year's Day: Ethel Peters. I didn't find it. There was no listing for a Scrabble club either. I called a game store in the Pleasantville Mall and asked the kid who answered about Scrabble clubs. He asked me if I didn't mean Dungeons and Dragons clubs and laughed.

That left Plan C, which was calling every church in the phone book. Midway through the list, I spoke with the Reverend Hubert Miller of Sunrise United Methodist Church on Indiana Avenue.

"Yes," Reverend Miller said in response to my standard question. "We're the Scrabble church. The club meets on Tuesday nights in our basement."

I asked for the name of the club president or secretary.

"I guess they're both me. I don't just provide space for the club. I actually got it going."

I asked him to stay put and then drove over to Indiana Avenue. If it hadn't been for the rain, I would have run; the church was that close.

Sunrise United Methodist was bigger than I'd pictured. It was a stone building with a crenulated tower in place of a steeple. The big black double doors at the top of its stone steps were locked. I found an open door, also black, on the side of the church and down a flight. Next to the door was a glass-enclosed bulletin board. It contained fliers for a number of meetings: a divorced parents support group, a retirement planning seminar, a gamblers anonymous chapter, and even a worship service of sorts. It was a winter solstice service, which was to feature "communal free movement with percussion."

Hubert Miller was seated in a small office just inside the door. It was a tiny office, given the size of his church. He had a brown beard, sandy hair, and a beak of a nose still red from the outside air. The half of him that showed above the desk was wearing a cable knit sweater. A dripping yellow rain jacket was draped across the room's only visitor chair.

"Throw it over here," Miller said of the jacket. "You the Scrabble guy?"

The scrabbled guy, I thought, but I didn't feel up to making even that pale joke. Miller, in contrast, was in a great mood.

"It's a very underrated game," he said. "I think of it as full-contact crosswords, but it also has its contemplative, strategic side. It's like chess for right-brained people."

He couldn't have heard the news about Theresa Rendeja. Even if he'd only known her casually, hearing she was dead would have damped him down considerably. The secret of his happy ignorance lay on the desktop, the new home of the yellow rain slicker. Sticking out from beneath the jacket was today's *Atlantic City Post*, still in the plastic sleeve some thoughtful paperboy had used to keep it dry.

To test my deduction, I said, "A friend of mine, Theresa Rendeja, told me about the club."

"Ah, yes, Theresa. She's come along quite a bit as a player. And as a member of the group. She's still too dark and quiet, but she's made progress."

"Do you award points for socializing?"

"Not in our little tournaments. But I keep a running tally in my head. I'm not here to promote a particular board game, after all. My job is to help people, even if all I can do for them is get them away from their worries one night a week."

"I noticed the fliers posted by the door," I said.

"They're not half of what we're into. Anything to keep the franchise open, that's my motto. Like most shore churches, Sunrise never had that big a year-round congregation. It was designed to accommodate the summer crowds. That was seventy years ago. Nowadays most tourists are worshipping at those chrome and glass cathedrals along the boardwalk. So I do what I can to keep the facility in use."

Miller was a man who could talk and observe at the same time. "You're not really interested in Scrabble, are you?" he said.

"No," I said. "I'm interested in information. I need the name and address of a woman Theresa met through your club. The woman is about sixty, with thinning, reddish hair. She's used the name Ethel Peters, but it's probably an alias."

"What's this all about? Why don't you ask Theresa about this woman? You're not some possessive boyfriend, are you? You're not jealous of a casual friendship Theresa made? Is that what's been bothering her lately? Have you been giving her grief about belonging to a silly club?"

"I'm not Theresa's boyfriend. We worked at the same casino. Theresa took part in a plan to rip the casino off. I think the woman she met in your club got her involved in it."

"That's impossible. Theresa? Wait a minute. You said she worked at the casino. Did she get canned? Is that why she was so down last night?"

"No," I said. "Do you know why she left here early?"

"She seemed anxious. Jumpy. And then Ethel didn't show up." Miller paused to recollect. "That's what Theresa was waiting for. I couldn't put my finger on it last night. She was waiting for Ethel."

"Ethel Peters?"

"That's not the last name she gave me. Did Ethel take part in this scam?"

"Yes," I said.

"God help her. She was part of our gamblers anonymous group, too. That's why she first came to Sunrise. I thought she was doing well."

"What's her last name?"

"How are you involved? If what you've told me is true, isn't it a job for the fraud squad?"

"No," I said, "the homicide squad."

I extracted Miller's *Post* from beneath his jacket and then from its plastic wrapper. I laid it flat on the desk and pointed to the little story on the bottom of page one. Miller read it in the time it took him to bow his head and raise it again.

"I think Theresa's murder may have something to do with the casino rip-off," I said. "I think Ethel knows the connection."

"Shouldn't you be telling that to the police?" Miller asked.

"You tell them, after you've given me Ethel's name."

"It's Taylor. She lives in Brigantine."

Nine

Brigantine occupied the barrier island north of Atlantic City. It was serviced by a single causeway near Atlantic City's marina district, a setup that created constant traffic jams but gave Brigantine a sense of isolation few Jersey shore towns possessed.

Traffic wasn't a problem on this particular rainy January morning. I drove north on Brigantine Boulevard with marshland on my left and slightly drier beach property on my right. Thanks to its proximity to Atlantic City, Brigantine had always been less a resort than a bedroom community, a quality that had only been intensified by legalized gambling. That morning, Brigantine reminded me of Hamilton, one of the neighbors of my hometown, Trenton: streets of little homes, Italian restaurants, and Catholic churches somehow lifted bodily from suburbia and set down on the edge of the dunes.

The address Hubert Miller had given me was in a block of nearly identical bayside homes called Mulliner Street. The buildings made me think of the little plastic houses from a Monopoly set, jammed into a long row in anticipation of a trade up to a plastic hotel. Some kind of trade was long overdue for most of the houses on Mulliner. They had a deserted, defeated look that was the temporary effect of the ugly day magnifying the permanent problem of an undignified old age.

Ethel Taylor's house had at least been painted recently. Its board and batten siding was a sage green that stood out dramatically among all the weathered, peeling white. Ethel answered her door so promptly that I thought for a second the Reverend Miller had called to warn her of my visit. I tossed that deduction on the ash heap when Ethel failed to recognize me. Whoever she was expecting, it wasn't her favorite bartender.

"Yes?" she said, blinking at the gray, wet day. Her head was bobbing slightly as though she were on the verge of sleep, falling forward slowly and then jerking back.

I told her my name. I added the name of my casino to prod her memory. "We spoke on New Year's Day."

"New Year's Day?" Ethel repeated warily. This time I got a whiff of bourbon.

"I've come to talk to you about Theresa Rendeja."

Ethel asked, "Who?" Then her rheumy eyes betrayed her, spilling tears that ran down her immobile face. She reached up to touch them and then said, "You'd better come in."

The darkly papered front room overflowed with furniture, but it didn't look like Ethel's furniture. It was new and cheap, a sofa, a love seat and chairs with imitation wood frames and gaudy, removable cushions that looked tightly stuffed but turned out to be largely filled with air. Between Ethel's sofa and my chair was a coffee table made of the same thinly disguised pressboard. On it was an empty juice glass and a bottle of Maker's Mark. There wasn't maraschino cherry in sight.

As she sat down, Ethel filled the glass. Before the sofa had stopped squeaking, she'd drunk off a third of the bourbon. Her head was still doing its little nodding dance. I figured I had about five minutes of her attention, no more.

"You've heard about Theresa," I said.

"Read about it in the *Post*," Ethel said. "First thing this morning. I've been crying ever since. How did you know that Theresa and I were ... acquainted?"

"I was on the casino floor when you passed Theresa the stacked deck."

I thought Ethel would kill a little time denying that, but she only said, "How did you find me?"

"Reverend Miller gave me your address."

Ethel didn't ask how I'd found my way to Miller. She cut right to the point as though our positions were reversed and she was afraid I'd shortly pass out on her. "What do you want?"

"I want to know who killed Theresa and why."

"Why do you think I can tell you?"

"Because I think there's a connection between the scam you dragged Theresa into and her murder. There has to be."

"There isn't," Ethel said. "I mean, there's a connection, but it's not an explanation. None of us, the people involved in the switch, would hurt a hair on Theresa's head. There was no reason to."

"Suppose Theresa threatened to turn herself in?"

"She would never have done that. She couldn't. She had responsibilities. It was one of the things that made her right for our work."

"You mean her brother?"

"Yes. Theresa would never do anything to hurt him. She would never have said anything to anybody."

"What's the connection that isn't an explanation?"

Ethel thought about it. "The money I paid her yesterday. Her part of our winnings. The paper said she was murdered by someone who was robbing her apartment. A man with a shaved head. The money we paid her got her killed."

It didn't even make a drunken sort of sense. "If the burglar was after the money, he had to have known it was there. He had to have been tipped by one of your teammates."

"No!" Ethel shouted, mad at me finally. "I told you, none of us would do that. We're technicians, artists, not animals. The worst of us wouldn't so much as twist another person's arm."

"How did you enlist Theresa, then? You must have forced her somehow."

"Theresa and I got to know one another socially."

"At the Scrabble club."

"That's what we played, dear, but it wasn't the reason we met. It was just an excuse for lonely people to gather. Theresa was very lonely. She didn't have anybody close to her."

"She had her brother."

Ethel topped off her drink. Her anger hadn't lasted any longer than the previous round. "That kind of someone is worse than no one. Raul was the reason her life was empty, but you couldn't tell her that. She wouldn't listen. He was the key to obtaining Theresa's help. I saw that from the start."

"Theresa's help with the blackjack scam?"

"Yes. She told me she was a dealer the first night we met. She was so naive."

"Are you saying she went along with you to get money for Raul's tuition?"

"His tuition? What did she tell you? That he was studying to be a lawyer?"

"An artist," I said. I didn't mention Chastine's writer. I knew I didn't have to.

"It was lawyer the first time Theresa mentioned him to me. We played little Scrabble tournaments at our weekly meetings. Three games or rounds each night, with the players matched by Swiss pairings, the system they use at chess tournaments. In the first round, you were pared with someone by blind draw. For the next two rounds, you played the person who had the score closest to yours in the previous round. That way, players of similar ability tended to play one another. Hardly a week went by when I didn't play Theresa in a second or third round.

"We'd talk, a little during the game and a lot afterward, during the soda and cookies part of the evening. One week she told me about her brother, the lawyer-to-be. Then, the very next week, he was suddenly a doctor-to-be. When Theresa realized what she had done, she told me the truth."

"Which was what?"

"That he might have been any of the things she dreamt of him becoming, but he'd chosen to be a person who uses cocaine. Theresa gave him all her money, poor girl, and dreamt of him becoming something else. It's hard to say which one was sadder, the user or the dreamer."

"How about the con artist who took advantage of Theresa's dreams? You told me in the bar you'd found a new family. You meant the friends you'd made in your club. It didn't take you long to sell your family out."

Ethel nodded. "That's how I lost my first family. I sold them off, bit by bit. Now I've lost another one."

I'd been listening to her speak of the Scrabble club in the past tense. Now I understood why. And I understood the connection that wasn't an explanation, the link Ethel saw between herself and the murder. It wasn't the money she'd paid Theresa.

"You didn't show up last night for your meeting."

"I couldn't," Ethel said. "I couldn't bring myself to."

"Reverend Miller said Theresa was waiting for someone. You. When you didn't show, she knew she'd been used. She went home, where she wasn't supposed to be, and got killed."

"Yes," Ethel said, her tears flowing freely now. "It was my fault."

Ten

I spent the rest of the long, wet day trying to trace Raul Rendeja. Ethel Taylor had assumed the guilt for Theresa's death—that part of the guilt I hadn't claimed for my own—but I was anxious to include the brother. He'd certainly blighted his sister's life, which made it natural enough to think of him as somehow involved in the crime that had ended that life. And Theresa had been waiting for a call from him on the day she'd died. I was sure of that.

She'd been waiting to tell him she had his money, the next installment on a debt she'd never pay off. Something had gone wrong. Raul hadn't gotten the happy news. Maybe he'd grown tired of the wait. Or too desperate to wait.

Raul hadn't been the man Theresa had surprised in her apartment, not unless he'd shaved his head since his portrait had been taken. And if Raul had been a regular visitor to the Bell Street Arms, as I was guessing, the nosy downstairs neighbor would surely have known him by sight. It was important for my structure of unsupported suspicion and conjecture that Raul be familiar with his sister's apartment and her schedule. That way, he'd have known where to send an accomplice and when.

The other detail that argued against Raul being the murderer was the fight Theresa had put up to save the money. She'd tried to save it for Raul, not knowing that it, or part of it, would have found its way to him eventually.

I tried to find my own way to Raul Rendeja. I asked for him at a drug rehabilitation center and two halfway houses, one in Atlantic City and one in Pleasantville, the nearby mainland town where Theresa had told me Raul lived. I tried the Pleasantville police station, using the same story: I wanted to find Raul so I could tell him what had happened to his dead sister. It was a true story as far as it went. If I was right about Raul, he didn't need to be told how his sister had died. But I thought he should know what she'd sacrificed for him.

I never came close to finding Rendeja. He wasn't known to the bureaucrats and workers in the drug user support industry. Or to the police. Not yet.

The next morning I reported to work so I could be fired properly. I'd picked up an authentic cold during my wanderings in the rain, which pacified Manny, my supervisor. Robert Guineri, when he showed up at my station around ten, was harder to satisfy.

"This has been a hell of a bad week for people named Rendeja," he said as an opener.

"People?"

"First Theresa and now her brother Raul. He was found dead early this morning in the Hotel Underwood."

I recognized the local nickname for the area beneath the boardwalk, the place where teenagers had sex and the homeless slept. "How did he die?"

"Drug overdose. Looks like he hit the lottery or something and couldn't stand the prosperity. He not only had a skinful, according to my contact, he also had a small collection of hundred dollar bills in his pocket. Any thoughts on that, Keane?"

"None that haven't occurred to you."

Guineri said, "What occurs to me is that the brother dying on top of the sister getting offed violates the laws of probability. I think the brother must have been involved in the robbery and killing in some way. But I guess we'll never know for sure."

It wasn't an outcome I'd ever been able to accept, not if there was the smallest chance of knowing. Not even when common sense screamed out for me to keep my mouth shut.

"Anything written on any of those C-notes?" I asked, remembering the bill Ethel had flashed at the bar. As a nod to self-preservation, I added, "Theresa had gotten one as a birthday present. Ask about lavender ink."

Guineri hauled himself off his stool and left me. Half an hour later, Manny was waving a phone at me. It was the security specialist.

"One of the hundreds said 'Happy Birthday' in lavender ink," he said. "But I checked Rendeja's personnel records. Her birthday was way back in November."

"So she hung on to it."

"How is it you knew about this present in the first place?"

"I contributed," I said and hung up.

St. Jimmy

One

I wasn't there for old times' sake. I was working on an investigation that had taken me from New York City to the Jersey shore. Maybe I should say that the investigation had trailed me to Jersey, that I was actually running away from it. Things were going badly, and I needed a breather. So I'd followed a slim lead to the shore, ending up in Seaside Heights, a hot spot in the string of towns between Asbury Park and Atlantic City.

A hot spot in the summer, anyway. It was now October, and the winterizing of the little resort was well advanced. I didn't mind. I've always preferred the shore on those days when the gulls outnumber the people. Walking along on that particular day, I could almost imagine how beautiful it must once have been. It was still beautiful, of course. The ocean wasn't really changed by the gaudy frills tacked onto its hem. But it was easier to look beyond the midways and amusement piers with the lights off and the only sounds coming from the birds and the waves. Even the old beach homes, the three-storied, turreted monstrosities that had grown with as little planning and restraint as the families who built them, looked less absurd, standing dark and silent. Given years of off-seasons to work with, the ocean had grayed and weathered them, giving the houses the same dignity you can see in a piece of beer-bottle glass polished by the surf.

I walked the boardwalk south out of Seaside Heights, still in no particular hurry to get back to my real job. The boardwalk ended, and I had to make do with sandy cement. Around the same time, the houses I passed became less eccentric, and I knew I was entering Seaside Park, a slightly newer, quieter community.

I almost passed the house before I recognized it. I stopped and turned to face it, while it patiently returned my gaze like a familiar face in a crowd.

89

Remember me? I didn't cross the street for a closer view. I didn't have to. I knew it was the right place, even though I hadn't been sure, a moment before, that I'd find it. I remember you, I thought.

The house was three stories tall but still managed to look squat. Only a plain porch and rather small windows—all shuttered now—broke up the facade, which was covered in once-white shingles. Nothing distinguished the house from its neighbors on either side. Nothing except the memory of a minor evil that had once occurred within it. I searched its weathered face for some small scar left by that night, but all I saw was the grim resignation of a house that had faced the Atlantic squarely for fifty years.

Nor could I find a bronze plaque or a wooden sign or a piece of weathered paper to identify the place as a landmark in the history of detection. I was thinking of the marker in London that commemorates the first meeting of Sherlock Holmes and his friend and biographer, Dr. John H. Watson. My plaque would have read "In this house, Owen Keane met his Moriarty."

Two

It was the summer following my junior year in high school. I'd agreed to represent my parish at a new Catholic retreat house for teenage boys because it was free and because it was located at the Jersey shore. "Agreed" is putting it too mildly. I'd angled for the chance. In addition to clean underwear and a bathing suit, I carried along a well-thumbed dream of spending a week at the shore, a dream fired by too many detective stories based on another, more glamorous coast. I should have left that particular article at home.

I found the house easily and stood for a moment examining it and pretending not to notice the four guys on the porch. I felt the heat my walk from the bus stop had built up in me and attributed it, self-consciously, to their quiet stares. After a moment, I picked up my bag and smiled my way through the group. One of them said hello, a skinny, red-headed kid.

The inside of the house was dark and almost cool, the result of some dead architect's sleight of hand. The front room was large, spanning the whole width of the house. Its twelve-foot-high, water-stained ceiling and peeling wallpaper spoke of a better day past. I walked slowly around the room, ending up at an ornately mantled fireplace.

"You're lucky you weren't down here in May. That was the only central heating we had." The speaker, a large man dressed in T-shirt and trunks, stood in a doorway at the back of the room. He was barefoot and tanned and what was left of his hair was black and curly.

"Welcome to Intrek," he said. "I'm Brother Stephen. You must be Owen Keane." He crossed the creaking hardwood floor and offered me a large hand.

I smiled nervously and tried to match the pressure of his grip.

"So you're the one they sent to check me out." His smile looked naturally broad and he spoke with enough north Jersey in his voice to make him sound like a tough guy from the late show. "We'll have to make an extra effort to impress you, so I can get some paying customers next summer."

I knew his effort to impress me had already begun, and I was still impressed.

"Have you ever been to a retreat before, Owen?" he asked.

"No," I said.

"Well, if you had, you'd be expecting a lot of prayer sessions and services and periods of silence, things like that. Intrek is different. We'll have Mass on Sunday, of course, but other than that, we'll mostly talk. You'll get tired of hearing your own voice, I can promise you that.

"Most people out in the world are too busy or too lazy to keep up with the things that are happening to them, to think them out. Do you know what I mean?"

"Yes," I said.

"For the next week we'll be examining our worlds, trying to decide who we are and where we're going. One week isn't too much to set aside for that, is it?"

"No," I said.

He noticed something in the corner to my left, something I'd managed to miss during my brief examination of the room. "Hey, Pat. Say hello to Owen Keane."

The man addressed was lying on the sofa under sheets of newspaper. He sat up now in extreme slow motion. His sandy hair curled fashionably over his ears, but he wore cuffed black pants, a white dress shirt, and black shoes. His regular features were small, as was the smile with which he ignored Brother Stephen's request that he say hello to me. I felt the coolness of the room in the small of my back.

"Whose Bermuda shorts are those?" he asked me.

"My brother's," I said, unable to word the easy lie.

"May I see your book?" He pointed to a paperback I carried in my shirt pocket. "Raymond Chandler," he read. "*The Simple Art of Murder*. The kid's a classicist," he said as he lay back down.

"Pat's a teacher from my school in Redbank," Brother Stephen said in a low voice that suggested a confidence between us. "I made the mistake of signing him on as a cook. Just remember that you're not down here to put on weight."

"Right," I said.

"Good. You've got time for a swim before our formal introductions."

I decided on some informal introductions instead. I left my bag in a corner and returned to the porch. The four loungers I'd seen on my way in were still watching the beach. One of them nodded to me as I stepped from the house.

"Can you catch a pass?" he asked.

"Pretty well," I said, my capacity for lying back from its coffee break.

"You and Bill are our receivers. I'll quarterback. My name's Doyle." He stood up to shake hands. He was a head taller than I was and heavier, blond-haired with the faintest trace of a moustache and a smile that curled up at the ends like a cartoon cat's.

"Who are we playing?" I asked.

Doyle gestured toward the ocean and the redhead interpreted. "What Brother Stephen calls a formal introduction is really a touch football game. The five of us are playing the five kids from Stephen's school in Redbank. They're out swimming now. My name's Jimmy. That's Bill and that's Rocky."

"Everybody calls me Rocky."

The speaker was dark featured and stocky, so he might actually have had the nickname. But he'd made the claim with so little confidence that I wondered if he might be assuming a new identity for the week. Bill stood apart from the others, studying the horizon. He was thinner than Doyle and blonder. He looked like he'd been at the shore for months.

"I can throw a pass, too, you know," he said to the ocean.

"I know you can, Billy," Doyle said. "Let's size them up first, all right?"

"Size them up? They're all freshmen or sophomores."

"Okay," Doyle said amiably. "Then we can take turns at quarterback. Let's just see first."

He looked to me for approval, so I said, "Sounds good."

"Have you been down to the water yet?" Jimmy asked me. "I feel like a walk."

I left my sneakers on the porch and followed him across the hot asphalt to the beach. The sand felt almost as warm to my bare feet.

"Be back by four," Doyle called after us.

The beach was crowded with blankets and bodies, and we worked our way down to the water single file without speaking. The water temperature was a foretaste of arthritis. Nevertheless, I walked ankle deep through the surf while Jimmy stayed on the smooth sand above. We headed toward a stone breakwater half a mile away.

"Do you know Doyle?" I asked.

Jimmy smiled. "I feel like I do, even though I just met him today."

"Huh?"

"He's the guy who knows everything practical from instinct. For him, puberty was a bad weekend a year or two back. Go ahead and laugh," he said, sounding pleased, "but you've met him before, too. Every high school has at least one. The Doyles dominate the proceedings by being whole people in a crowd of bits and pieces."

That last line sounded rehearsed, but I laughed anyway. "I know what you mean," I said.

"He and Bill came together," Jimmy added. "I think from Camden."

"Where's Rocky from?"

"God knows." His smile disappeared. "I didn't mean to put him down. Or Doyle either," he said quickly.

I was surprised by his sudden penitence. "Tell me about yourself, then," I said.

I watched him as he talked. He was about my height, five ten, but even thinner, as thin as Doyle's summer moustache. He had large blue eyes made larger by his glasses. His hair was short and curly, and his face and arms were freckled. I had classified him by his short hair and glasses on the porch and mentally thrown in my lot with Doyle and Bill, but I realized as I listened to Jimmy's sketchy autobiography that he had singled me out as a friend.

"I'm hoping to go on to St. Peter's in New Brunswick when I graduate," he was saying. "Dad still wants it to be Rutgers, but that doesn't sound right to me. I don't know what I want to do with my life. I've still so many questions. All dad can think about is me getting a job. He's afraid if I fall in with the Jesuits I'll end up one myself. It took a lot of persuading to talk him out of the money for a week at the beautiful Jersey shore. But I wanted it."

"For the ocean?" I asked.

"Partly." He smiled self-consciously. "I thought Brother Stephen might be able to answer some of my questions."

"Good luck," I said.

"You don't think he's that bright?"

"I don't know if there are any answers."

I sounded rehearsed now myself, which made me self-conscious. Jimmy added to the feeling by considering me closely. I stooped to pick up a shell and tossed it, unexamined, to an approaching wave.

"That's what attracted me, anyway," Jimmy resumed, "that and the name of the retreat."

"Intrek? What's it supposed to mean?"

His shy smile deepened. "A journey into ourselves," he said.

Three

That same evening, after the football game and a cookout, we had our first discussion. Later, Doyle would call it our first seance, capturing in a word my own impression of the evening. I was a nine-year veteran of Catholic school and used to religious discussions conducted from neat rows of desks in sunlit classrooms. Brother Stephen's disorienting approach was to seat us in a circle of chairs, each facing everyone, and to ignore the advantages of electric light. As the evening passed and the room grew darker, the faces around me lost the little familiarity they'd gained during the afternoon.

I expected Stephen to begin by asking each of us for a short autobiography. Instead, he selected a victim at random and assigned him someone else in the circle to describe. I was given one of the kids from Stephen's high school in Redbank. There were five of them, and during the course of our week I would never see one without the other four. I only knew now that they dressed badly, wearing dark socks with their sneakers and tucking in their shirt tails, and that they were worthless at football. I happened to know the full name of the one I'd been assigned, but beyond that, I was lost.

"His name is Carl Moldt," I began. "He's from Redbank. He looks like a nice guy"—desperate, I fell back on Bill's guess about the age of the Redbank group—"a typical sophomore." That brought smothered laughter from Moldt's buddies. I gave up.

I was hoping that Jimmy would be assigned Doyle. I was curious to see if he would repeat his observations of the afternoon in front of the entire group. Instead he was given Pat, the lay assistant.

"His name is Pat," Jimmy began. "He likes games, especially chess. He puts on a cynical front, but it's just a facade, one that believers often adopt these days."

That speech was greeted by a moment of silence. Brother Stephen smiled broadly. Pat's eyes, half closed from the moment we'd sat down, were now fully open.

Pat was included as a biographer as well. His subject was Owen Keane. The brown eyes narrowed again as he examined me briefly.

"He suffers from the curse of all Watsons," Pat said slowly. "He sees, but he does not observe." He startled me by suddenly meeting my gaze. "What's that on Mr. Moldt's left hand, Doctor?"

I looked across the circle to the shadow where Moldt was trying to hide himself. "A class ring," I said.

"Not unlike the one you're wearing. That might have told you that he will be a senior in September, not a sophomore. Master Keane is also without much knowledge of the world, or else he would never refer to another person as typical. That's all, I think."

I watched the floor during the rest of the exercise and for the first few moments of Stephen's talk. I had already heard it in any case. It was a rerun of the greeting he'd given me that afternoon. He'd gotten to the part about "examining our worlds" when Jimmy interrupted him by raising his hand.

"Don't you mean our world, Brother Stephen?" Jimmy asked. "It's the same one for all of us, isn't it?"

This unexpected question brought new life to the group, signaled by a general shifting about.

"I meant our individual experiences of life and the unique challenges each of us face," Stephen replied. "You don't think we're all alike, do you, Jimmy?"

"I think as members of the Mystical Body of Christ we are," Jimmy replied.

Again there was a moment of silence. If Jimmy had mentioned the Knights of Columbus as part of his argument he would not have surprised me more.

"We can't discuss a moral framework for some of us or most of us," Jimmy continued. "There's only one for all."

I looked over to Brother Stephen and found him smiling again. "I can see this is going to be an interesting week," he said. "Suppose we just set out on a journey without a destination in mind and see where we end up. How would that be, Jimmy? On the way we may all learn a thing or two. Does that sound okay?"

"Yes, Brother Stephen," Jimmy said.

Stephen nodded and continued his introduction. I watched Jimmy's smile as the monk droned on. Without knowing why, I didn't like it.

Four

Pat and I walked the first block from the house without speaking. In the darkness between street lights I looked for a break in his introspection but never saw one. He strode down the gravel-strewn sidewalk effortlessly in his ridiculous black oxfords, while I hurried with painful, barefoot steps beside him. At the start of the second block, I stepped off the concrete and onto the now cool sand.

"Tenderfoot Keane," Pat said, "toughest man east of New Jersey."

It was the evening of our second day and Brother Stephen's routine was firmly established. We rose early for breakfast and our first discussion session. At eleven we were released to swim or to do whatever we could get done before five. In the evening, we'd have two more talks. Between these sessions, Stephen paired the group off for get-acquainted walks.

I'd been looking forward to my walk with Pat and the opportunity to offer unsolicited bits of myself. His detachment and sarcasm had won us all over, in spite of his cooking and clothes. I was disappointed when—at the end of another silent block—he chose a topic for our talk.

"I don't know what gets into that kid," he said. "I really don't. He hangs around you, do you know what his problem is?"

He meant Jimmy, of course. His performance in our discussion groups had been a growing embarrassment to me. The talks had begun smoothly, with topics like drugs and sex and the war. Stephen would consider any point of view, but his rough emphasis was clearly placed on irresponsibility and consequent unhappiness. To please him and fill the time, Doyle and I and some of the others would challenge him on minor points, always backing down when the sun got high enough for swimming.

Jimmy had broken our comfortable pattern. His questioning, timid at first and then demanding, cut through our situational ethics to doctrine and dogma. He disrupted Stephen's obvious direction, forcing us from his broad hypothetical streets and into the labyrinth of the Catholic Church.

"What's the matter with him?" Pat asked.

"He's just asking questions," I said, hoping to kill the subject.

"The Trinity, for God's sake, and the Immaculate Conception! Who worries about the Immaculate Conception at age sixteen?"

"I've asked those same questions myself," I said.

"Really?"

"I mean I've thought about them," I said. "Speculated."

"Jimmy doesn't speculate. He wants to know. That's what I can't understand. He actually expects an answer."

"Brother Stephen answers him."

"That's a recorded message. 'The number you have reached has been disconnected since 1545.'"

We paused to watch a girl cross the street ahead of us. Her white shorts looked all but disembodied in the darkness. Pat studied the ground for another block, and I began to think we had left Jimmy behind.

Then he said, "The kid makes me nervous."

I was mad now myself. "He wasn't questioning you."

"That last name of yours isn't exactly descriptive. Let's just say I'm uncomfortable around people who discuss their emotions openly."

"Jimmy discusses ideas."

"His ideas are emotions. That's a short definition of a fanatic, should you ever need one. What do the other guys think of him?"

"They don't mind him," I said. In fact they made fun of him when we were on our own, calling him "Saint Jimmy."

We stopped next to a large swimming pool five or six blocks from the house. The motel it belonged to was square and stuccoed and ugly. There was a sign on the side of the building, lit by the last of three bulbs.

"Salt water pool, filtered and heated," I read aloud. "Why would anyone drive all the way down here to swim in a pool?"

"You've obviously never lived in fear of unseen things with claws," Pat said. "We'd better start back. There's no point in upsetting Stephen further."

"I thought he wanted discussion."

"I'll try to make it simpler for you. Do you follow baseball?"

"A little," I said.

"You're just a dabbler, aren't you? Never mind. Stephen's not a theorist, he's not some guy sitting up in the press box wondering why things happen. He's a first-base coach. He's accepted the rules of the game and he's trying to get as many kids as he can around the bases. He's used to kids who don't want to go and kids who've found another game to play, but a kid who wants to play baseball and still asks why it's ninety feet to second and not thirty-one or a hundred and ten, Stephen just can't understand."

"Why do you think it's ninety?" I asked.

"It makes the game work," he said after a moment.

I listened to the sound of the waves coming over the curve of the beach for most of the walk back. I thought of the poor way I'd defended Jimmy to Pat and the others. I thought of Pat's picture of Brother Stephen. Mostly I thought of the girl in the white shorts, heading off alone for the ocean.

When we were a block from the house, Pat turned to me. "I guess I should talk with Jimmy," he said. "Sorry I got so carried away. You're from New Brunswick, aren't you?"

"Trenton," I said.

Five

The next day brought the first bad weather of the week. The sky was overcast, and, without the sun, the sand felt damp and the ocean breeze cold. The stretch of beach in front of the house was as empty as I'd seen it in daylight. Jimmy and I had it almost to ourselves.

Because of the weather, the others had gone off to the boardwalk at Seaside Heights in pursuit of the girls who had forsaken the beach. Jimmy had been neither invited nor interested, and he'd decided, without asking me, that we would have a talk. That suited me, as it happened. I'd made up my mind to set Jimmy straight on the way he was acting before any more of the week was spoiled. I saw this as a favor—almost a duty—that I owed him because he thought of me as his friend. Even though I knew it was for his own good, it was difficult for me to start.

My first problem was simply finding a break in the traffic. Talking with Jimmy meant listening most of the time. As we spread out our towels and settled on the hard sand, he presented highlights from a lecture on grace he'd tried to deliver in our group discussion that morning. Brother Stephen had come so close to telling him to shut up that the rest of us had been sitting at attention. When Stephen managed to control his temper long enough to dismiss the group early, the general reaction had almost been disappointment.

I lay on my back and watched the sky while Jimmy talked. In spite of the breeze, the clouds seemed to be fixed above us. The overcast was solid and covered with little bumps and cracks. It looked like a badly plastered ceiling, discolored by age and smoke.

Jimmy hadn't noticed my inattention. "Brother Stephen wants to talk about lying," he was saying, "or stealing as though they're isolated ideas that pop into your head all by themselves. 'Don't lie because it's bad.' What does that mean to anyone? In some situations, it might be good to lie. What meaning does it have without some unifying scheme? None. If you take it out of the context of grace and the refusal to accept grace, what does it really mean?"

"It means don't lie because it's bad," I said, propping myself up on one elbow. "Why bring in something that none of us understand and most of us wouldn't buy if we did?"

Jimmy was a little surprised by that, my first stated objection to one of his rhetorical flights. He thought about it for a moment. "Because not buying it is a lot worse than lying," he finally said.

I sat up so I could face him squarely. "Look," I said. "I'm not saying you're wrong for believing that. I actually think more of you for it. But you're wrong to drag it around in the open like you do. I'm telling you this for your own good. Really."

He made no effort to interrupt me, which was disturbing. He sat cross-legged with his hands on his knees and a small smile on his face. It seemed to me that he knew what I would say, that he'd been waiting for me to say it. The smile made me speak less gently than I'd intended.

"You're making an ass of yourself, do you understand that? These guys we're with aren't a bunch of fifth graders down here to memorize the Baltimore Catechism. They're here for a good time. If Brother Stephen can get them to think about where they're going or what they're doing, that's fine. It's part of the deal. But they don't want to listen to you talk about grace or the Holy Ghost or anything else. It's embarrassing, Jimmy. There are certain things you think, that we all think, but we keep inside. You don't wave your religion at people. If you do, people think you're strange, they talk about you ..."

"Behind your back?" Jimmy prompted.

"Yes," I said. "And it doesn't make you a martyr just because you can't get along with these guys. You have to learn to keep your mouth shut."

I'd said more than I'd planned to and said it less kindly. I lay back down on my towel.

Jimmy let me stare at the cracked gray sky for the time it took three waves to arrive. Then he said, "You talk about these things like they're just opinions."

"Well," I said, "since we can't know for sure, aren't religious beliefs like opinions?"

"I know for sure," Jimmy said.

The boast was typical Jimmy, and it brought me up off the sand for round two. I never opened my mouth. Jimmy had spoken softly, almost in a whisper. I was surprised to find that his face was red and his eyes were wet behind his glasses. He was upset, just when I'd decided that I couldn't upset him.

"I'm going to tell you something," he said, speaking softly. "I haven't told anybody before. Not even my folks. I'm telling you because I think you'll understand. You might not want to, but you will."

"What are you getting at?" I asked.

"God talked to me," he said. He looked at me steadily as he spoke, but his head was bowed slightly as though he expected me to laugh. "If you don't want me to go on, I won't."

"Go ahead," I said.

"It happened this spring, one night this spring. I was in my room, lying on my bed, reading." He smiled again, briefly. "Alistair MacLean, not St. Augustine. I was reading and barely staying awake and suddenly the room was lit up, like a flash had gone off, only it was bigger and continuous. I couldn't see anything in the room around me or even the room itself. I didn't close my eyes; the brightness didn't hurt them.

"In the middle of the brightness, I saw a flame. It was brighter than the pure white light around it. It was small at first, like the flame of a candle, but it grew larger slowly and came closer, until it was right in front of me. I could feel the heat on my face. Then a voice spoke to me. I didn't hear the voice. The words were in my mind like my own thoughts, but not in my own voice. Then it was over and the flame and the light were gone instantly, as though someone had pressed a switch.

"I didn't sleep at all that night. It was a mild night, but I couldn't get warm."

He watched for my reaction and then turned to face the sea. I didn't know what to say. I was suddenly cold myself. The few people around us were gathering up their things and leaving. The ceiling of cloud seemed much lower. On the open beach I had the irrational feeling that I was somehow shut in.

Jimmy turned back to me. "Now maybe you can see why I want to know these things. It isn't a dead subject for me, or something to ignore in polite company. I have to know, Owen. I *can* know.

"I've told you because I think you can appreciate it. I think you're a believer. You're the only one I've told. I trust you. The others wouldn't understand, not even Brother Stephen." He stood up. "Thank you for listening," he said.

"Wait a minute," I said. "Aren't you going to tell me the rest? Aren't you going to tell me what the voice said?"

Jimmy seemed surprised. "I can't," he said as he left me.

Six

I walked the beach for some time after Jimmy had gone. It seemed to me that I'd be unable to continue with Intrek, or rather, it seemed that Intrek itself could not continue in the face of Jimmy's revelation. I didn't arrive at that idea after careful thought. I simply had the feeling that something had occurred which made continuing impossible. The projector had broken down in the middle of the film. A principal actor had walked out during the performance of the play. When I later learned that our routine had been broken, I wasn't surprised, even though Jimmy had had nothing to do with it.

I returned to the house at dinner time and found the group assembled in the living room. Pat rose from the sofa as I entered.

"Philo Keane, society sleuth, returns," he said. "Now I can make my announcement. Brother Stephen has been called back to Redbank for a budget conference. I am in sole command. It ill befits a commander to cook, so I'm canceling dinner. I'm also canceling the evening discussions. In their place, I recommend that you observe human social interaction. I suggest the boardwalk. They have food there. Take money. Company dismissed."

All eyes were on Jimmy at the end of the speech, the group's elation being held in check by the expectation that he would somehow screw up the deal. Jimmy was disturbed—a red steak was rising on his forehead—but he was just as obviously disoriented.

Pat took advantage of Jimmy's momentary confusion and delivered a master stroke. "By the way," he added, "I'll be available for private discussions for anyone interested in hanging around."

Jimmy brightened at that and the glow spread around the room. Five minutes later I was on my way to the boardwalk in the company of Doyle and Bill and Rocky, the last five dollars of my spending money in my pocket. I was willing to blow every penny to get away from Jimmy and his vision.

It wasn't fully dark, but the lights of the amusement pier were blazing away. My three companions walked quickly, laughing and shoving each other. It was hard to believe that this was their second trip of the day to the lights, harder to believe their optimism, since all their previous expeditions in search of the opposite sex had ended in failure.

Doyle addressed my thoughts. "Hope springs eternal, Keane. We saw some possibilities this afternoon. Definite possibilities. Tonight we'll have an added advantage. In the dark, the girls won't be able to see old Rocky so well."

Rocky didn't laugh, and Doyle failed to notice. That didn't surprise me.

We were all still really strangers and speaking out against anyone in the group, even in a kidding way, was a risk, an unnecessary exposure. Doyle, the premature man, spoke with a contempt for our opinion of him that conquered everyone. His favorite target was Jimmy, and, to please Doyle, the other two mocked him in turn.

"I can see Jimmy's confirmation," Bill said, smiling in anticipation when his at bat came. "The church is packed. Kids, sponsors, parents. The bishop is walking up and down the center aisle, asking questions. He calls on Jimmy. The kid answers for four solid hours. Everyone else gets up and leaves and the kid's still standing there, explaining Extreme Unction."

"You miss the essence of Jimmy," Doyle said, silencing Rocky's laughter and snuffing out Bill's smile. "The bishop never gets to ask Jimmy a question. Jimmy asks the bishop. Then he asks the bishop about his answer and then about the answer on his answer. The bishop finally gives up and resigns, and Jimmy has to anoint himself."

The boardwalk at Seaside Heights was already busy, but the crowd was still mostly kids wearing the bathing suits of the afternoon. The evening crowd, kids, too, but older, was just starting to arrive. It was my first trip to the Heights, and I was impressed. For a span of a few blocks, the boardwalk widened to Atlantic City width and put on a show that made me forget Jimmy.

In those days the pin ball and skeet ball machines still filled the arcades, the machines as old and worn as the weathered boards beneath our feet. Fast food meant pizza by the slice served by prisoners our age trapped in tiny, steaming stalls. The row of small stands that lined the land side of the walk was dominated by games of chance: wheels of fortune, bingo, darts, ring toss. Carnival distractions that came once a year to most places were fixed here in gaudy storefronts lit like a town square at Christmas. The brightest lights of all belonged to the single amusement pier, its outline topped by a roller coaster that seemed to hang out over the ocean.

We walked toward the pier, Doyle in front, nodding his head with surprising subtlety to indicate some girl who had met his standards. I saw many more who met mine, well tanned girls dressed in light colors that glowed in the gathering darkness. They were a hopeless sight for me. I knew I would never interrupt a strange female's evening walk, having only just begun to speak to girls I'd known for years. But I wasn't really worried about having to try. I was comforted by our numbers and by the noisy presence of Rocky, who scattered the game as we walked.

When we reached the amusement pier, Rocky and Bill took advantage of a short line to take a ride on the roller coaster. As soon as the bullet-shaped cars of the small train began to move, Doyle pulled at my arm.

"Come on, sport," he said. "This is our moment."

"Where are we going?"

"From despair to hope. We're doomed with those two clowns, but together you and I have a chance. Stick close to me. Thank God you didn't wear those Bermuda shorts."

I followed Doyle while he hunted, wishing all the while that I'd stayed to talk with Pat. He approached two very dark brunettes who were waiting in line for pizza. I followed cautiously a few steps behind. One of the girls was striking and overdressed, her black hair elaborately curled and brushed back in an arrangement that suggested a mane. The other girl was thinner and plainer, as plain as the gold cross she wore—my counterpart, I realized, the disposable companion. She acknowledged our relationship with a small smile, after which she looked down at her cross.

The actual encounter was over quickly. Doyle justified my faith in him by using a subdued opening line, something about pizza. The exotic lioness turned around and looked him over slowly. Then she turned back to her friend.

"The older ones come out a little later," she said.

Doyle banged my arm and we left. When we'd reached a safe distance, I expressed my relief by laughing. I hadn't intended to insult Doyle, but I did. He blew up.

"What are you laughing at? You little shit! You couldn't even open your goddamn mouth. I should've left you with Rocky and brought Bill. He's a stiff, but at least he likes girls. You probably wish you were home with your boyfriend, that goddamn faggot altar boy."

I was completely surprised by Doyle's attack and completely threatened. It never occurred to me to stand up to him. I only wanted to win back his good opinion. Without thinking, I tossed him Jimmy. "He's no friend of mine," I said. "He's crazy."

"Yeah," Doyle said. "Crazy about you."

"About religion," I said. "He's seen God. He thinks God appeared to him, in a flame or something, and talked to him. That's why he's been such a pain."

About that time I started to think again. It was Doyle's expression that checked me. His red-faced anger had been replaced by surprise and amusement. "Tell me more, sport," he said.

I turned and walked away, expecting Doyle to follow me or call after me. All I heard him say was "Jesus."

I didn't go back to the house for several hours. Instead, I walked the beach, just above the surf. The sky was still overcast, and the darkness unrelieved. I came upon other wanderers with little warning and passed noisy groups on the beach unseen. I'd started my walk kicking myself for having mentioned Jimmy's secret, but before long I was safely back on my own side. I convinced myself that my position, somewhere between the Jimmys and the Doyles, was the worst one possible. I was doomed to wander unknowing, envying the people who knew.

When I did go back to the house, I found it quiet and dark. There was no sign of Pat or the others. Jimmy was asleep upstairs. I thought about waking him to warn him. I let him sleep instead.

Seven

The next day started quietly, with nothing to remind me of the evening's disaster except a bad feeling that wouldn't go away. Brother Stephen was back and presided over breakfast. He was in a talkative mood—Redbank was going to have a good year in football—and he never got around to asking about the previous evening. No one offered to tell him, the most likely volunteer being unavailable for the duty. Jimmy had come down with something during the night. I'd awakened to the sound of him vomiting in the bathroom. Stephen's remedy was simple quarantine. That made the day easier for me.

Everything about the day was easy. Our morning discussion was the smoothest of the week. Even Rocky contributed, outlining his views on pre-marital sex, to everyone's enjoyment. Stephen was so pleased, he sent us out to the beach a full half hour early. I didn't go. It wasn't that Doyle and the others weren't friendly. Doyle had surprised me by not mentioning Jimmy's vision or anything else about the evening before. I approached him as he and the others set out for the ocean and asked him to forget what I'd said.

"Don't worry about that," he replied, banging me on the shoulder.

But I did worry. I camped on the porch for the rest of the day, trying to read my book of private eye stories. I should say that reading the book was only my cover, my disguise. I was really guarding Jimmy, who was still upstairs in bed. I wasn't sure why I was guarding him. I was only sure I would fail.

Jimmy missed dinner that night, but he came downstairs for the evening discussion, pale and restless. This last condition spread throughout the group. I paid less attention than usual to Brother Stephen's opening remarks. His subject was the limits of civil disobedience, by which he meant the protests that were beginning to sound against the Vietnam War. He paused when he noticed that the room was getting dark.

"Light the candle, Pat," he said. "It's getting too easy for Rocky to fall asleep."

He stretched as he spoke, and Rocky laughed loudly to prove he'd been awake. We all watched Pat as he moved slowly to the mantle and lit the large white candle. Its flickering light made the room seem darker.

"That may look like a holy candle," Stephen said, "but it isn't. I won it up at the Heights for knocking down milk cans with a softball.

"Anyway, to get back to our topic, I'm sure you can see where I'm heading. Acting on your own conscience, even when it contradicts the establishment, can be a noble thing to do. But it's a tricky point. We, as individuals on the street, only have so much information about what's going on. Sometimes we have to give the government or the Church or some other institution credit for having a broader view. What seems to be wrong to us as individuals may be right for our country. Sometimes the first and greatest sacrifice an individual must make as a member of a group is to have faith in that group's broader vision."

He paused to let us think about this and to prepare our token objections. No one stirred. The five escapees from Redbank were studying each other's feet, as usual. Across the circle of chairs from me, Jimmy sat with his head down, his chin resting on his chest. I wasn't sure if he'd even been listening. I decided that I would have to be the one to speak. Doyle beat me to it.

"Suppose a person knows he's right and the group's wrong," Doyle said.

"How does he know he's right, Doyle?" Stephen countered.

"Some higher authority," Doyle said.

"Like the Church coming into conflict with the government, say?" the monk asked with interest.

Doyle thought about that for a moment. I mentally congratulated him on his question. Given a little more encouragement, our leader would happily fill the time left until our break with a set speech on conflicting loyalties in modern society. But I had mistaken Doyle's motive.

"I was really thinking of an authority higher than the Church," he said.

"I don't understand," Stephen said.

I did. I tried to catch Doyle's eye, but he was considering the dark ceiling, overplaying the part of a man struggling with his thoughts.

"I guess I'm asking about the possibility of God speaking to us directly," Doyle said slowly. "We had something like that at our school. Do you remember that, Billy?"

Bill nodded emphatically and took up the tale, speaking so quickly that I knew he'd been dying for his cue. "A guy in the class ahead of us had a vision. He was in bed one night, and God appeared to him in a burning bush."

I looked across the circle, but only for an instant. Jimmy was staring at me with wild, unbelieving eyes.

"God talked to this kid," Bill was saying, "only He didn't really talk. I mean the kid didn't hear anything. The words just kind of popped into his head. The next morning when the kid woke up, his bed was all wet."

Jimmy stopped the nervous laughter that followed by standing up and knocking over his chair. I stood up, too, as he ran out through the front door. I hesitated for a moment and then followed him into the night.

"Come back here you two!" Stephen yelled after us, the command overlaid by the slam of the screen door behind me. I could see Jimmy on the beach as I crossed the road. He headed north toward the Heights, running splayfooted in the loose sand. I ran straight down to the water and then north along the hard, packed sand at the edge of the surf. The slope of the beach brought Jimmy down to me as he ran out of wind. I grabbed the back of his shirt, intending to ease him to a stop, but he jerked around and swung at me. I ducked, and the force of his swing carried him into the water.

He sat up with sand on one side of his face and black water roiling over his legs. "Leave me alone," he said.

"Get up. You're acting like an idiot."

He stood and took two steps away from me. "Leave me alone," he said again. "By myself."

I stood my ground. Jimmy turned and stumbled north. I knew I couldn't go back without him, so I followed at a distance. A brilliant full moon shown down through a broken cloud cover. Bits of cloud were moving swiftly past the moon, creating the ancient illusion that the moon itself was sailing across the sky. I felt a kinship with the moon just then. We'd both been made dizzy by the rush of things around us.

When I looked down from the sky, Jimmy was gone. I cursed out loud and began to run toward the distant lights of the amusement pier. Between them and the sand was a belt of darkness. I concentrated on it, trying to pick out some movement or color.

Then I saw him, running toward me. I stopped and waited for him at the edge of the surf, held in place by the sound of Jimmy's breathing. It was high-pitched and painful and driven. His face, when he came near me, so clearly showed his terror that it passed that terror onto me. He was by me before I could shake free of it.

I let him go, waiting in his tracks for whatever had chased him back to the house. I strained to make some shape of the darkness below the neon lights, to hear the sound of a footfall above the deep rolling of the surf. I stood there, frightened, until the calm rhythm of the waves told me I had been outflanked.

Eight

I didn't see Jimmy again that night. Brother Stephen met me when I got back to the house. He told me that Jimmy was too upset to see anyone. Stephen himself was mad and bewildered in equal parts. The anger glistened on his forehead and soaked his dark T-shirt. His thin hair was standing out from his head in places. He smoothed it constantly and without effect while we talked.

He asked me to explain the evening. I told him everything except the details of Jimmy's vision. "I'm to blame," I concluded.

He seemed to agree. He sent me to my room. "Try and keep your mouth shut for a change," he told me.

That turned out to be easy. No one bothered me that night. The next morning I found that nobody would talk to me. The five Redbank kids had no idea what was going on and no desire to know. Doyle and Bill and Rocky gave me the silent treatment in anticipation of Brother Stephen's formal sentencing.

After breakfast, I sat on the front porch and stared out at the beach. I'd brought my book of Raymond Chandler stories with me, but I never opened it. Instead, I ran and reran the previous evening through my mind, punishing myself with the memory of Jimmy's face across the circle of chairs. When that lost its edge, I backed up to the evening on the boardwalk and the moment when I had betrayed Jimmy. Then I ran the two scenes together, beginning and end, betrayal and loss. That's when I first felt there was something wrong, something missing. The two ends wouldn't quite fit together.

I was still working on it when Stephen came out of the house. "Jimmy wants to talk with you," he said. "I think it would be a good idea to take him for a walk."

Jimmy came out a few minutes later. He looked red-eyed and miserable, but he tried to smile. We walked down to the beach together without speaking. He chose the same route we had taken on the first day, south toward the small breakwater. The sun was already uncomfortably bright on the wave tops. I'd left my shirt on the porch and I could feel the heat of the day on my shoulders. With our old route came our old roles: Jimmy spoke and I listened.

"I'm sorry for the way I acted last night," he began. "I still wasn't feeling well, I guess. I just wanted to tell you that I forgive you for telling Doyle. I understand the pressure, I think, and the temptation."

He walked a little ahead of me, so I couldn't watch his face as he spoke. "I told you earlier that you're a believer. I was wrong about that. You're someone who wants to believe. It's not the same."

That was his parting message, the small, harsh thing he wanted to say. I was almost disappointed. From my place a step behind him, I watched the soapy remains of the waves as they washed around my feet. Jimmy had used the word "temptation." That was the problem with the story of Jimmy's miracle: It was too tempting. No one who heard it could resist passing it on.

"I did tell Doyle about your vision, Jimmy," I finally said, "and I'm sorry. But I wasn't the only one spreading it around. You told someone besides me. Who was it?"

He stopped and looked at me, a minor victory. His swollen eyes wouldn't meet mine. "No one," he said.

"I didn't tell Doyle any of the details of your story, where it happened or about the voice being in your head. But he knew all that. He got it from somebody else. Who?"

Jimmy turned away without answering and started back toward the house. I stayed at his shoulder.

"What scared you last night on the beach, Jimmy? Was somebody out there? Who was it? Who else did you tell?"

He walked more quickly, as stiff-legged as a toy soldier, kicking sand back at me with every step. I followed him as he worked his way between blankets and folding chairs, taking the shortest route possible back to the house. I knew I was losing my last chance.

"What did the voice tell you, Jimmy?"

He surprised me by stopping again. "You already know," he said.

His answer froze me long enough to give him a small head start. He was still a few paces ahead of me when we came in sight of the house. Then he turned to face with me with the same wild look I'd seen in his eyes on the moonlit beach. He resumed his stiff walk before I could reach him, swinging small, clenched fists at his side. There was a car parked in front of the house, a brown Chevrolet. A short, broad man with red hair was leaning against it. Jimmy crossed in front of the car and got into it without speaking to the man. I called out from the street as the stout man started the car. Jimmy never turned his head.

Nine

I went into the house to look for Brother Stephen. Instead I found Pat, in the glassed back porch that he used as a pantry. He was sitting on a large box, holding an empty tumbler. His sandy hair, which had always been casual, now looked unkempt, and his hooded eyes were glassy. A wine bottle was on the floor next to his right foot. Once I spotted it, I couldn't take my eyes off it. The bottle sat in a square patch of sunlight, and the golden liquid sparkled.

"Have you never seen a bottle of wine before?" Pat asked.

"He's sent Jimmy away," I said, still staring at the wine.

"We sent him," Pat said. "I called his parents last night. It's nine in the morning, and I'm having a drink. Now you can stick your teeth back in your head." He splashed some wine into his glass defiantly. "What did Jimmy want to tell you this morning?"

"He wanted to forgive me."

"Did he tell you what frightened him on the beach last night?"

"No," I said. "But I think I know." I did know. I'd had all the pieces but one, and the last piece was shining on the floor in front of me. "You frightened him last night," I said.

Pat's surprise looked genuine. "I never left the house."

"The idea of you frightened Jimmy," I said. "The idea that you'd told the others about his vision."

"I don't know what you're talking about."

"Jimmy told someone besides me. The guys knew things I hadn't told them."

Pat accepted that with a small nod and asked quietly, "Why me?"

"Right up to the end last night, while Doyle and Bill were going through their act, Jimmy never took his eyes off me. He was sure I'd handed him over."

"You had."

"So had someone else, but Jimmy never looked at him. He'd forgotten about him. About you." I extended my right foot and touched the wine bottle with my toe. The bottle rocked slightly. "The night Brother Stephen was gone and the rest of us were at Seaside, you and Jimmy shared a bottle of wine. That's why he was so sick yesterday morning and why he didn't remember telling you about his vision until he was out wandering on the beach."

Pat smiled. "Remembering scared him? It doesn't sound like enough."

"It was enough for Jimmy. He realized then that you didn't believe him, that you didn't believe in anything. That idea scared him."

Pat considered the argument for a long minute. Then he reached again for the wine bottle. "Now I know you," he said. "You're Mr. Keen, the old-time radio detective. The 'tracer of lost souls.' Your baggy Bermuda shorts fooled me."

He poured a little wine in his glass and set the bottle back down. "Always remember that it's more genteel to fill a glass slightly. How many times you fill it slightly doesn't seem to matter."

I turned to go.

"Wait, Inspector," Pat said. "Hear my confession. I did give Jimmy a little wine that night. Maybe more than a little. I was just trying to make him less strident, trying to pass the evening. I never dreamt he'd tell me that tale of his. I was still a little gone when the others got back. I couldn't resist telling them. Doyle knew already, of course, but I was able to add to his knowledge. The next day, I repented of it. I asked Doyle to forget it, but he didn't."

He finished his wine and examined the empty glass. "Are you going to tell Stephen?"

"No," I said.

"Thank you. Don't go yet. There's one more thing for you to consider, one more inference to draw. Suppose you're correct. Suppose Jimmy was frightened last night on the beach by the idea that this house is a sham or the universe is godless or whatever. What does that tell you about his vision?"

It was a problem I hadn't considered, two more ends that wouldn't meet. I'd solved a small mystery and ignored a larger one. Jimmy had been spoken to by God. He couldn't have been terrified by the idea of no God. He couldn't have doubted for a moment. But I had seen the terror myself.

"Jimmy lied about the vision," I said. "He made the whole thing up." That's what Jimmy had meant when he'd said that I already knew what God had told him. "Why did he do it?"

"Perhaps he wanted it too much. You're an honest man, Keane. I feel sorry for you."

"Jimmy's lying doesn't make you right," I said.

Pat reached down for his bottle. "Give it up, shamus. You'll never crack this one."

"I can try," I said.

Ten

They were vain words and even silly ones, coming as they did from a detective in baggy shorts who had failed his client and hopped the first bus home. But I was glad, looking back over the years, that I'd said them. As I stood in the street watching the old house, it occurred to me that I was still trying to live up to those words, more than a decade later. That idea made me feel better about myself and my many failures. The feeling made my trip to the shore a success.

I said good-bye to the house. It couldn't tell me if Brother Stephen was still coaching first base or if Jimmy had recovered from his journey into himself. I'd never tried to check up on Jimmy. I didn't have anything to tell him. I still hadn't tracked down and cornered the thing that had scared him that night on the beach, although I'd felt it near me since and seen it reflected in other faces and in the yellowed pages of books.

It was waiting for me now, in fact. I started back to my car.

ON PILGRIMAGE

One

We'd run through rain showers on the drive from North Jersey to Doylestown, Pennsylvania, and they'd rinsed weeks of dirt from my car. Amanda and I paused to admire it in the grassy field where it was parked with about a hundred other cars and vans and trucks. A break in the clouds was bathing them all in a brilliant morning light, but none shone brighter than my new used Saturn coupe.

"It's very red," Amanda said. "I like it."

I decided that what she especially liked about the Saturn was being outside it. She'd been unusually quiet on the drive down from Morristown, even though our being together that day was pretty much her idea. She'd originally arranged to do the "Pilgrimage for the Cure," a fund-raiser for breast cancer research, with her father, my old friend Harry Ohlman. When Harry had been forced to drop out at the last minute, Amanda had tapped me, her Uncle Owen. That I was only an honorary uncle, and a black sheep one at that, had seemed to hit her a few minutes into our drive, when she'd begun answering every question I could think of with a monosyllable. Or that reticence might just have been due to her age. She was now officially a teenager and resistant to all adult interrogation.

Amanda had certainly grown in the months since I'd last seen her. She was almost as tall as her mother—as I remembered her mother being. Mary Ohlman, another old friend, had been dead eight years, killed by a drunken driver. I couldn't look at Amanda without thinking of her, even though the daughter's blond hair had refused to darken to the mother's brown, as I'd been expecting it to do all her life.

The field where we stood belonged to Delaware Valley College, a tiny school on the outskirts of tiny Doylestown. Our "pilgrimage" would

114

take us to the nearby Shrine of Our Lady of Czestochowa. At least I was hoping it was nearby, as my longest regular walks were to my mailbox and back.

All around us as we wound our way to the registration area were ominous signs, very thin men and women in warm-up suits and running shoes, jogging about or stretching against parked cars.

Amanda caught me checking out the competition and said, "Relax, Uncle Owen. We're doing the five K course, not the ten K. That's just three miles. And we're in the walking group, not the running group. And there's no time limit."

She might have gone on to tell me about the oxygen stations they'd set up for me and the other forty-year-olds if we hadn't rounded a parked van just then and happened on a couple in a very tight embrace. He was tall and dark and she was petite and golden-haired. That was all I was able to observe before my scandalized companion hustled me along.

Just as we reached the shadow of an SUV, we heard the man say, "Kimberly," sighing it, like the first word of a song.

"Please," Amanda said. And then, louder, "Get a room."

I asked where she'd picked up that expression, but she only laughed in reply. We were in the registration area by then. Volunteers were handing out coffee and donuts. For us non-runners, I decided and went off to collect some. When I found Amanda again, she had a disgusted expression on her face. It made her look more like Harry than Mary for once.

"Get a load of that," she said, pointing at her own shoulder to something behind her back. I looked and saw a woman in a wheelchair, her body wasted by something, probably the disease we were there to fight. Beside her, holding her hand, was a tall dark man in a gray track suit.

"That's the guy we saw kissing the blond. Do you believe it?"

"Are you sure?" I asked, though I was fairly certain she was right.

"I'm sure. His girlfriend's standing over there." She pointed in the other direction with her donut. "Pretending she doesn't know him."

I thought of Harry again. His record in the fidelity department hadn't been a good one. I wondered how much Amanda knew of that ancient history, especially after she added, "Men are pigs."

I said, "We don't know anything about it. We don't even know if the woman in the wheelchair and that guy are married."

"Here's our chance to find out. They're getting into a registration line.

And look, the blond's getting into a different line. Naturally. You follow the couple and see how they register. I'll tail the blond."

"Sounds like my line," I said, officially joining the pigs. "Why don't we mind our own business?"

"When did you ever do that?" Amanda countered. "What kind of detective are you?"

The amateur kind, I thought, which meant I wasn't a real detective at all. But I didn't point that out to Amanda, my longtime fan. I valued her good opinion too much.

"I'm on it, chief," I said instead and went to join my line. My hesitation had let two others slip in between me and the man pushing the wheelchair, but I was close enough to hear the names he gave the volunteer behind the table: Jack and Rhea Asher.

"Mr. and Mrs. John Asher," the woman in the wheelchair amended, as though to answer any lingering doubts I might have had.

"Well?" Amanda asked when I rendezvoused with her in the crowd of waiting pilgrims.

"Husband and wife," I said.

Amanda turned me around so she could pin the cardboard square that bore my official number to my windbreaker. "Did you hear what he called the blond when they were sucking each others faces?"

"Kimberly," I said, being careful not to croon it.

"Well, she's not Kimberly anymore. The name she gave just now was Cecilia Gibbons."

Two

Shortly after that, a woman in a Yankees cap began addressing the crowd through a bullhorn. After officially thanking us, the shrine, the college, and five or six corporate sponsors, she got down to business.

"We're going to begin in a few minutes. The runners will go off first, followed by the walkers. The routes are clearly marked, but I want to go over them with you.

"Both the five K and the ten K routes start right behind me, at the college gates. And they both head west on Butler Avenue. At the corner of Butler and Ironhill Road—about a mile from here—the five K course turns to the right. Don't worry; there's a water station marking the turn.

"The ten K course continues west on Butler to North Street, where it jogs to the right and picks up Park Avenue. The course then follows Park north to Ferry Road, which is the road the shrine is on. About a half a mile after Park joins Ferry, Ironhill Road comes in, too, so all the five K participants will be rejoining the ten K people at that point. You'll all head east together on Ferry to the shrine."

Amanda, my expedition leader, had been following along on a map she'd taken from a small backpack. I was hoping the backpack also contained our lunch.

"Remember to pace yourselves. Both courses cross a little valley—Peace Valley—so they're downhill at first and then uphill. And the shrine is on a hill of its own. Save something for those hills.

"One last thing," the Yankee fan said. "None of the roads we'll be using today has been completely closed for us. We have the right-hand lane only. So you'll be facing oncoming traffic the entire way. Stay well to the right of the centerline, and you won't have any problems.

"Now I'd like to have all runners at the gates, please."

Amanda had put away her map by then and was scanning the crowd. "There they are," she said, nodding discreetly toward the Ashers. "And Kimberly Celia is staying close to them. I don't like it."

The situation was losing its charm for me as well. "Forget it," I said. "It's nothing."

We'd always played at finding mysteries in the everyday, she and I. At least it was a game for her. For me, it was more a cast of mind. A disability, I sometimes thought. But I wasn't in the mood to play that morning. Without Harry around, I was the responsible adult. Or thought I was.

"It can't be nothing, Owen," Amanda said, dropping the uncle, which she did from time to time. It certainly wouldn't have gone very well with her condescending tone. "This 'Celia' wouldn't have used a false name if she was just along for the walk. She's up to no good."

A blast from an air horn started the runners moving. And Amanda. She crossed to the woman in the wheelchair. A moment later, she'd struck up a conversation. My only protest was to drag my feet joining them. By the time I got there, Amanda and the woman were old friends, and I was a relative again.

"Uncle Owen, I'd like you to meet Rhea and Jack. They're doing the ten K walk."

"We're going to try it," Jack said, grimacing slightly. I guessed him to be in his late thirties and uncomfortable, perhaps with the idea of pushing a wheelchair six hilly miles. His track suit and shoes looked brand-new, and his skin was pasty, even for April. His eyes were hidden behind dark glasses, so as I shook his hand, I noted instead his small ears, each pierced but undecorated, and his large, sullen mouth. It had been wiped clean of any trace of the kiss we'd seen.

Rhea said, "I told Jack we'd see how it goes." Like her husband, she wore a shiny nylon jogging suit, fresh from some rack. At the neck and wrists, a bulky sweater protruded. Against its heavy turtleneck, her face seemed very thin, all cheekbones and bright blue eyes. When I'd first seen her, I'd thought her lustrous brown hair a survivor of her illness. Now I saw it was an expensive-looking wig.

"We're not going to do ten K unless we find some nice people to help Jack push."

Amanda jumped all over that hint. "We'll help, won't we, Uncle Owen?"

Another potential volunteer was standing not far away. From behind the shelter of a group of identically dressed women, whose sweatshirts identified them as "Dayla's Divas," Celia Gibbons was watching us openly.

Watching Amanda and Rhea, actually. Amanda had said something I hadn't quite caught about a chain that hung from Rhea's turtleneck collar.

"It's not a necklace," Rhea said, pulling the chain from inside her jacket. "It's my engagement and wedding rings. My fingers are too thin now for me to wear them safely. I don't want to have them sized because then I won't be able to wear them when my weight comes back. So I keep them on this chain."

Leaving it to my sometime niece to say the correct, complementary thing, I looked back to Celia.

Her gaze was fixed on the dangling rings, I thought, and her expression was a mixture of surprise and anger. Then she caught my eye and quickly looked away.

Three

I was still thinking of Celia's expression as we joined the others at the starting gate. The surprise I'd seen in it bothered me more than the anger. It was as though Celia was shocked that Rhea should be showing off her rings—and by extension her marriage—to a stranger. Why? Because Celia considered that marriage a sham? Was Rhea's offense that she was clinging to her marriage? Or to her life?

Another air horn blast roused me from that disturbing thought. We were off, shuffling and jostling at first as we merged onto Butler Avenue under the watchful eye of the Doylestown police, who were holding back the traffic in the eastbound lane so we could cross it. The westbound lane— set off by orange cones—belonged to us, but it was too narrow at first for the crowd. Amanda and I walked shoulder to shoulder behind Jack and the chair, serving as a breakwater against the tide of faster walkers bumping past us on either side.

After half a mile or so, the crowd had stretched itself out. We were able to walk beside the chair, which meant to its right. Rhea found the slopping road uncomfortable and preferred to be as near its crown as the orange cones permitted.

Amanda stopped to retie a shoe at one point and then came jogging up to whisper in my ear. "Ten people back."

I knew without asking or looking that she was giving me Celia Gibbons's current location.

During Amanda's brief absence, Rhea had found two new recruits: Jane and Larry Hoyer, retired teachers from New Hope. Like many of the people we'd seen that morning, the Hoyers were walking memorials to a cancer victim. They each wore a pink sweatshirt decorated with the smiling photograph of a young woman. It could have been Jane Hoyer in her youth, but it was almost certainly the couple's dead daughter.

Jane took over pushing the wheelchair immediately. Pushing and lecturing Amanda on our destination.

"You've never been to the shrine? Oh, you're in for a treat. It's a beautiful place. It was built to commemorate Poland's Millennium, which was in 1966. Did you know that? Our Lady of Czestochowa is the name of a famous painting of the Blessed Virgin and the Christ Child that ended up in a small village in central Poland. Czestochowa, of course."

"Once a teacher always a teacher," her husband said in an aside to me.

The pair were a confirmation of the belief that a husband and wife grow to look like one another over the years. Both were snub-featured, short, and round. Both saw the world through eyeglasses with heavy plastic frames. Both wore their hair in an early Beatles bowl-cut, Larry's thinning at the crown.

"According to legend," his wife was saying, "the painting was done by St. Luke on a piece of wood that had been part of a table belonging to the Holy Family. Supposedly, it was found in Jerusalem by St. Helen, who also found the true cross."

"She later bought the Brooklyn Bridge," Larry whispered.

"According to tradition," Jane continued, "the painting reached Poland as part of a dowry for a royal marriage. A Polish prince married a princess from Constantinople.

"Eventually the painting ended up in a shrine in Czestochowa. Then in the late Middle Ages, the shrine was sacked—I don't remember by who— and the painting was damaged. The slashes made by a sword are still visible on the face of the Virgin. You'll see them when we get to the shrine."

"How did the painting get to America?" Amanda asked.

"It didn't," Larry said. "The one they have at the shrine is a copy."

"An exact copy," his wife said.

"Right," Larry shot back. "They were able to find another piece of wood from that table from Nazareth. St. Joseph made a new leaf every time Jesus added an apostle."

Jane laughed with the rest of us at that. Then she started in again. "The American painting was done by an art professor from Poland. And the shrine was designed by a Polish-American architect and dedicated by a Polish-American Archbishop, John Krol, and the president back then, Lyndon B. Johnson."

"The B stood for Bronski," Larry assured Amanda.

"She knows better," Jane said. "My husband snuck in Bronski because it was my maiden name. So I'm proud of being Polish when I come here. Who wouldn't be?"

Rhea had been so quiet, I thought she might have fallen asleep. But now she said, "It's a shame you don't know more about the prince and the princess, the ones whose wedding brought the painting to Poland. I'd like to hear more about them. About their lives."

"Oh, honey," Jane said, "I don't think anyone knows much about those two. They're just part of the legend of the painting, a kind of blank spot in the story. You can fill it in however you like."

We'd arrived at Ironhill Road, the turnoff for the five K course. I stifled a sigh as we passed it. Then Amanda was tugging at my sleeve. I turned and saw the false Celia Gibbons jogging up behind us.

"Mind if I join you?" she asked. "The people I was walking with turned off back there."

"If you join this group," Larry said, "you have to help push our friend Rhea."

"I'll be happy to. My name's Celia, by the way."

We all introduced ourselves, Larry and Jack shaking Celia's hand. She favored them each with identical stiff smiles. She had a broad face given to dimples, but not a girl's face. It was the face of a young woman in her prime, its only bad features the eyebrows, which were so severely trimmed they looked stenciled on.

Jane said, "You have to help push and you have to tell a story."

Several voices said "What?" to that, mine being one.

"I just thought of it. I mean, I had two thoughts come together. I was remembering what I'd told Rhea just now, about the story of the prince and princess being a blank you could fill in any way you liked. That was the first thought. The second was that we're pilgrims on a pilgrimage like the characters in Chaucer's *The Canterbury Tales*. Larry taught that book every fall for thirty years."

"Forty years," Larry said.

"Chaucer's pilgrims tell each other stories to pass the time. And I thought we could do that, too. We could each tell a story about the prince and the princess who got the painting. Of Our Lady of Czestochowa," she added for Celia's benefit. "Don't worry. You'll get the idea. I'll go first."

Four

Before she started her story, Jane passed off the job of pushing the wheelchair. The first one to step up was Amanda, but Rhea surprised us all by vetoing her.

"Not the child. Not while we're on the city streets. I'd be too nervous.

Let's save her until we reach the grounds of the shrine. We'll need her young legs then. I hear there's a hill there that will be a real challenge."

"A very steep hill," Jane said.

Amanda shrugged and passed the job to me. I was immediately conscious of how uncomfortable the trip had to be for Rhea. Every crack and bump in the road were transmitted to my hands through the chair's metal framework. Its occupant was seated on a cushion, but her feet and hands had to be receiving the same jittery feedback.

I was so preoccupied with finding the smoothest possible path that I barely heard the opening part of Jane's story, which had to do with the fairy-tale courtship of the prince and princess. But I did get a feel for Jane's storytelling style. It suggested that we were all rammy children and it was past our bedtime. When the pavement finally improved and I was able to listen along, the royal couple were married and living in Kiev.

"The prince's old father died," Jane was saying, "and the prince and princess became king and queen. Naturally, they wanted to have a child, like every couple wants to have. Only being a royal couple, they had that much extra pressure. But the years came and went and no child.

"So the princess—the queen, I mean—knelt before the picture of Our Lady, which hung in the castle's chapel, and prayed and prayed for a baby. Every morning at Mass she prayed, until one morning, after a year had passed, she found she was with child.

"By and by, the most beautiful baby was born. A girl, but such a beautiful girl that the king and the queen and everyone in the kingdom forgot that they'd been hoping for a boy."

"A little more to the left," Rhea whispered to me. "It's flatter up there. It tires me to be leaning over all the time."

Her instructions took us very close to the oncoming traffic. We were on North Street by then, and it lacked a center line. Perhaps to compensate, the orange cones were more numerous along this stretch, but they didn't seem like much protection.

I looked up from one cone in time to see a white van coming toward us. The two men in the front seat were both wearing sunglasses as dark as Jack's, so their eyes were hidden. But it seemed to me that they were staring right at us. Staring us down, in fact, for crowding the center of the road.

By the time they were gone and my breathing had returned to normal, Jane's story was approaching its second and true crisis.

"Then the beautiful little princess came down with a terrible fever. All the doctors in the kingdom were summoned, but none could make her well. Everyone in the castle walked on tiptoe, and the lanes all around were covered with straw to muffle the sound of the carts and wagons.

"Finally, the queen decided that she had to seek the intercession of Our Lady. So she and all her court went on a pilgrimage to Czestochowa. The painting was there in its very own shrine. The queen had built it in thanksgiving when her daughter was born. So it was the natural place for the queen to go.

"She and her ladies-in-waiting prayed for three days and three nights. On the morning of the fourth day, word came from Kiev that the beautiful princess had been miraculously cured."

Her voice caught a little on those last two words. I wondered how many days and nights Jane had prayed for a miraculous cure for her own daughter, perhaps at the very shrine where we were heading, the one she knew so well. No cure had come, but she was on her way to that shrine again. That in itself was a miracle, it seemed to me.

Jane ended the story with the approved formula and in a steady voice: "And the three of them lived happily ever after."

But when I glanced over, I saw tears streaming down her face.

Five

Amanda was at Jane's side at once, one arm around her. But it was Larry Hoyer who really saved his wife.

"My turn," he said, ignoring the tears and the consolation. "I happen to know the true story of the Polish prince and the princess, the king and queen of all Poland, eventually, and several other kielbasa-eating provinces. And they didn't have one daughter. They had eleven. The king was going to stop after one, then after two, then three. He was going to stop after every daughter, but his wife, the former princess, was from the Middle East and did this dance with veils."

"Larry," Jane said. She was only sniffling now, and her arm was around Amanda.

"What? Every time she danced, she'd drop a veil. And every time she did, they had a daughter. But she'd only brought eleven veils from Constantinople, and after she'd dropped the last one, that was it, game over."

"Larry," Amanda said, capturing Jane's intonation exactly.

"Once the daughters stopped coming, the king thought his troubles were done, too, but they'd only just started. Twelve women in the house, all with royal prerogatives. No more nights at the lodge, no more polka parties, no more bowling, which was the national pastime back then. It was 'do this' and 'don't do that' all day long, and every door to the castle guarded, by the princesses, working in shifts.

"That was how the original shrine in Czestochowa came to be sacked by Mongol hordes, by the way. Instead of being at the head of his army, the king was stuck at a dance recital."

We'd turned onto Park Avenue, which was starting out flat enough. There was a hill ahead, though, as we all could see. Above it, the dark clouds were gathering again.

As though able to follow my gaze from her seat in front of me, Rhea said, "More rain coming. Is my poncho back there?"

"Back where?" I asked and then saw it tucked inside a pocket on the back of the chair's seat. "Yes, it's here. Do you want to put it on?"

"Not yet."

Given Rhea's ESP, I was hesitant to look over at Celia and Jack. But I did steal a quick glance. The two were walking side by side very naturally, a little way off from Amanda and the Hoyers.

Rhea didn't catch me checking on her husband, but Amanda did. She'd been watching him and Celia, too, evidently. The disgusted way she shook her head when our eyes met was a perfect imitation of her father.

Larry had meanwhile gotten the oldest princess up to marrying age.

"It was the big wish of her father that she should get married and move out of the castle. And for a while, it seemed like that was a sure thing. The princess had met the Crown Prince of Portugal. They'd hit it off and set the date. But then the prince's father, the King of Portugal, had thrown in a monkey wrench. He'd heard of the miraculous picture of Mary and Jesus, the one the queen had brought from the East all those years before. And he demanded that the painting be part of the dowry of princess number one.

"Now our hero had a problem. When word got out that daughter number one would get the painting, daughters two through eleven started squawking. Each one wanted the painting for herself. And if she couldn't have it, she didn't want any of her sisters to have it. It started to look to the king like he'd never get any of them married off.

"He decided he would kick the problem upstairs. He'd ask Our Lady. He went down to the castle's chapel—the painting had been moved back home after the shrine had been sacked—and prayed and prayed. In fact, he fell asleep praying, which happened a lot in the days before television. He didn't wake up until the next morning, when sunlight was streaming though the chapel windows.

"The king saw right away that a miracle had happened. Instead of one painting of the Madonna and Child over the altar, there were two. That is, there was one hanging in the normal spot and a second, identical picture leaning against the tabernacle.

"The king put the second painting in with the loot he was shipping to Portugal. And before he knew it, daughter number one was married and living in Lisbon.

"By then, daughter number two was engaged to the Prince of Scotland and demanding her own dowry painting. So the king went back to the chapel, prayed, fell asleep, and whammo. When he woke up there was an exact copy of the miraculous painting leaning against the tabernacle.

"This went on every year until, finally, princess number eleven was on her way to Norway, her painting under her arm.

"Then peace and quiet reigned in the castle for the first time in thirty years. The king should have been happy, but he wasn't. He was worried about the queen, afraid she'd be lonely now that it was just the two of them. So he went looking for his wife. He found her on the highest turret of the castle. She was waving good-bye to daughter eleven, whose honeymoon caravan was still in sight.

"The king took the queen's hand and kissed it, and a funny thing happened. He smelled turpentine. He looked down at the fingers and saw there was paint under the nails, the same color blue as Mary's dress in the painting that was now on its way to Oslo."

I looked over and saw that Larry's own wife's hand was wrapped around his.

"Right then the king knew where the miraculous paintings had come from. And he knew everything was going to be all right. They'd miss their daughters, but they'd all be together again someday. In the meantime, the king and queen would be together. They'd live happily ever after, in fact."

Six

We were approaching another water station, the ground beyond it littered with paper cups dropped by runners too intent on a personal best to hit a garbage can. Rhea suggested that we stop.

Her husband pointed out that we'd already dropped behind, which was true. The group ahead of us had opened a gap of over a hundred yards. Incredibly, there were still people behind us, despite our leisurely pace. They were so far behind, though, that they could only have been late starters.

Jane Hoyer jumped in to counter what she seemed to see as criticism of the woman in the chair. "We're doing fine—you're doing fine, honey," she added to Rhea. "We don't need to get there at any special time. The shuttles back to the college run until three."

We were enjoying our paper cups of tepid water by then. Rhea asked, "Are any of those shuttles equipped to handle my chair? Did you ask about the buses, Jack?"

"We talked about that, Rhea," the dark man said. "If there isn't a handicapped shuttle, I'll ride back and get our car. It won't take me twenty minutes."

Amanda pulled me away from the group and began to pick up dropped paper cups, motioning for me to do the same. So my back could feel as good as my feet, I thought at first. But it was really an excuse for a secret conference.

"It sounds like Jack is planning to strand Rhea at the shrine while he supposedly goes back for the car. Whatever's going to happen may happen then."

"Nothing's going to happen," I said, though that wasn't how I was feeling. For one thing, it now looked like it could rain at any moment. Pour, in fact. The dark clouds were twisting and tumbling above us.

"Did you notice that white van?" Amanda asked. "The one with the two guys in sunglasses? On a cloudy day?"

"I saw it go by."

"It's gone by *twice* and slowed down both times."

I'd trained her too well. Luckily, I'd spent a lifetime listening to other people's reasonable explanations of things I found threatening or sinister. I put that experience to work now.

"Traffic's one-way today, thanks to us. Any delivery or repair guys who miss a turn have to go all the way around again."

Amanda's answer to that was cut off by a recall order from Larry. Team Rhea was on the move again, with Larry pushing the chair. At first. We hadn't gone very far before he was waving Amanda over to take his place. Amanda pointed to Rhea and shook her head no. Larry put a finger to his lips and repeated the summons. Without consulting me, Amanda dropped a few steps back and then slipped up behind the chair. She and Larry accomplished the handoff without breaking stride or—more amazing—giggling.

"Might as well warm the kid up," Larry whispered to me when he was well away from the chair. "Rhea will never know the difference."

He was wrong about that. His wife started the scheme unraveling by asking who wanted to be the next to tell a story. Those of us who hadn't told one began looking around for someone else to volunteer, Rhea included.

She said, "Come on now," encouragingly and then cut herself off. "Where's the child? Where's Amanda?"

Larry was already hurrying back to the chair, but it was too late. Rhea had twisted around enough to answer her own question.

"I told you *no*," Rhea said, her voice trembling. "I asked you to wait until we were away from this traffic. How could you do this to me? Look how you've frightened me. Look at my hand shake."

"My fault," Larry said. "I had to stop to tie a shoe. I'll take over."

"No," Rhea said. "I want Jack. Jack come over here. You've been ignoring me long enough. Come push for a while. Bring your friend to help. This hill is getting steep."

Amanda retreated to my side, still blushing like only the really fair can. Everyone could see the glow, even Rhea. The sight of Amanda so upset seemed to calm the woman at once.

"I'm sorry, Amanda," she said. "I'm sorry everyone. I don't want to spoil this beautiful time. It's the sickness that makes me act this way. It's not how I really am. Do you forgive me, Amanda?"

"It's fine," Amanda said, even more embarrassed now, if that was possible.

"You tell the next story," Rhea suggested. "Then I'll know you're okay."

I expected Amanda to say no to that with her next breath, but she hesitated. She was looking at Celia, who had accompanied Jack to the place of honor beside the wheelchair. Amanda didn't like that. And I didn't like the look on her suddenly blush-free face.

"Okay," she said.

Seven

"My story takes place after the prince and the princess have been married for a few years," Amanda began. "After they'd become king and queen of Poland. But before the painting of the Virgin and Child had been moved to Czestochowa. It was still in the castle's chapel, and the king and queen saw it every day.

"They were very happy at first. For years. They had a baby, a daughter. For a while, that made everything perfect. But then things changed.

"The problem was, the king didn't want to be a king. He'd always wanted to be a painter. But being the only son of a royal family, he hadn't had a choice. It was okay at first because he really did love the queen and his daughter. But then the job got to him. Doing something he hated doing day in and day out got to him. And what made it worse was, every morning at Mass he saw the beautiful painting over the altar and it reminded him that he'd been born to paint beautiful things like that and he wasn't doing it."

Like the Hoyers before her—and every other storyteller for that matter—Amanda was dropping some personal history into her fiction. Family history, I should say. Harry, her father, was the only son of a successful lawyer. He'd been pressured into becoming a lawyer himself and eventually taking over his father's firm, even though he'd wanted to paint.

I'd wondered earlier, back at the college when Amanda had been dismissing men as pigs, how much she knew of her father's infidelity, his stupid response to his career frustrations. Now I had my answer. That is, I thought I did. I thought I knew where Amanda was heading. Given the way she was staring at Jack and Celia, I would have bet my car on it.

"The queen had a Spanish lady-in-waiting, the daughter of a nobleman, a count. The count's daughter was very beautiful, with her dark hair and eyes and olive skin. She stood out in the northern land of Poland so much the king couldn't help noticing her. And she noticed him. Pretty soon they were lovers, meeting in a room in the highest turret of the castle."

Jane was giving Amanda a serious second look, while her husband was smiling and nodding.

"Best story so far," he said.

Amanda's true audience, the pair walking behind the chair, didn't appear to be paying attention. Nevertheless, she soldiered on, moving from family history into pure invention.

"For the king, the affair was just something to take his mind off how unhappy he was. He was weak and foolish, but he had no intentions of leaving his wife and baby and deserting his people. The lady-in-waiting knew this, but she had ideas of her own. She wanted to be queen. She knew there was only one way that could happen.

"So she started to think of ways to kill the queen. She slipped out of the castle one night and went to the shop of an alchemist. She bought hemlock from him and hid it away. Her plan was to poison the queen's tea, but before she could do it, the Mongol hordes attacked."

"All right," Larry said. "This could be a movie."

"The Mongols laid siege to the castle in Kiev. The king and his men fought bravely, but the Mongols forced their way inside.

"The lady-in-waiting saw her chance. She grabbed a sword and ran to the room where the queen was hiding with her baby. And she killed the queen, cutting her across the cheek with one of the first blows. Then she took the baby and ran away.

"By then help was arriving."

"The Polish cavalry," Larry suggested.

"The Polish cavalry," Amanda said. "And they drove the Mongols off. The king was wounded, but alive. When he found the queen, he and everyone else thought the Mongols had killed her and carried the princess away.

"Then the Spanish lady came out of hiding with the baby. She claimed to have saved it, and everyone called her a hero. The king asked her to care for the royal princess and, when he was well again and out of mourning, he asked the lady-in-waiting to marry him.

"So everything had worked out just the way she'd wanted. On the morning of her wedding, she went down to the chapel knowing she was going to live happily ever after, with another woman's husband and baby and title.

"The chapel hadn't been touched by the Mongols. It was crowded with all the nobles who had survived the attack. They all sighed when the bride came in; she was so beautiful in her white dress. She knelt down next to the king, and the bishop began the wedding ceremony. When he asked if anyone knew of any reason why the king and the lady should not be joined in matrimony, someone called out, 'The painting!'

"Everyone in the chapel looked up at the painting above the altar and gasped. On Mary's cheek, a gash was appearing, right where the dead queen had been slashed across the face.

"When she saw the miracle, the lady-in-waiting started to scream. Before anyone could stop her, she'd run out of the chapel. They found her in her chamber, dead, the hemlock she'd bought for the queen still on her lips."

After Amanda had finished, no one spoke for a moment. Then Jane took my hand and whispered, "Good luck with that one."

Eight

My first reaction to Amanda's cautionary tale was shock at her nerve. The second was the thought that it would be a hard act to follow. That seemed to be the consensus among our fellow pilgrims, none of whom volunteered to go next.

Before our troop leader, Jane, could do more than drop a hit or two, the long-awaited rain finally began. It wasn't the downpour I'd been expecting, but it was steady and cold.

We stopped so Jack and Celia could help Rhea into her poncho. The Hoyers huddled under an umbrella, which had previously dangled on Larry's belt. Amanda and I had ponchos of our own, I was surprised to learn. Bright red ones. They'd been in her backpack, taking up the space I'd hoped had been filled with sandwiches. As I pulled my head through mine, I saw Jack offer his poncho to Celia.

"Too late," she said, shaking her head to demonstrate how wet her blond hair already was. Her enjoyment of the shower heightened the contrast between her and the woman huddled in the chair.

"Let's get moving, you two," Rhea said. "Before we drown."

We were still on Park Avenue and still on its final, steep hill. Ahead I could see the intersection with Ferry Road, the shrine's road, at last.

"Celia, you haven't told your story yet," Jane prodded, the words well spaced out as she was breathing hard.

"I can't think of stories," Celia said. "If I tried, I'd just end up telling someone else's over again. Amanda's probably. Only I'd tell it differently. Not have the king be so weak and dumb, maybe. Maybe try to understand more why he did what he did. Why he took up with the Spanish lady, I mean. I wouldn't have it be because he didn't like his job. That didn't seem real. He's the king, right? So he could paint or do whatever else he wanted.

"There had to be another problem between the king and the queen. I think maybe she stopped paying enough attention to him, maybe after their daughter was born. Stopped caring about him and how he was changing and the problems he was having, with Mongol hordes and things.

"So maybe she asked for it, what happened to her, the queen. I don't mean getting killed or slashed across the face, but losing the king's love to the Spanish lady. Anyway, that's how I'd tell it."

Amanda didn't like this reworking of her story in favor of the cheating husband. I could tell that from how stiff-legged her walk had become.

Then the husband piled on. "I'd tell it differently, too," he said. Or tried to say. His breathing was almost as labored as Jane's.

"For heaven's sake, Jack," Rhea said. "Let someone else push me if you're going to talk. Celia, do you think you could make it to the top of this hill?"

"Of course."

Amanda was squeezing my arm. I interpreted the pressure to mean, "Keep an eye on her."

Rhea was prompting her husband. "You were saying, Jack?"

"I was just going to say that I'd tell Amanda's story differently myself. I wouldn't make the Spanish lady such a villain. She was just trying to be happy like everybody else and to make the king happy. Maybe she wasn't trying to hurt anybody, not intentionally."

If Jack had kept up on that line, Amanda would have been positively goose-stepping with indignation. But his wind had given out. We were all breathing harder by the time we turned onto Ferry Road and the grade flattened.

A drenched volunteer at the intersection was waving us on. "You're on the home stretch," she said. "Don't give up now."

A long column of walkers was strung out ahead of us and an equally long line of traffic was coming the other way. Most of the cars had their lights on now. The wheelchair was closest to the traffic, as it had been all morning, Celia behind it. Jack was beside the chair and Amanda and I beside him. The Hoyers were to my right, walking awkwardly under their umbrella.

Rhea spoke up then, her voice somehow carrying easily above the sound of tires swooshing past on wet pavement. "I would have changed the part of Amanda's story about how the queen died. I would have had her struck down by one of the Mongols. Fatally wounded, but still alive when the lady-in-waiting found her.

"Lady-in-waiting," she repeated and laughed. "What a perfect title for the 'other woman.' The other woman is always waiting. Waiting in the wings. Waiting for her chance. It's what she does best.

"Where was I? Oh yes. I would have the lady-in-waiting find the queen wounded and dying. The queen would know all about the affair in my version. It hurt her badly, of course, but she kept silent. Out of love for the king.

"Now she knows she's about to die. Nothing can save her, no doctors, no miracles. As her last act, she gives her baby to her rival. She knows that she's giving her husband away as well. And that's what she wants. She wants the man she loves, the man who has given her so much happiness, to be happy himself. That's all she cares about at the end, his happiness. She doesn't want him to live out the long years alone."

Jane Hoyer was sobbing openly, but I only had a second to notice that before things started happening.

Amanda was squeezing my arm again and pointing. Coming toward us slowly—following a long gap in the traffic—was the white van. I could just make out the two men inside against the glare of the headlights.

Celia was saying, innocently, "The chair is pulling to the left. Is your poncho caught in the wheel?"

Already the chair was dangerously close to the wrong side of the road. And the van was suddenly accelerating.

I caught Amanda's arm as she started for the chair and yanked her back, passing her to Larry. Jack seemed transfixed by the sight of the oncoming van, which was knocking aside cone after cone. I brushed past him and ran in front of the chair, waving my arms, the red poncho flapping up and down like a signal flag.

At the last second, the van swerved away and disappeared down the hill.

Nine

It was a dispirited group of pilgrims that turned onto the shrine's drive and began to climb the last hill. The Hoyers, still clinging tightly to one another, had dropped back a few yards. Jack and Celia were staying farther away from one another than they had all morning, neither saying a word to anyone. Rhea was slumped in her chair.

The exception to the general gloom was Amanda. She was wearing a small, tight smile that I alone understood. The others might have attributed it to her having finally gotten to push the wheelchair, which she was moving along with a will. I knew her high spirits were due to the feeling of a job well done. She'd spotted an evil plot and foiled it, she and I.

So I should have been pretty high myself, but I wasn't. I was too busy thinking about what had happened, trying to make sense of it. When the shrine finally came into view, I was so distracted that Amanda had to call my attention to it.

The main building was big and white and modern, with a concave front and stubby, set-back wings decorated in stained glass and golden panels. A spire, which looked like a stack of elongated blocks, stood to the right of the shrine. The two structures seemed to be connected only by a raised plaza, which was reached from the drive by a double staircase. Coming off either side of the floating plaza were long wheelchair ramps that turned and ran down both sides of the building.

The design of these ramps caused our group to break up at last. Jack stepped up and relieved Amanda, saying, "No point in you folks walking all the way back to where the ramp starts. We'll say good-bye here. And thanks."

He directed that thank you to me. If his gratitude puzzled Amanda, she didn't show it. She was too busy hugging a barely responsive Rhea. And worrying, one more time.

While the Hoyers took their turns saying good-bye to the woman in the chair, Amanda whispered to me, "Is she safe now?"

"Thanks to you," I said.

Celia was already on the steps, her final message to us a cryptic wave.

As Amanda and I started up those same steps with the Hoyers, Jane said, "The rain has stopped."

"Now that we're almost inside," her husband grumbled.

His wife ignored him. "And look. The sun is coming out. Just in time for your tour."

The sunlight, which burst through so strongly it made the white concrete all around us painful to the eye, seemed to revive Jane. She happily acted as tour guide for Amanda, leading her into the shrine's main sanctuary while Larry and I trailed behind. I caught Larry looking at me several times as though he wanted to ask me something, but he never did.

It was lucky for us that the sun had decided to return, since the architect had apparently intended light to be an important part of the sanctuary's decoration. Sunlight backed the stained glass, of course. And a shaft of it illuminated a gigantic sculpture that hung above the altar, a triumphant Christ flanked by angels with trumpets. In addition to being the focal point of the space, the frieze was one of the world's largest picture frames. Set in its center like a square jewel was the reproduction of the miraculous painting of the Virgin and Child.

In Larry's story, the Virgin's dress had been its traditional blue, but in the painting, it was black and red. Jesus, so out of scale that he looked like a doll, was also in red. Both figures were dark-skinned and unsmiling. Mary seemed especially wary, not looking me in the eye, but staring off to my left.

The Hoyers knelt down together in the sanctuary's first pew. Amanda joined them, perhaps to say a prayer for the grandmother she'd lost to cancer. I wandered outside.

There I found Rhea Asher, alone on the front plaza. Her back was to the shrine, which meant that her view was of Peace Valley, the little valley we'd crossed on our walk. The rooftops of Doylestown were visible on the next hill.

She was isolated, exactly how Amanda had feared she'd be. It was the perfect moment for Kimberly, a.k.a. Celia Gibbons, to spring from the shadows for a second attempt. I sprang from the shadows, or rather strolled from them, instead.

"Owen," she said when I arrived at the railing next to her. She'd lost her plastic poncho and bounced back a little from the walk and the rain. "Not religious or just overwhelmed by the place?"

"Both," I said. "Where's Jack?"

"Gone to get his car."

Not "our car," I noted.

"You got off easily," she added.

I pictured the van bearing down on us and decided I had. Rhea was thinking of something else.

"You never had to tell a story," she said.

"Nope."

"Tell me one now to help me pass my wait."

I wondered which wait she meant but shook the question off.

"All right," I said.

Ten

I considered using a fairy-tale framework for my story as the others had done, rewriting the parts for kings and queens and princesses. But it seemed like too much work. And I didn't know when Jack would show up and end the interview. I did choose an apt beginning, though, one that was a homage to Jane Hoyer, whose storytelling idea had proven as valuable as Amanda's suspicions.

"Once upon a time, a married man was having an affair. The other woman was sure she'd get him away from his wife eventually, when some obstacle was overcome, maybe when his child reached a certain age or a promotion came through. She'd gotten a pledge to that effect from the husband in the form of two rings, and engagement ring and a wedding band."

Rhea reached up to the chain she wore around her neck.

"But then the other woman got sick. She got cancer. The married man stood by her, though he didn't leave his wife. The other woman knew he wouldn't now.

"Worse, she'd somehow discovered that the wife knew all about the affair, had found out about it, probably when the other woman's illness had started to require so much of the husband's time. The wife had not only forgiven her husband, she'd encouraged him to support the sick woman, who otherwise would have been facing her cancer alone.

"That kindness might have been the thing that was too much for the other woman to bear. Or it might just have been the thought that the wife was healthy and had the man they both wanted. The other woman decided to break the marriage up in the only way left to her. She decided to kill the wife.

"A cancer walk she'd been planning to do with the husband gave her her chance. She learned that the wife was going to tag along, under a false name, to help out or maybe just to keep an eye on things. Though forgiving and kind, the wife was also human. The other woman worked out a murder scheme using the walk. It meant killing herself as well, but she knew by then that she was going to die anyway. She hired some men to drive a van into the chair at the moment the wife was pushing it. But things didn't work out."

A hawk was soaring above the valley, though it wasn't much above eye level to us on our hill. I wondered what the bird made of all the human clutter and movement beneath it.

Rhea said, "What a farfetched story. A ridiculous story. Why would you even think of something like that?"

I mentally listed the various clues. The first had been Kimberly's use of a phony name. Then the look of surprise on her face when Rhea had shown off her rings. Kimberly shouldn't have been surprised that Jack's wife had a wedding ring, but she had been. And not just because Jack and Rhea's marriage was as good as dead, as I'd thought at the time. But because it had never existed.

I thought next of the gap Rhea's water stop had opened between our group and the walkers ahead of us and her insistence on staying near the crown of the road so she'd be close to the oncoming van. When the critical moment had come, she'd made the chair veer even farther left by pressing the brake on that side, causing the pulling that Kimberly had noticed. More damning was the panic and fear Rhea had shown earlier in the walk when she'd realized that Amanda was pushing her chair. Amanda, who was as tall as Kimberly and as blond and who might easily have died in Kimberly's place, struck down by the van driver who'd been instructed to wait until a petite blond was pushing the chair.

But I didn't mention any of that. "It was your stories," I said. "Yours and Jack's and Kimberly's."

Rhea didn't ask me who Kimberly was. But she was still looking at me defiantly.

"I don't mean stories, really," I continued. "I mean your variations on Amanda's story. Kimberly's was a defense of the cheating husband, or so I thought at first. It was really a confession. She was telling us how she, the wronged wife, had neglected Jack and brought on all their troubles.

"His variation was a defense of the other woman. You. He had no idea what you were really up to." But he knows now, I thought. There'd be no further attempts on Kimberly's life.

"What about my story?" Rhea asked. "The dying queen who gives her husband away. Are you saying that didn't touch your heart?" She was looking past me now, like the Madonna in the shrine.

"No," I said, "it didn't. You laid it on too thick. The part about the other woman, how she's always waiting in the wings, that came from the heart. The rest of it rang false. When you were talking about the queen not wanting her husband to live out his life alone, you were telling us exactly what you did want for Jack. What you'd planned for him. You wanted him to lose both of you."

"The animal," Rhea said softly. "The noble animal. The pair of noble animals. What a child she is. How could she think I wouldn't know what she looked like? That I wouldn't have made it my business to know? And could she really imagine he wouldn't tell me that she was planning to come today? He almost bragged about it, he was so proud."

She looked me in the eye again. "Does Amanda know?"

"No."

"I should never have let her tag along. I didn't realize how much she looked like Kimberly until I saw them together. By then it was too late to send Amanda away.

"Promise me you won't tell her about any of this." The huge blue eyes were pleading. "She's younger than the rest of us. So much younger. She'll remember me longer. Maybe another eighty years. I don't want her to remember me like that."

I thought of the words Rhea had used when she'd apologized to Amanda for speaking to her harshly: "It's the sickness that makes me act this way. It's not how I really am."

"I won't tell her," I said.

Eleven

Amanda was quiet on the shuttle ride back to the college. And less obviously triumphant. That disappointed me. I was afraid she was thinking ahead to the long ride to Morristown in the Saturn, stuck beside a man she really barely knew. I'd started to feel like a real uncle over the course of the walk, and I hated the thought of being demoted again. Perhaps for good.

The little coupe was one of the few cars still parked in the muddy, rutted field. We stood examining the car as we had hours earlier. I steeled myself for another remark from Amanda on how red it was, a signal that our easy familiarity was over and we were back where we'd started, searching awkwardly for something to say.

Instead, she asked, "How can people who love each other end up wanting to hurt each other?"

For a second I thought that she'd figured it out, that she was asking how Rhea could have loved Jack and still have tried to hurt him. Then I realized that Amanda had drifted back to a much older crime, to what her father had done to her mother.

"Tell you what," I said. "Whichever one of us figures out love first reports back to the other."

"Deal," she said, and we shook on it, a pack that bound us for years and years.

She held on to my hand and tugged me toward the car. "Didn't we pass a McDonald's near here?" she asked. "I'm buying, Uncle."

A SUNDAY IN ORDINARY TIME

One

W elcome to St. Joseph the Worker," the woman behind the lec
tern said. "Today is the Twenty-fourth Sunday in Ordinary
Time."

Ordinary time, I repeated to myself, ignoring the rest of her greeting.
That term, I knew, was just the Catholic Church's way of saying that it
wasn't Advent or Christmas, wasn't Lent or Easter. But it was also far
from an ordinary time, an ordinary Sunday.

For one thing, I was in a church, a place I didn't often visit. And I wasn't
the only special-occasion congregant. The old, sixties vintage building had
an Easter crowd on this ordinary, September Sunday.

And the church had American flags prominently displayed, a common
feature back when I was a kid that had gone out of fashion since. Many of
the people around me were similarly decorated, with flag pins and red,
white, and blue ribbons. One old man, whose red-rimmed eyes had met
mine when I'd entered, held an actual flag in his big fist, the kind of toy
flag kids waved at parades. In ordinary times.

The hymn with which we greeted the celebrant was "America the Beautiful." The line about "heroes liberating strife" caused the woman beside
me to begin to sniff. When the choir reached the last verse and sang about
"alabaster cities undimmed by human tears," the woman's sniffing
became sobbing. I patted her shoulder.

The celebrant was a boy priest named Plezniak. He had a dazed look, as
many of us did. Tired and dazed in his case. After reading us the gospel,
he left his pulpit, descended from the altar, and stood in the center aisle,
looking suddenly small and squat in his green vestments.

"There are many reminders of this terrible week in our church
today," he began. "The flags, the music, the tears. Not that any of us

here in Carteret need additional reminders. We only have to walk outside and look to the north to see the smoke from the World Trade Center fires."

It was more of a haze now, certainly not the billowing plume of the prior week, just a whitish brown smudge in the sky beyond Staten Island. Several people had told me that they could smell the fire when the wind was right, but I'd been spared that. The normal smells of this old North Jersey city, the ones coming off the stretch of water called the Arthur Kill and the aroma of the nearby oil refineries, were still too new and overpowering.

"To be honest, though," Plezniak continued, "there can't be any place in America that needs a reminder of what has happened. They can't see the smoke in Ohio or New Mexico, in Minnesota or Oregon, but the people there are thinking of New York and Washington and a field in Pennsylvania this morning, as we are. Their hearts are in those three places, as ours are.

"I'd planned to speak on evil today, on the continuing presence of evil. But I've decided not to. On this Sunday, we don't need to be reminded that evil exists in the world any more than we need a reminder of the rescue efforts going on across the bay."

He paused for so long I thought that might be it. Then he started in again. "All week we've gotten calls at the rectory from people wanting to know what they could be doing to help and calls from people who were just trying to find a way to get through each day, a way to deal with the pain and the confusion. And I found that I was giving the same answer to both types of caller, the ones who wanted to help and the ones who needed help. The answer was that they should find some positive thing close to home to do."

The priest had a very unseasoned face, its youth accentuated by his hair, which managed to be both short and unruly. But this morning his voice had the wear of ages in it.

"It's the same answer I would have given a month ago to a person overwhelmed by the evil in the world. I'd have said to such a person, 'Turn off your television, stop wallowing in despair and helplessness, leave your home, and find one thing you can do to make the world a better place.'

"A month ago that kind of call was rare. Most of us were too distracted by our own worries and dreams to give more than a passing thought to the evil in the world. This past week I suspect that many of us had a hand on the phone at one time or other, ready to make a call to someone, anyone, who could help us with our pain.

"In a moment we'll continue our celebration of an event, Christ's death and resurrection, that offers us the hope of tremendous good coming out of crushing evil. That hope can and will comfort us.

"But don't discount the power of small, insignificant acts of goodness to counteract a crushing evil. If you find yourself in despair today or in any of the days and nights ahead, turn off your television, go out into the world, and find your own personal act of goodness to perform."

Two

At the very end of the Mass, the lay reader returned to her lectern to read us the parish announcements that we could have read just as well for ourselves in the bulletin if we'd cared to. When she'd finished, Plezniak stood, drawing us all to our feet. He started for the center of the altar to say the final blessing, stopped midway, and turned to face us.

"On the subject of small acts of goodness, the family of Martin Kolczak is organizing a neighborhood search today. As many of you know, he's been missing since Friday. They've asked all volunteers to meet in the church parking lot after this service. Let us pray."

I hadn't heard about Martin Kolczak, but then I hadn't been paying much attention to local news. When the Mass ended, I filed out with the crowd and wandered toward the corner of the parking lot where the volunteers were gathering.

Not that I was volunteering for anything. I not only doubted the power of small acts of kindness to counteract a tremendous evil, I had reason to believe, based on a lifetime's research, that small, kind acts, done at the wrong time and in the wrong place, could actually spark the evil. But I'd never been able to resist a mystery, and I was reluctant to give up the sense of community I'd felt in the packed church.

There was plenty of that feeling on display among the milling volunteers. Although the crowd was much smaller than the one that had attended the eleven o'clock service, it was also much more sociable. People were hugging one another, shaking hands, calling out to neighbors and friends. Not that the mood was upbeat. The gathering had the feeling of a wake, but an odd one, a wake at which all the mourners were also family.

None of the members of that family spoke to me at first, which was okay. A vicarious feeling of community was as much as I ever hoped for. But then, just as we were being called to order, someone tugged at my elbow. It was the woman whose shoulder I'd patted at the beginning of the service. She was a small woman whose lined, sallow face and dark, sunken eyes took me back to my childhood parish, reminding me of the mothers and grandmothers of my Italian friends.

She whispered, "Thank you," and then turned to face the speaker.

He was standing in the bed of a pickup truck, holding a bullhorn that he never got around to using, a thirty-something guy in golf shirt and khaki safari shorts. I decided that his build and boot-camp haircut and general air of authority marked him as an off-duty cop, but I never bothered to verify the guess.

"Attention everybody. Let's get settled. We need to get started as soon as possible, to make the most of our daylight."

The crowd unsettled at that, perhaps because of the suggestion that this good deed might take the whole day.

When the buzzing died down, the man on the truck said, "First I'd like to thank you all on behalf of Irene Kolczak, Martin's sister." He gestured to his right, to a figure all but hidden by the crowd.

"Just to recap, Martin Kolczak is an eighty-year-old Alzheimer's victim who wandered away from his home on Dewey Avenue on Friday afternoon and hasn't been seen since. His immediate neighborhood has been searched pretty thoroughly without result. Today, with your help, we're going to expand that search to include the entire city."

That sounded more ambitious than it really was. Technically a borough and not a city, Carteret had a population of only about twenty thousand.

"Our plan is to divide you into teams of two. Each team will be given one or more city blocks to canvas. You're to knock on doors, talk to people, show Martin's picture around. We've pictures enough for all of you; is that right, Betty?"

Betty's offstage voice said it was.

The cop then echoed Father Plezniak. "Over in Manhattan today, there are a lot of people walking around with pictures of loved ones they're trying to find. We can't help those people. Probably no one can. But we're going to make a difference right here in Carteret. We're going to find Martin Kolczak."

Three

The man with the bullhorn broke the crowd in several lines, each leading to volunteers with an armload of paper. It was the moment to wander off, but I joined a line instead. The sallow-skinned woman followed behind me. While we waited, she gave me the unauthorized version of the Martin Kolczak story.

"An actuary," she said. "Before he retired. Worked for an insurance company for forty years. A big man at St. Joseph's. Everybody knows him. How could he just disappear?"

That was the question that had gotten me into line. My confidential source had her own theory.

"Something fishy about it. A man wanders off in broad daylight and no one notices. And that sister of his, who was supposed to be watching him, where was she? Asleep, I heard. Taking a nap. Three o'clock in the afternoon. Nice work if you can get it."

The little woman had no sooner damned the sister for sleeping on duty than she upped the charges against her. "But who's to say she was napping? What could be easier than leaving the door unlocked and looking the other way? Or sending the poor guy on an errand? Two minutes out the door he forgets where he's going, maybe forgets the way home. You know he has plenty of insurance, him who worked with it all his life."

Actually, I thought it just as likely that Kolczak had no insurance. I'd known enough mechanics whose cars were wrecks and doctors who smoked. I didn't mention them to the little woman who shuffled along at my side. Something had caused her to reexamine her position without my help. Maybe it was that whitish brown haze to the northeast, hovering over all of us like an admonition against pettiness. Maybe the unkindness of her words had finally registered, had been able to register because of the peculiar quiet of this day. Or maybe the change of heart was simply due to the unobstructed view of Kolczak's sister we'd gotten as our line had inched forward.

"Shame on me," my confidant said. "Shame on me."

At first glance, you wouldn't expect Irene Kolczak to inspire such contrition. She was one tough looking woman, maybe in her sixties, maybe in her seventies. Her dyed and lacquered brown hair made it tough to judge, as did her face, which was broad and flat-cheeked and largely unlined. Her nose was also flat—if she'd been a man I would have suspected a football injury. Her small eyes were unhopeful and her lips ungenerous. Though the day was mild, she wore a leather car coat and held the collar of it closed with fingers that had been misshapen by something, possibly arthritis.

Sooner than I'd expected, we were at the head of the line and I was being introduced to my partner. I'd resigned myself to the company of the little Italian woman who was dogging my steps, but the volunteer working our line split us up, pairing me with a woman who looked young enough to be a student somewhere.

When we introduced ourselves, she repeated my name, Owen Keane, several times, committing it to memory. Her name, Moira Wyszynski, suggested the kind of mixed breeding that was North Jersey's saving grace. She was dressed in jeans and a lightweight sweater trimmed in faux leopard fur. Her full lips were painted lavender, though the cosmetics company had surely given the hue a more interesting name. The same shade appeared her nails, which flashed every time she raised her cup of Starbucks coffee. Her eye makeup, in contrast, was plain old black, but there was plenty of it. Her light brown hair had blond highlights that looked like they'd been made with a florescent marker, and it was cut in the current fashion, which called for the strands to curve inward toward her face, their ends always threatening to enter her mouth.

That threat was made all the more real by a characteristic of Moira's mouth, which was that it was very seldom closed. But I didn't pick up on that right away. The frazzled volunteer who gave us our final briefing—Betty, the photo authority—did most of the talking.

"Here's a photograph for each of you. And here's a map with your streets marked in green. You'll be on Randolph Street, the two and three hundred blocks. The phone number of the police is written on the bottom of your sheets. Call them if you have any trouble. They know we're going to be out today. The other number rings in our command center. Call that if you find Mr. Kolczak or anyone who's seen him or if you have any questions. You have a cell phone, right?"

I looked to Moira, who was nodding.

"That's it then," Betty said. "Good luck."

She started to turn to the next team, but my partner held her in place with a hand tipped in lavender. Bending slightly so she could look the shorter woman in the eye, Moira said, quite slowly, "We will find him."

Four

That rash promise was the only slow thing I ever heard Moira say. Before we'd driven a block—in her little Korean car, at her insistence—she'd told me that she was native of nearby Montclair, that she was twenty-six, that she worked as an assistant buyer for a department store chain, that she'd only recently moved to the Carteret area, and that she'd heard about the search on a local radio station.

To be fair, she'd given me a chance to speak, asking me where I worked—Home Depot, as an assistant everything—and how long I'd lived in Carteret. That last question had been prompted by our inability to find Randolph Street.

"I just assumed you were a native," Moira said as we straightened ourselves out with the aid of the Xeroxed map Betty had given us. "I figured they'd teamed me with an old hand 'cause I'm a newbie."

"I've only been here a couple of months," I said. I might have gone on to say that I'd picked Carteret because I'd once known a man by that name and liked him. I might even have remarked on an interesting coincidence, which was that the man I'd known had suffered from memory loss, like Martin Kolczak, though Carteret's had been caused by a hunk of shrapnel. But Moira didn't give me that much air time. She'd found us on the map, and we were off again.

As she drove, Moira discoursed on Alzheimer's. "Know much about it, Owen? I looked it up on the Internet last night. I thought it might be useful to have some background."

"Good thinking," I said, smiling to myself at how quickly she'd gotten comfortable with my first name, how comfortable she was with the idea of being alone for the day with a stranger twice her age. She was more than comfortable with the situation, she was in command of it, lecturing more than briefing me as we careered along.

"Alzheimer's affects about four million Americans. It's basically a disease that kills brain cells. It's progressive, too. You loose your recent memories first, then your long-term memories, then your ability to function at all.

"Alzheimer's victims are all prone to wandering off, like Mr. Kolczak did. They might do it because they're disoriented or frightened or just restless. Or they might feel they have to go to work or fulfill some other commitment, maybe a commitment that's twenty years in the past."

So much for the Internet experts. Moira had her own theory about the cause of Kolczak's disappearance. "I think it had to be the terrorist attacks. I mean, I watched the tape of that second plane hitting a dozen times, didn't you? I've heard that watching it over and over is bad for you, but I'm not so sure. Because anything you watch over and over again, even a horrible thing like that, you get used to. You get numb to.

"But imagine you're Martin Kolczak, with no short-term memory. The television stations keep showing that moment of video, and each time it's new to you. So you never get used to it, you never develop those emotional calluses. Tell me that wouldn't drive you into the street."

The problem with her theory was that it denied the possibility of a beneficial cumulative effect—numbing—while positing a harmful one. If Kolczak had been forgetting the attack between viewings of the video record, he could never have reached the point of overload. He would never have progressed beyond the stunned disbelief we'd all experienced in those first terrible minutes. Not unless there was some emotional memory at work, something unimpaired by his disease.

I didn't voice the objection since Moira didn't open the floor to discussion. Instead, she shifted back to the question of our pairing.

"I bet they put us together because of our ages. They want each team to be able to relate to anyone who answers the door, no matter what age the person happens to be. So I should talk to the young ones. And you should talk to the, ah, …"

"Seasoned ones?"

One look at Randolph Street convinced me that I'd be going hoarse in a hurry. The age of the street was reflected by its curbs, which were stone and almost buried under the patched pavement's many layers. The houses represented some kind of intermediate stage between the row homes of a city and the stand-alones of a true suburb. They were detached, but only just, three stories high counting attic dormers, and narrowly fronted. Their cellars stuck up out of the ground a few feet, as evidenced by the tiny windows around the base of each house and the half dozen steps required to connect their front doors to the rolling sidewalk.

Our mode of operation, established at the first house, was for both of us to squeeze up these steps, as narrow as they were steep, and ring the bell. Then, depending on the age of the person who answered, one of us would fall back. I was pleasantly surprised to find that I was doing the falling more often than not. The old houses were turning over, evidently, and the post war generation, Martin Kolczak's generation, was giving way to a much younger one.

Younger and more ethnically diverse. Moira might have better used her time on the web brushing up on her Spanish and Ukrainian. Luckily her facility for English, combined with a theatrical flare, got her through every time. From the bottom step of staircase after staircase, I watched her all but act out Kolczak's disappearance, admiring her body language certainly, but also her enthusiasm.

My own was waning. The people I was talking to were sometimes hard of hearing, sometimes vision impaired, and never very interested in my questions. One man was actually belligerent.

He answered his door in a sleeveless undershirt and rumpled trousers, carrying a newspaper, also rumpled. He must have been Kolczak's age, but he was in better shape mentally. Physically, too, probably. Though his skin was sagging generally, there were still muscle underneath it.

Every house we'd visited had a flag out, even if it was only the paper one the local weekly had provided. This house had several and something I was willing to bet was unique on all of Randolph Street. In one front window hung a little banner of sun-faded silk, maybe a foot long and six inches wide. On it were sewn two stars, one above the other, the top one gold and the bottom one blue.

The man in the undershirt let me get through half of my spiel before he cut me off by thrusting his newspaper at me. "Everything that's going on and you're worried about one old crazy? Get out of here!"

Our only other exchange of note took place near the end of our second block, at a house whose brick had taken on a heavy coating of stucco at some time in the past, making it look like a badly iced cake. A flag staff had been mounted on the front door frame and quite recently; where the molding had been chiseled away to make a flat spot for the base, the raw wood was unweathered and clean. So was the flag that moved in the gentle breeze, nudging Moira as she rang the bell.

There was nothing remarkable about a brand-new flag, not this week. We'd sold out of flags at the Home Depot in the days following the attacks. It wasn't until Moira froze in the act of pushing this particular flag away from her face that I started paying attention.

The man who'd opened the door was young and thin and frightened. He had every reason to be frightened on this particular Sunday, since he was very obviously of Middle Eastern descent. However hard my week had been and Moira's, they can't have compared with his.

His age made him my partner's to question, but for once the power of speech deserted her. I smiled and held up Kolczak's photograph.

"Sorry to bother you. We're looking for a man who wandered away from his house over on Dewey Avenue. Have you seen him?"

The young man hadn't taken his dark eyes from my smile. It must have held up, because he finally dropped his gaze to the photograph. Then he shook his head and, almost bowing, shut the door.

Five

That encounter left Moira subdued. But she'd recovered by the time we'd checked the last house on our last block.

"I just don't feel like giving up, Owen," she said as we started back for her car. "How about we try another street?"

"I don't think so."

Her eyes were quite blue, a fact more disguised than highlighted by all the mascara. They flashed at me now. "Do you want a ride back to the church or can you walk?"

"Not without my cane," I said, trying to raise a smile. I added, to redeem myself, "I'm not giving up. But we're not going to find Kolczak by knocking on doors."

"How then?"

"By asking questions. I've had a little experience finding people."

"The ones who get lost in the lawn and garden department?"

Before I could correct her impression of my life's work, she let up on me. "Sorry. I'm sure you haven't always been at Home Depot. Were you some kind of investigator?"

That sounded vague enough to cover me. "Yes."

"So how did you find people?"

An accurate description of my technique would have mentioned chasing every red herring and charging down every blind alley that came along. I summarized. "I tried to get to know the missing person, to understand them. I got inside the person's head."

"The inside of Martin's head is a blank slate."

"Not blank yet. He left the house for a reason. If we can figure out why he left, it could tell us where to look."

We'd reached her little Hyundai. Moira jiggled a ring that held enough keys for a dealership and said, "Give me a for instance."

"Okay. You said an Alzheimer's victim might wander off because he thinks he has to go to work. It could be as simple as that."

"Somebody must have thought of that already. And why wouldn't someone at his workplace have noticed him?"

"He wandered off on a Friday afternoon. The office might have been closed when he got there. He might be sitting there now, waiting for it to open."

"Office? For all we know he was a brick layer."

"He worked for an insurance company," I said, giving away my only piece of inside information.

It turned out to be a sound investment, since it tipped Moira my way. "Who could tell us where his old office is?"

"His sister," I said. "Irene."

If I'd been on my own, I would have been second-guessing all the way to Dewey Avenue. For example, there was a good chance Irene wouldn't be at the address she'd shared with her brother. She might still be in the parking lot at St. Joe's or at the "command center" we'd heard about, where we wouldn't be able to question her without first explaining ourselves to the people running the search. Or the Kolczak house might *be* the command center, in which case we wouldn't find Irene alone.

But Moira was convinced that she could talk her way past any obstacles. I found her confidence so infectious that I just listened to the cryptic rhythms she punched up on the radio and enjoyed the ride.

As it turned out, we didn't have to put Moira's confidence to the test. Irene was at home, her only company a neighbor lady who retreated to the kitchen to make coffee when Irene reluctantly invited us in. We sat in a living room I'd been in a hundred times before in other remote corners of New Jersey. It was the architectural equivalent of an old gym shoe: aromatic, broken down, and comfortable.

"You really should report to the command center," Irene told us. "Over in the church basement. I asked them not to have it here. I couldn't stand all the coming and going."

She still looked as hard as her varnished hair, but her voice was gentle, with the slightest trace of a *W* every time she pronounced an *R*.

Moira said, "We'd like to try a different approach, Irene. We'd like to figure out why Martin left."

Irene got so defensive so quickly that I wondered if there might be something to the gossip I'd listened to back at the church lot.

"Why he left? What do you mean? Do you think somebody did something to him?"

"Of course not," Moira said soothingly. She surprised me then by giving an earlier theory of hers an airing. "Except maybe the terrorists. I mean, we've all been upset. Did the news reports of the attacks bother your brother?"

"They made him restless. So I turned them off. Then he forgot what had happened."

"And settled down?" Moira prompted.

Irene nodded, but I could tell she was still thinking about it. Meanwhile Moira was signaling me to jump in.

"We thought your bother might have left because he felt he had to be somewhere," I said. "Like his job."

"They thought of that," Irene said. "But the insurance company where he worked, Consolidated, went out of business ten years ago."

"Where did he work before that?" Moira asked. "He may be using very old memories."

"Nowhere but Consolidated. Except for the defense plant where he worked during the war. But that was over in Union, where we lived back then. It made ball bearings."

"Let's stick with Consolidated for the moment," I said. "Did anyone check the building where the company used to be located?"

Irene blinked at me. "I don't know. I'm not even sure where it was exactly. I was still living in Union when Martin got the actuary job. I was taking care of our mother. I didn't come back here until after she passed. Not even then. Not until after Martin got sick."

It was a thumbnail autobiography if I'd ever heard one. The woman with the hard face and the gentle voice had been a caregiver all her life. First for her mother and then for her brother.

"Who would know where the building was?" I asked. "Do you know the names of any of your brother's coworkers?"

"No," Irene said. And then, "Wait. He got a Christmas card from one of them every year."

She padded off, and I noticed for the first time that she'd traded her shoes for carpet slippers. When she returned, she was carrying a little red basket that contained the Kolczak family's tiny cache of nearly year-old Christmas cards. Few as there were, it took Irene some time to sort through them with her gnarled fingers.

"Here it is. I always save the envelopes. Walter Odle. His address is 333 Carteret Avenue."

Six

On the way to Carteret Avenue, I asked Moira if she thought our hostess had acted strangely.

"Caregiver fatigue," she said. "I read about it last night. People who care for Alzheimer's patients wear out in a hurry if they don't empower themselves, don't give themselves permission to still have a life."

I spent the remainder of the short drive wondering whether I'd ever met a person less empowered than Irene Kolczak.

Walter Odle was working in the little front yard of his bungalow when we pulled up. He was somewhere between Moira and me in age, which meant he must have been a fairly junior member of the insurance company Kolczak had left fifteen years ago.

Odle was a short guy who needed more exercise than the chrysanthemums were giving him. His smile was genuine from the start, but it got positively warm when Moira mentioned Martin Kolczak.

"How is the old guy? I really miss him. I didn't work with many white guys of Martin's generation who were as friendly to me as he was."

Odle's face literally drooped as my partner explained the situation. "Alzheimer's? Martin? I did not know that. Trouble with Consolidated going under, besides me getting tossed out on the street, was that it scattered everybody, broke up the network. I don't hear the news."

"We're here because of Consolidated," I said. "We think Martin might have gone to his old office."

"Thinking he's still in harness? That makes sense. Trouble is, the office is gone. They tore the building down when they expanded the turnpike exit a few years back."

Moira's nails pressed my arm. "Martin may not remember that. He could be wandering around looking for that building. Walter, where was the building in relation to the exit?"

Odle was pulling off his gloves. "I'll show you."

As we drove, Odle reminisced in the backseat. "Good old Martin. He was the guy who organized all the office birthday parties and the going-away parties. I always thought he did it because he didn't have any family, so he'd adopted the whole office. I never heard him talk about any sister.

"You know, I actually thought of Martin last week right after the attacks. I figured an old war-horse like him would be chafing to be back in uniform kicking butt. I felt like kicking some butt myself, and I was never in the service.

"Turn right up here and look for a place to park."

Parking was easy. The turnpike exit was squeezed on all sides by commercial properties and their parking lots, none of them full. The business closest to Consolidated's former location was a Holiday Inn, so we started there, showing Kolczak's picture around as we had on Randolph Street.

After that, Moira worked the tollbooths while Odle and I scrambled around on the stony ground beneath the elevated ramp that carried traffic between the turnpike and the exit. We found evidence of human habitation under there in the form of flattened cardboard packing cases and cold fire pits, but it predated Kolczak's disappearance. There was no one around to question.

Next we worked a little strip mall across from the exit. Moira did most of the talking, which left my mind free to think about the lunch I wasn't having. Eventually, though, it got thinking about something Odle had said in the car.

I asked him about it outside a discount shoe store. "Did you say that Kolczak had been in the service?"

"Right. During the big one, World War II. He was in the Marines. Talked about it all the time. Saw action somewhere in the South Pacific. Tarawa, I think."

I turned to Moira, but she was too quick on her feet to need the dots connected for her. "Owen, didn't Irene tell us that Martin worked in a defense plant during the war?"

"No way," Odle said. "He signed up the day after Pearl Harbor. Didn't get out until after they dropped the Bomb."

"What does that mean, Owen?"

Another part of my technique as an investigator was to resolve all discrepancies, no matter how trivial or peripheral they seemed.

"It means we talk to Irene Kolczak again."

Seven

The caregiver wasn't thrilled to see us back on her doorstep, though she was gracious to Odle. The attention she showed him was largely due, I decided, to his faithfulness with the Christmas cards. Moira, as usual, was in charge of the conversation. Before the discreet neighbor lady could pad off to the kitchen in search of the coffee that never seemed to arrive, Moira had asked if there'd been any word from the command center. Irene shook her head, and Moira moved us on to new business, meaning me.

"Ms. Kolczak," I began, "you told us your brother worked in a defense plant in Union. When was that exactly?"

She did her blinking bit again. "When? During the war. All through the war. Martin moved us there in 1941. We'd always lived here in Carteret, but he wanted us with him in Union, my mother and me. He worked at the plant from 1941 until V-J day. Then he moved back here."

"But you and your mother stayed on in Union?" Moira asked.

"Martin thought that was best," Irene said. For the first time, I heard some serious bitterness in her voice. "Mother had had the first of her strokes. Martin didn't think she could get used to a new house."

Odle was struggling to catch up, but he was polite about it. "So your brother was never in the Marines?"

"Martin? No. What made you … Did he tell you he'd been in the war?"

Odle looked to Moira and then to me before saying, "He might have given me that impression."

"Why would he do that Ms. Kolczak?" I asked.

Her eyes wouldn't meet mine. "He might have wished he had been. But he got an exemption from the draft so he could take care of my mother and me."

Odle was shaking his head. "And here I was thinking of him marching into some recruiting office last week, an eighty-year-old veteran volunteering to fight the terrorists. And all the time he'd made up his big war record. He'd just been pretending to be the man he wished he had been."

"What, Owen?" Moira asked. She'd noticed my vacant expression.

"Suppose that's exactly what he did last Friday."

"Did what?"

"Tried to enlist. You said an Alzheimer's victim might wander off to fulfill a commitment, maybe one that's years out of date. Suppose Martin couldn't make sense of the terrorist attack because of his disease, but it reawakened some emotional memory of another time this country was attacked."

"December 7, 1941," Odle said.

"Right," I said. "Martin didn't march down to a recruiting office then, and he regretted it the rest of his life. In fact, he spent a large part of that life pretending he had enlisted. Now suddenly he's back in 1941 emotionally. And he has a chance to right that old mistake."

I'd lost Odle. "Don't you think a recruiting office would have reported an eighty-year-old disoriented guy who showed up talking about whipping the Axis?" he demanded. But then, he was new to the team and our methods.

Moira wasn't. "He wouldn't have gone to a 2001 recruiting office. He would have gone to a 1941 recruiting office. Irene, do you remember where the local recruiting office was in 1941?"

"No," the old woman said. "Who would remember that?"

"I think I know someone who might," I said.

My hunch took Moira and Odle and me back to Randolph Street, to the house of the old man in the undershirt who'd told me to get lost. His name, according to the label on his mailbox, was Balerno, and he was still dressed in his Sunday casual attire. He wasn't pleased to see Moira and me again, and he was plain mystified by Odle's presence.

"What the hell?" he asked.

"Hi there," Odle said back, giving a little wave.

I said, "Mr. Balerno, we're still looking for Martin Kolczak, the Alzheimer's patient who wandered off. We think he might be so confused that he's mixing up the terrorist attack and Pearl Harbor. We think he might even have tried to find a Marine recruiting office. We need to know where the local one was located in 1941."

"What makes you think I can tell you that?"

I pointed to the little faded banner with the two mismatched stars that hung in the window beside the front door. "You're a World War II veteran, aren't you? That's the kind of banner families hung in their windows back then when they had someone in the service. Your family had two servicemen, and one of them didn't come back, so his star is gold."

"My brother Sammy," Balerno said. "North Africa."

He had eyes that were barely visible between craggy brows above and bags below, making me think of flowers trying to fight their way through cracks in old concrete. Flowers because they were blue eyes, almost as bright as Moira's, and gleaming a little now.

"I don't know why I dug that banner out of the drawer last week when I was putting up the flags. Just seemed right. Maybe I was back in 1941 myself. So I can't laugh off this crazy idea of yours. What did you say the wacko's name is?"

I told him.

"Kolczak. He have a sister? Name of Irene?"

"Yes," Moira said.

"Let me get a shirt on. I'll be right back."

Eight

The Hyundai was noticeably less peppy with four of us squeezed inside it. Balerno's directions took us back the way we'd come, toward Dewey and then on past it. The latest addition to our troupe showed his age as he guided us. He had a tendency to cite landmarks that were no longer there, as when he told Moira to park near a now nonexistent bakery at the corner of Washington and Atlantic.

"The recruiting office was right next door," Balerno said. "I remember the Dutchman who ran the bakery bringing out hot rolls and coffee to the guys waiting to sign up. Best rolls I ever had."

He looked as though he could still taste them. I almost could myself; we were that far past my lunchtime.

Though the bakery had been torn down to make way for a windowless pharmacy, the building that had housed the recruiting office was still there. It was a storefront with an old cast iron facade whose fluted columns were rusting their way through a century of paint. The most recent occupant had been a beauty parlor, but it had folded back when Moira was in high school.

Balerno wiped at one grimy window while Odle tested the locked door. "Martin didn't get in here," the latter said.

We fell back on canvassing then, Balerno and I working one side of the street while Odle and Moira took the other. Half an hour into it, I heard my name being shouted and saw Odle waving to us. He was outside a Chinese restaurant.

Moira was inside. She'd been ordering fried rice to go when the young man behind the counter had noticed the picture of Kolczak she was carrying and mentioned that he'd seen him.

"Tell him, Francis," Moira said to her new old friend.

Francis, a smiling young man in a Hawaiian shirt, was happy to repeat the story for me. "It was Friday evening. I was coming in to work the dinner shift. I saw this old guy tottering along Roosevelt Avenue headed west." He pointed to the photocopied likeness again. "That's the guy, I'm sure of it. I remember wondering where he was going all by himself."

We all stood there wondering about that, the four of us and Francis, crowded in the restaurant's little red and black waiting area.

Balerno said, "He was headed out toward my neighborhood. It's west on Roosevelt."

Moira actually jumped. "So is Union. It's west of Carteret."

"Northwest," Balerno grumbled.

"But if you were driving there," Odle cut in, "you'd go west on Roosevelt and pick up something else, Highway 27 maybe, to take you north out of Rahway."

"He was heading to Union," Moira said. "He was trying to go back to work at that defense plant."

"You've got it!" Odle all but banged her on the back. "Where's a phone? We've got to move the search."

"What defense plant?" Balerno demanded.

Odle and Moira were near to dancing. He said, "The one where Martin spent the war years. We just have to find out where that was."

"Maybe Irene could tell us," Balerno said, warming to the idea.

"Right," Moira said. "We have to go back to Dewey Avenue."

Francis would have come with us if he hadn't had to watch the counter. As it was, he insisted on us each taking away a carton of fried rice, no charge.

I had mine safely tucked away before we'd driven the block and a half to the Kolczak house. The rice was my compensation for having been demoted from head idea man by our overall commander, Moira. She and Odle had the thing all worked out by the time a not-too-shocked Irene Kolczak admitted us for the third time. That is, she wasn't shocked to have Moira and Odle and me turn up again. Balerno was a surprise, but not, I thought, an unpleasant one.

"Ronnie," she said. "It is Ronnie, isn't it? Ronnie Balerno?"

"It sure is, Irene," Balerno said.

The sister had company as usual, but this time it wasn't the shy neighbor lady. It was Betty, the volunteer who had given us our original assignment.

"There you are," she said to Moira and me. "I've been waiting for you to call in. I just stopped by to tell Irene that we've heard from all the other teams and that none of them found any trace of Martin. How did you know I'd be here? Have you found something?"

Bringing Betty up to date with as much extraneous detail as possible was a job Moira could really sink her teeth into. And did. I sat in a quiet corner, feeling discontented with the turn events had taken and wondering if the feeling had any basis other than jealousy.

Meanwhile my partner had reached her peroration. "We need to send the volunteers over to Union. That's where we'll find Martin."

"But the volunteers were all released as soon as they reported in," Betty said.

"It's just us then," Odle said, not sounding altogether unhappy about it. He'd be making up a team name for us next. Team Kolczak maybe.

"Do you remember where this defense plant was?" Balerno asked Irene from his place of honor beside her on the sofa.

"It was on Stuyvesant Avenue," she said. "I think I could find it again."

"We'll need another car," Moira said.

Betty volunteered hers, and everyone started stirring. It was my last chance to object, and I took it.

"I don't think Martin was headed to the defense plant when Francis saw him."

"Why not?" Moira asked, showing her opinion of my opinion by not resuming her seat.

"We have to be thinking in terms of an unfulfilled commitment, something undone that would have nagged at Martin all these years. Like the military service he never did. His work at the defense plant doesn't fit that pattern. That was a job he took on and finished. We should be thinking about something he didn't finish, a promise he made and didn't keep."

All eyes turned to Irene. She wouldn't return anyone's gaze, not even Balerno's. I was sure then that there was an answer and that Irene knew it. I thought I might know it, too.

"Irene, you told us that Martin got a draft deferment so he could take care of you and your mother. Did he have to do that? Did you two depend on him?"

Speaking very slowly, Irene said, "My mother had a job before we moved to Union. She'd had to find one after my father died. I was still in school."

"And then, after the war, your mother had her first stroke. You were taking care of her alone because your brother had moved back here."

"Yes," Irene said. "Martin went to night school during the war. That got him a good job with Consolidated. He sent us money."

"But he didn't move you and your mother back."

"No."

"How long did your mother live?"

"The last stroke took her in 1972."

"And you cared for her all that time?"

"Yes."

"How much help was your brother? What did he do besides sending money?"

Irene answered me with a single tear that rocketed down her flat hard face.

Balerno saw the suicide tear and didn't like it. "What are you getting at with this?"

"Martin Kolczak made a commitment to take care of his mother. He used it as a way to dodge the draft. When the war was over, he turned his back on that promise. He left Irene to care for their mother, and he came back here to restart his life. That broken promise may have eaten at him all these years. When the terrorist attacks brought back the feelings of 1941, that unfulfilled commitment to his mother may be what Martin remembered."

Nine

Moira showed true executive ability then. "No problem, Owen. We can hit both places, the defense plant and the Kolczaks' old place in Union. Is the house still there, Irene?"

Irene thought it was.

"Good. We'll stop there first. You'd better ride with me, Irene."

That meant the very attentive Balerno would be riding with her, too. Odle and I were relegated to Betty's minivan, with me in the first of its two backseats.

That was appropriate, since I was still feeling as though I'd moved to the backseat of the investigation. No one had taken my latest epiphany very seriously. I wasn't entirely satisfied with it myself. I spent the first part of the drive west on Roosevelt wondering whether I'd leapt too far or fallen short.

As I tuned out their conversation, Betty was telling Odle that she was a nurse specializing in the care of the elderly and that she'd just been trying to convince Irene it was time to consider a nursing home for her brother. When I checked in on them again, she was thanking Odle for getting involved.

He made light of it. "I've gotten more help than I've given today, believe me. All week I've been looking for some little job I could be doing to take my mind off things. Nothing's worked very long, except this hunt for old Martin. It could go on all night, and it'd be fine with me."

From there they fell into discussing whether the healing processing could already have begun, less than a full week after the tragedy. I stuck with Odle's prior observation, thinking that the search for Martin Kolczak had certainly made me feel better. Even the monotonous business of knocking on doors and showing his picture had helped.

And suddenly I knew that I hadn't leapt far enough back in the Kolczaks' little living room.

I grabbed Betty's shoulder. "Flash your lights. Get them to pull over."

It took a combination of lights, horn, and Odle waving out the window before the Hyundai finally pulled into a Hess station. I figured out how the van's sliding door worked and called back over my shoulder, "Follow us."

Balerno and I made quite a load in the little import's backseat. He and Moira were both looking at me expectantly. Irene's expression had an element of dread in it, but then I had a history of asking her uncomfortable questions. My latest was a softball: "Where is your mother buried?"

"St. Gertrude's Cemetery. In Rahway."

The town where we currently sat. "Have we passed it yet?"

"No. It's just up the road."

"Show us."

Moira was waiting for an explanation. I gave her an excuse. "It's on our way."

I'd often observed one characteristic of urban New Jersey cemeteries, which was that they were tightly packed. Always before I'd thought of it as a final indignity, a final gyp: People who'd been forced to live their lives jammed shoulder to shoulder with strangers now had to face eternity in the same crush. On this particular Sunday, I had a different reaction. It might have been due to the week we'd all struggled through or the age I'd reached, but as our little procession entered St. Gertrude's, I felt the people buried there were lucky to have the company. The community.

The place was huge and hilly and not without the occasional very mature tree. Irene's formerly sure directions became tentative and inaccurate. She got a little defensive about it, too, as though we'd condemn her for not being a regular visitor, this woman who'd spent her life waiting on others. I was about to say something to her when Balerno pronounced absolution by simply reaching out and patting her arm.

She settled down then and led us right to the grave, or as close to it as the cars could get. We trooped down a gentle slope on foot, the six of us, all scanning the place for Martin. Other than Team Kolczak, there were only a few people about. None of them was the man we were after, which caused some grumbling in the ranks.

"What are we doing here anyway?" Balerno asked when we'd reached the Kolczak plot. He was reacting to another of Irene's stingy tears, which had been squeezed out of her by the sight of the old upright headstone.

On it were the names of Irene's mother, Marie, and her barely mentioned father, Gregory, who'd died in 1939.

My unspoken answer to Balerno's question was that we were there because Odle's soliloquy about finding some small thing to do to take his mind off the death and suffering across the bay had redirected my thinking. I still believed that Kolczak's unfulfilled obligation, the broken promise that he'd left his home to make right, involved his neglected mother. But I no longer saw Kolczak's solution in terms of some dramatic recreation of the past. I was thinking now of some simple act. Like tending a grave.

The Kolczak plot had certainly been tended by someone. I stooped down to examine it, noting that the grass had been pulled up for an inch or two around the base of the headstone. The grass that covered the grave was as even as if it had been mowed that morning. The stone itself had been brushed. A little greasy soot remained in some of the smaller crevices, but the face and the larger letters and numbers were very clean.

"Martin's been here," I said. "This grave's been cleaned up recently."

"You're nuts," Balerno said. He was standing on the plot to my left. "This one over here's just as neat."

"So's this one," Odle said from my right. "It's funny, when we first drove in, I was looking over the graves and thinking they didn't get much maintenance. But back here it's great."

Moira and I exchanged glances. "Owen. You don't think—"

"I do. You go back up the slope and I'll go down." Balerno and Odle had gotten the idea and were moving off in their opposite directions. I called after them, "Find the first untended grave."

Betty and Irene stood near the Kolczak stone, watching as the four of us moved slowly away, our steps tracing an invisible cross that grew larger and larger. I'd examined six graves, all as neat as the first, when I heard Odle cry out.

He'd worked faster than I had, getting all the way into a new section of graves whose stones were set perpendicular to the Kolczaks' row. When we reached the spot where Odle stood crying, we found an old man sprawled on the grass, his head against a slab of polished pink granite.

His clothes were grass- and sweat-stained, his hands dark with dirt and dried blood, especially around what was left of his nails. Where he'd brushed his wispy hair away from his eyes as he'd worked, his face was also the reddish brown of the soil. Everywhere else it was an unnatural white, the color of the bone that was so pronounced beneath the wasted skin.

I'd been carrying his picture around all day, and I still had trouble recognizing the man as Martin Kolczak. I might not have recognized him, in fact, without the testimony of his sister's tears, which now flowed freely.

Ten

Odle tried to find Kolczak's pulse and failed. I tried and failed in turn. It took Betty, the medical professional, to detect the fluttery rhythm. By then Moira had phoned for an ambulance and Odle had retrieved the afghan Betty kept on her van's third seat. He and I used it to cover Martin to his chin. Our long afternoon was giving way to evening, and the air was getting cool.

As soon as Balerno had gotten Irene calmed down, Betty and Odle started in on the subject of nursing home care for her brother. The unanswerable argument was lying before her under the rainbow-colored spread and Balerno was crooning in her ear about having a life of her own, but still Irene hesitated. The pull of her old life, her only life, was that strong.

I left them to it and climbed the slope to where Moira was waiting to guide the emergency medical technicians. I found her in a narrow patch of sunlight between long shadows cast by the stones and the trees. Her face was turned toward the sun and her eyes were closed, but she somehow identified the sound of my step.

"Owen, is that you?" she asked without opening her eyes. "Can you feel the sun on your face? There's still the tiniest bit of warmth in it."

"I feel it."

"Last Wednesday I was outside somewhere and I felt the sun on my face; remember how beautiful the weather was? I was just standing there soaking it in and suddenly I felt so guilty. I mean, all those people buried under the rubble of those towers, and there I was getting off on the feeling of sunlight on my face.

"And then I thought, 'No. I'm not going to feel bad about this. And I'm not going to stay out of the sun because none of those people will ever feel the sun again. That's just the opposite of what I should do. Because those people can't, I'm going to hold my face to the sun every chance I get. And every time I do it, I'm going to remember them.'"

"That's a good idea," I said.

Her eyes snapped open then, catching me smiling at her. But she didn't call me on it. "How many graves do you think he cleaned?" she asked instead.

"I don't know."

"I've been doing a little calculating. Based on how far the four of us got from that central grave and how squeezed together they are, he might have cleaned a hundred. That's an unbelievable number, even when you divide it by the two days he was missing."

"Then don't divide it by two days," I said. "Divide it by the thirty years he spent avoiding this place."

"Damn," she said. "It makes you wonder what penances we're all putting ourselves through without realizing we're doing it."

For some reason that thought carried her to the subject of my career. "Now that I've gotten to know you, I'm having a hard time picturing you at a Home Depot. What's that all about?"

"I happen to look good in orange," I said.

The alternating notes of a siren sounded in the distance.

"That's it then," Moira said. "It's over. Tomorrow we go back to whatever stupid thing we were doing with our lives. You go back to explaining the difference between Phillips head screws and regular screws, and I go back to deciding whether next spring's Capri pants should have cuffs or slits."

"Definitely slits," I said.

"I'm serious, Owen. How can we go back to that? Why should we?"

I turned my face toward the last of the sunlight. "Because they can't."

The Headless Magi

One

If Marjorie should call back, tell her *The Bells of St. Mary's* is on Channel 9 at eleven. That always cheers her up. Though why a movie about a nun getting tuberculosis should cheer anyone up is beyond me. May be some Catholic school issues there."

The speaker was a nun herself, but not the least bit tubercular. Even a mild chest cold would have prevented her from bustling about the tiny office as she was doing, collecting hat and coat and mittens, while keeping up both ends of our conversation.

"That's the scariest part about being a religious: walking through a crowd of strangers, knowing that about half of them were taught by nuns and that some percentage of those have been harboring dreams of revenge ever since. No wonder I prefer sweat suits to habits."

Sister Agnes Kelly was a sparrow-like woman, which is to say, small and apparently frail, with a self-consuming energy, bright eyes, and a sharp nose so prominent that it seemed to be what her entire face had set itself to achieve. The room in which I sat and around which she ricocheted was the headquarters of just one of her many ministries: a crisis phone service she'd set up in an old rectory turned Catholic Life Center in a quiet corner of quiet Elizabeth, New Jersey. The service was called Adullam Line, after the cave in the Bible where David hid from a jealous King Saul and where all the "discontented gathered themselves unto him."

"I hate to leave you here alone, Owen, fresh out of training. Not that my training amounts to much. Honey over at Domestic Justice—that's another crisis line, you know—always says that my training consists of the laying on of hands, and she might be right. But a person has the knack for listening or he doesn't. That's what I say."

164

Anyone who spent much time in Sister Agnes's company would develop a knack for listening, like it or not, I thought. Aloud I said, "I'll be fine."

"Speaking of Honey, she got an interesting call the other night. What?" she interrupted herself as my three-word message got through. "You'll be fine? Of course you will. But I usually have someone sit in with novices on their first night. It's just that it's so close to Christmas, and my other volunteers have families. I mean, I'm sure you do, too, Owen. A nice family. Somewhere."

She sidled then, physically—toward the door—and conversationally. "Like my nieces who always want me to come to their Christmas pageant." She pushed back coat and sweatshirt sleeves and squinted at her watch. "For which I'm now late. Not that I'll miss more than three percent of the total running time. I can remember when a Christmas pageant was two kids in paper halos knocking on inn doors and one chorus of 'Silent Night.' Now it's *The Sound of Music* with shepherds.

"That reminds me. If an out-of-town guy should call looking for a room for his very pregnant wife, offer him the couch downstairs."

Two

When the last echoes of the front door's slam had faded away, I went from enjoying the quiet in the second-floor bedroom turned office to missing Sister Agnes in a heartbeat. I coped by centering the old black rotary telephone on the contact-paper mahogany of the desktop and drawing two binders closer to hand. One was what Sister Agnes called the *Code Red Book*, though its cover was black. It contained phone numbers for emergency agencies and social services in Elizabeth and the cheek-by-jowl communities in this damp edge of North Jersey's urban sprawl. The second binder was known as the *White Book*, and it actually was white. Within it, yellow tabs divided instructions for dealing with various types of calls.

I had a book of my own, a private-eye paperback by Ross Macdonald, but I was saving that for later, when I knew I'd be fighting sleep. So I opened the white binder and began to page through its overview of human misery, wondering what I'd be dealing with before the end of my shift.

The *White Book* handled the big ones first: suicide, physical abuse, substance abuse. I flipped through those quickly, especially the last one, which might have set me thinking about a scotch on the rocks. The next categories, depression, loneliness, and anger, were also familiar to me. I'd experienced them all in the two years since I'd quit a steady and relatively respectable job in New York City and moved back across the river to my native Garden State.

Job problems was the next tab in the binder, but I didn't linger there either, having had enough personal experience in that area to counsel an entire union. In part, my history of job failures stemmed from the type I chose: uninvolving, undemanding jobs that left me free mentally to explore my own interests. Those interests accounted for the bulk of my career difficulties. I was an amateur detective, to state things in the most flattering way possible. Or a compulsive meddler in mysteries that were none of my business, to give the opposing view.

The next tab bore the legend friendship, and I did pause there, friendship being a subject I'd been thinking about a lot this Christmas season. Why so few took and why the ones that did endured so much. Those issues weren't considered in Sister Agnes's notes, which were mostly suggestions on making friends that read like advice you'd give your five-year-old if he came home from school and announced that no one liked him. Take an interest in other people. Smile. Change your socks.

The next tab, religion, likewise promised more than it delivered. Here Sister Agnes's emphasis seemed to be on not offending anyone's religious sensibilities, however bizarre. All the pussyfooting created the impression that belief in God was just another delusion that had to be humored, like the idea that President Reagan was reading one's mail. An odd attitude for a nun's notes to reflect, but then I was finding the early eighties to be an odd time in general.

The *White Book*'s final section was a catch-all of lacks relating to poverty: lack of food, lack of shelter, lack of clothing. All things I was too close to experiencing firsthand to want to read about. So I shut the book and turned to examining the room, the water stains on its papered ceiling and the collage on the wall opposite me. It was made up of dozens of human faces, cut from newspapers and magazines and taped up at random.

Then the phone rang. I reached first for the spiral notebook that served as the office log and then for the handset. "Adullam Line."

It was Marjorie, one of Sister Agnes's regulars, a woman with too many kids and not enough of anything else, including friendly ears. She didn't seem to mind breaking in a new pair of those, especially after I passed on the news about *The Bells of St. Mary's*. She wanted to talk about her oldest daughter, who was skipping school, so I listened, saying "uh-huh" occasionally while outside my window a car with a powerful stereo passed every ten minutes, as regular as a police cruiser on patrol, which it might even have been.

As I listened, I went back to examining the wall of pictures across from me, looking for a face that matched Marjorie's very tired, somewhat nasal voice. I found the right one near the upper edge of the mosaic, a glossy color shot of a stout woman with clear blue eyes and a square jaw. It occurred to me that Sister Agnes had taped the pictures there for that very purpose: so her volunteers could put faces with the voices, making it easier to think of the callers as human beings and not just disembodied woes.

When Marjorie signed off, it was so close to nine on the dot I deduced that some favorite television show or old movie was about to start. Maybe *Going My Way*.

I was deep into the adventures of Lew Archer, private eye, when the phone rang again. This time the caller was a man, an angry man.

"This the crisis line?" he asked, sneering the crisis part.

"Right," I said.

"What'dya call it? Adullam?"

"Yes."

"What's that supposed to mean?"

I told him the story of David, hiding in the cave from the wrathful King Saul and being visited there by troubled Israelites, who preferred David's judgment to the king's, which is what had bummed out Saul in the first place.

"That's damn stupid," the man said.

"Is it?" Ask open-ended questions, the *White Book* advised. It was easy advice for me to follow, a man for whom all questions were open-ended. I noted the time in the log, expecting a hang-up. The man hadn't offered me a name, so I gave him one, writing "Saul" next to the time.

"You're taping this, right?"

"Nope," I said, "no tape." Sister Agnes thought taping would break Adullam Line's implicit promise of confidentiality. Not to mention breaking our budget.

"I'm supposed to believe that?" Saul demanded.

"Your call," I said, the laconic voice of Archer still fresh in my ear.

It turned out to be the right tone to take. Saul started telling me, hesitantly at first, about his ex-wife. She'd talked him into a divorce, claiming an unhappiness that was pushing her toward suicide. He'd given her the divorce and most of their joint possessions in the settlement. Too late he'd learned that she hadn't been unhappy at all, largely due to the attentions of the young man she'd been seeing for a year and more. Now the boyfriend was living in Saul's house, sleeping in Saul's bed, watching Saul's television.

I found I was staring at the collage, at a black-and-white picture of a balding guy with intense eyes that stared back into mine. Sister Agnes had cut him from some medical ad, I decided. He was the doctor who recommended the latest wonder drug. The more I listened to Saul's clipped anger, the more I wondered which he missed more, his wife or his Magnavox. I sensed that he'd been happy to go along with the divorce at the onset. Now he was very unhappy. Because his wife had finished the game with more chips? Because she'd gotten them through trickery? Or was it because all the possibilities he'd seen in divorce hadn't panned out, starting with the chance to see himself as a man who had made a noble sacrifice?

I was trying to connect the dots, a tendency of mine that Sister Agnes had warned me about during my training. I reached for the *Code Red Book* and found a phone number for a counseling service for divorced men and another for an anger management class. Not much to offer, but then Adullam Line's major service had already been delivered. Someone had listened to Saul's side of things, which had calmed him considerably.

When he ran out of gas completely, I had him copy the phone numbers down. We were encouraged to arrange for call-backs, so I suggested that he sleep on things and call again.

"Will you be there?"

"Someone will be," Archer said.

I got up to stretch and make a pot of coffee. Sister Agnes bought hers in five-pound cans from Thriftway. It was the last thing she should scrimp on, I thought. Then the phone rang again.

This time the voice was very young and very frightened. "Help me," it said.

Three

"You gotta help me."

I stifled an impulsive "I will," which would have violated Sister Agnes's second most sacred rule: "Never promise help until you've identified the problem. Then don't promise."

"Tell me about it."

My FM radio calm was wasted on the caller, who was nearing hysterics. "Ain't no time for talking. We gotta save him. Now."

"Who?"

"My brother. Benjy. He's gonna snatch him. He said he would and he's gonna do it. Tonight. I know."

"Benjy's going to snatch—"

"Benjy's gonna get snatched. Shit. Listen to me. I'm talking, and you ain't listening. Shouldn't have a guy on this phone that don't listen."

Oddly, my incompetence was having a calming effect on Benjy's brother. "You new at this?" he asked, concerned for me now, it seemed.

Something in his voice told me that he wasn't new to his end of it, new to dealing with problems too large for him or anyone else. I said, "Yes," quickly, anxious to keep us in the pocket of calm we'd blundered into. "I just started."

"Shit," the voice said. And then, "Sorry. But this ain't no call about boozing or paying electric bills. This is an emergency."

"I know," I said.

"If I wanted somebody who didn't know nothing, I'd call the cops. They'd really mess things up."

"Right," I said, taking my hand away from the *Code Red Book*. I reached for the log instead, wrote the time and asked, "What's your name?"

"John," he said, after the slightest hesitation. "But everybody calls me Jackie. What's yours?"

Sister Agnes had advised me to select an Adullam name, one that would protect my own anonymity. I'd egotistically considered David, after the biblical cave dweller and counselor, but now I impulsively gave my own.

"Owen? What kind of name's that?"

"South Jersey. Are you okay yourself?"

"Okay?"

"Somewhere safe?"

"I'm always safe. Don't worry about me. Russet don't bother me. He don't even think about me. I'm not his."

"Not his son?"

"Damn right not his son."

"But Benjy is?"

"Russet thinks he is. Momma told him he is. But Benjy don't look like any Russet to me. Russet's an alien. Benjy's human."

"An alien?"

"From space, like that one that comes out of your chest, rips you apart, and kills you. That's Russet."

"He's not really from space though. Is he?"

"You nuts and new both?" Jackie piped. "No, he ain't from space. But he ain't from South Jersey either. And he's big. Big and sweaty. Benjy's little and pretty. Russet can palm him, he's so little."

"Benjy's a baby?"

"Yeah, a baby. Momma told Russet that Benjy's his to keep him from beating her. But nothing keeps Russet out of a beating mood for long. The Nets winning a game's about the best thing. But the Nets don't win that many."

By then I'd relaxed sufficiently to scan Sister Agnes's photo lineup for a likely Jackie. The closest I could find was a pre-teen with large eyes and a seventies afro. But the photo kid was smiling, and there was more wrong with the picture than that. It had been cut from a glossy ad, cut generously enough to include a hint of bright green background around the kid's head. A sunlit field, maybe, in soft focus. A Kodak moment. There was nothing bright or soft about the moment Jackie was calling from.

"You there, Owen?"

"I'm here. Why does Russet want to take Benjy?"

"To hit Momma. To hit her without hitting her, worse than really hitting her."

"To punish her?"

"That's right, to punish her. Cause she likes Benjy more than him. Like who wouldn't? So he's gonna take Benjy away."

"And do what with him?"

"Lose him. Take him across the Hudson and leave him on the subway. Or just use the bay. This is the best place in the world for losing stuff. The Mafia know that. That's why they hang around here. You got Mafia in South Jersey, Owen?"

"Some."

"Yeah? Well, I bet when they want to lose a guy they bring him up here. Then he stays lost. We got a smelter near here that does guys all the time. They go in, but they don't come out."

"What's a smelter?" I asked.

"You don't know or you don't think I know?" Jackie shot back. "Smelter's a big black place with smokestacks. It's where Benjy's going if you don't do something."

"And you don't want me to call the police?"

"No. Momma won't say a word to them against Russet. Then, when they leave, he'll beat her again. No social workers either. Russet beats on them first and Momma second."

"But not on you?"

"I'm too fast for him," Jackie said, but without his earlier, easy conviction. "Benjy's no faster than a brick. He just lays in his crib smiling at you. This time tomorrow, Momma's gonna be kneeling next to that crib crying, 'cause it's gonna be empty."

An odd thing happened then. A siren started to wail—not in itself an odd thing in Elizabeth. But I heard two sirens, one through the thin walls of the old rectory and one over the phone, their risings and fallings perfectly matched. Jackie was very close.

"I can be there in a few minutes," I said, breaking Adullam Line's most sacred rule: "Keep your body out of it."

"You?" Jackie said. "You'd come here?"

"Yes."

"You are a rookie. Nobody's ever said that before. You'd come here right now, and Russet showing up any time?"

"Just tell me where."

"Wait a minute. How do I know you won't screw things up worse? Or get scared and run?"

"You'll have to trust me."

"Trust you? I don't even know you. Listen. I ain't got much time. Tell me something about yourself. Something bad."

"Something bad? Why would that make you trust me?"

"You trust me first, with something you don't want anybody to know. You trust me, and I'll trust you. So tell me something bad. Tell me about some time when you got scared and ran."

I didn't have to rack my brain for examples. "I was going to be a priest. I was in school for it, a school out west. I got scared that I wouldn't measure up, so I ran away."

"Ran here?"

Via a series of stops, I thought, some of which were further examples of my cutting and running. I said, "Yes."

"Shit, Owen, this ain't no place to run to. You run *from* here. You get the hell away from here."

"Let me help you then. And your mother and Benjy."

"I gotta think. I'll call you back."

"Wait. Don't hang up." I scrambled for some way to keep him talking. "I told you something about me. Tell me something about you."

"Something bad?"

"If you like."

The silence lasted so long I thought I'd somehow missed the click of the connection being broken. Then Jackie said, "Sometimes I'm Russet," and the line went dead.

Four

The policeman, one Sergeant Grabowski, was unhelpful. "Kidnapper name of Russet?" he asked in a voice only slightly louder than the static on the line. "Sure we aren't talking about a spud napper? Is that a first name or a last name? Wait, I remember. You don't know. Address? Also unknown. Ditto time and place of the crime."

I liked the ditto. I hadn't seen it coming, unlike the rest of Grabowski's spiel. In honor of the ditto, I tried to be patient with him. "The guy's been in trouble before for beating his girlfriend. Or maybe his wife. Somebody down there should recognize his name or the names of the two kids. Jackie and Benjy."

Grabowski was also patient, to give him his due. "It's going on eleven, Mister, ah, Keane. I'm a lot of all the somebody down here who's down here. And I never heard of any wife or girlfriend beater named Russet, first name or last. To speak the truth, we've so many of those creeps around this town that it would be hard to know half of them. But I'll ask around. Can I reach you at Adullam Line?"

"Or at home," I said, giving him the number of the phone in my tiny apartment.

"Got it," Grabowski said. "And give Sister Agnes my regards. Tell her Merry Christmas for me. Not Seasons Greetings. Merry Christmas."

"Got it," I said, but I never did pass on the message. The nun returned shortly afterward, aglow from the pageant or the cold night air. Before she'd gotten her scarf-of-many-colors unwound, she'd started to tell me about her evening.

"You would have liked this play, Owen. Really. It was a mystery, like you're always reading. The hero is a detective who's trying to find the true spirit of Christmas. He visits all the shops in a mall, which gave all the grades in the school a chance to sing a number. That padded things, let me tell you. In the end it turns out that the detective is really an angel. He takes off his trench coat and a long white robe drops down. This is after he's found one person out of all the ones at the shopping center who still remembers what Christmas means, which is exactly the ratio you'd expect at a Jersey mall."

Then she caught my eye and stopped. "Owen. Something happened while I was gone. Tell me, tell me, tell me."

I did, getting through all of Jackie's story and as far as Sergeant Grabowski's name before the nun interrupted me.

"Owen, Owen, Owen. You never called the poor police over that, did you? You did. What will they think of us now, of our credibility, when we need them in a real emergency?"

"This wasn't a real emergency?"

"No. It was a prank, like that call Honey got over at Domestic Justice the other night. I told you about that." She stopped and held a mitten to her open mouth. "No I didn't, did I? I started to tell you and got distracted. So I guess this whole thing was my fault after all. My mind will wander."

"What about the other call?"

"Oh. Some child called Honey and wove her a tale about his mother being attacked by her boyfriend for stealing some of his drug money so she could buy food for her babies. That part rang true, God help us, so Honey tried to get some details. The child told her his mother's name was Angela and that her boyfriend had cut her hands as a punishment and that they were red with blood and her dress was red with it, too.

"Honey was still taken in at that point, so I guess I can't be too hard on you, Owen, you being a rookie and Honey an old pro. She started to get suspicious when the boy wouldn't give her his name and address. He just kept piling on lurid details.

"Then he overstepped himself. He said he didn't know Honey well enough to trust her. Her asked her to tell him something bad about herself. Something she didn't want anyone else to know."

Sister Agnes didn't have to catch my eye this time. She'd been studying both my eyes, watching for my reaction. "Ah, ha. I thought so. He asked you the same thing. What did you tell him, Owen? Was it about your time in the seminary? Never mind; I don't want to know. Forgive my curiosity."

"Anyway, that was the tip-off for Honey. She knew then she was being strung along. The callers who ask you to say something nasty or to repeat some fetish word that turns them on are the classic time-wasters. Like the ones who ask our female volunteers what they're wearing. I always disappoint those guys," she added, tugging down the sleeves of her sweatshirt.

"This boy seemed very young to Honey to be into that kind of thing, but when she confronted him—gently—by suggesting that he was making up the bloody hands stuff out of whole cloth, he didn't argue with her. Didn't say another word. He just hung up. He would have given up with you, too, Owen. If you'd been more …"

"Rational?" I suggested, so embarrassed that the underheated room suddenly felt oppressively warm.

"Forceful," Sister Agnes said. "And don't be hard on yourself. We all make mistakes when we're starting out. When we've been at this for years, we make new mistakes. Go on home now. I've some paperwork to do and I can listen for the phone until the midnight relief comes on. It's Rhoda tonight, I think. She'll bring cookies and I'll cage some from her. All those dancing sugar canes at the pageant gave me the munchies.

"Be careful on the front walk; it's icy. Don't slip and land on you keester."

Yet again, I thought.

Five

Two nights later I had a social engagement, a rare event for me. It was a dinner at the home of friends who lived in Morristown, not a long drive from Elizabeth in a normal car, but quite the haul in a barely heated Volkswagen Karmann-Ghia. The friends were the Ohlmans, Harry and Mary, two people I'd known since my first year in college, which is to say, for almost fifteen years. A decade and a half. It was this amazing span of time that had gotten me thinking about friendship, the resiliency thereof, this Christmas season, or rather the Ohlman's invitation—pressed on me in the face of many subtle hints and outright refusals—had.

I would have been thinking of friendship as I drove—northwest on Eighty-two and then Twenty-four past Millburn and through Chatham and Madison and Convent Station, the towns getting nicer if not noticeably farther apart—if I'd been able to put Jackie out of my mind. I'd waited all day for a call from Sergeant Grabowski and had even casually dropped by the Adullam office on the off chance that Jackie had called back. But there had been nothing there for me, not even leftover cookies.

I'd been quick to accept Sister Agnes's pronouncement that Jackie's call was a hoax and I still doubted the story he'd told me, Russet the alien's imminent kidnapping of innocent Benjy, but I'd gone back to believing the call itself. By that I mean I now believed again that it had been a genuine call for help. I had just failed to determine what the real problem was. That failure and the nature of Jackie's unstated problem haunted me as I drove through frozen marshland, patches of ice in the weedy darkness beyond the road reflecting an elusive moon.

Suburban Morristown's zoning seemed to restrict builders to colonial homes, the bigger the better. Harry and Mary's was a nice brick example in a subdivision too new to have many trees. That was just as well, as those trees present were strung with enough electric lights to distract the airliners swarming Newark. An unfamiliar car was parked on the Ohlmans' slopping drive, a sleek Audi, but that didn't surprise me, Harry being as sentimental about cars as George Steinbrenner was about managers.

So I rang the front bell worrying only about whether I'd be able to make two hours of small talk with my old friends, the woman I had once loved and the man who had won her away from me. But as soon as the door opened, I knew I was in far worse trouble. I could hear Harry's deep voice a room or two away, speaking to someone who was not the couple's two-year-old daughter. And there was the look on Mary's face, the how's-Owen-going-to-take-this? look. I knew then I was being set up, not the way paperback detectives were set up, to take the fall for someone, but the way unmarried friends were. To fall for someone. Some stranger.

"It's not too late to run," Mary said. "I thought you might when you saw Beth's car in the drive."

"I'm not that fast mentally."

She didn't disagree with me. "Tenacity," she said as she hugged me. "That's your strong suit. Owen, you're frozen. That car of yours. Come inside."

I'd already noted that she was very warm. And soft, in a mauve cashmere sweater with a floppy turtleneck collar. As we did the little dance required for her to take my coat, I further noted her brown, calf-length skirt and matching boots. Her short, honey-colored hair was arranged more formally than usual, which had the effect of making her look older. All grown up. Or maybe it was the setting, the formal entryway, all warm wood and antique brass, with fresh greenery draped over its doorways and wound around the banister of the staircase that led to the shadowy second floor.

Somehow I'd held on to the present I'd brought for Amanda, the two-year-old. "Wrapped it yourself, I see," Mary, who was something of a detective in her own right, observed. "That's so sweet."

I was still holding the package as we entered the softly lit living room, where a fire crackled aggressively and smoked slightly.

"Damn fireplace isn't drawing right," Harry said as we shook hands. His large hand switched to smoothing his dark, thinning hair self-consciously the second I released it. He also directed my attention to the extra pound or two he'd put on by sucking in his stomach. "Should have preheated the flue. That column of cold air acts like a cork."

"I'm fine, Harry," I said. "How are you?"

Then Mary was introducing me to our fourth, who was seated on one of the twin love seats that faced each other at right angles to the hearth. "Beth, I'd like you to meet Owen Keane. Owen, this is Beth Wolfe."

Beth was a slender woman in a rust-colored knit dress that was doing what clinging it could with what was available. Her facial features were also slender, in a very regular, very classic way: her lips thin but not wide, her nose straight but not sharp, her cheekbones visible but not hollow. The elegance of the whole was offset by a dusting of old freckles on her very pale skin and by her eye makeup, which was a bit on the heavy side. All the eye shadow and mascara made her dark brown eyes look very dark indeed, as did the up-from-under look she gave me from beneath chestnut bangs. Her thin hand felt cold even to my frozen one, and her legs were not so much crossed as clamped, one atop the other. This icy reserve relaxed me as thoroughly as the double scotch Harry handed me. Beth wanted no more to do with Mary's ambush than I did.

Though my secret ally looked like a model, she was actually a teacher whom Mary had met while working as a volunteer for the local school board. Mary mentioned this in her introduction, also that Beth was a Jersey girl, a native of Metuchen, and a graduate of Drew, the school I'd driven past that evening about the time I'd been losing the feeling in my feet.

I was anxious to hear how Mary would summarize me to Beth, but that tale had evidently been spun before I'd arrived. So we passed immediately to small talk.

Harry, poker in hand, led off by demanding, "What are you doing to run down that crèche vandal, Owen?"

I begged his pardon.

"Over in Elizabeth. Somebody's been screwing with Nativity scenes. It was in today's paper. Probably a hit squad from the ACLU. I thought you'd be right on top of that. It sounds like your kind of case."

"Case?" Beth repeated, the question barely escaping the depths of the love seat.

"Sure. Owen dabbles in crime detection," Harry said. "Or palmistry. His technique is somewhat idiosyncratic."

He was close to undoing all the careful obfuscation Mary must have done on my behalf. Or so I guessed from her serrated expression, which Harry was taking pains not to notice. He was saved by the entrance of his daughter in footed pajamas, one tiny balled fist working one half-closed eye, her blond hair informal in the extreme.

"Amanda, honey, you're supposed to be asleep," Mary said, crossing to her. "Now that you're here, you can say hello to Beth. Can you say hello?"

Amanda could and did.

"And you know who this is, don't you? He brought you a present. Can you say who this is?"

"Uncle Owen," Amanda said.

The uncle part was news to me and to Harry, too. Mary must have been coaching her all day long in secret. Harry liked my new title about as much as Mary had liked his palmistry crack, which evened their score.

I liked my promotion in general, and Amanda seemed comfortable with it as well. She led me by the hand to the Christmas tree, the fire's rival as the room's principal source of light. She showed me where to put her unopened present—a snow globe containing an angel—and then identified various ornaments for me—balls and birds and bells and drums—letting me pick her up so she could point to the higher branches. We'd reached the star at the top when Mary arrived beside us.

"Your reprieve is over," she said, addressing Amanda or me or both of us. "Dinner is served."

Six

The Ohlman's dining room was dark blue and large. The table it contained was proportionally large most nights, but tonight it had lost more leaves than the front yard maples and was no bigger than a generous card table. An intimate setting for a somewhat restrained dinner.

Or maybe I should say constrained, conversationally at least. The food couldn't have been better, a brothy soup supporting chopped green onions followed by a tossed salad garnished with nuts and cranberries followed by beef tips on rice, the beef the most red, unground meat I'd had in months. Harry kept a series of wine bottle circulating, for his own benefit chiefly, but they didn't do much to help the talk.

The problem was suitable subject matter. The Ohlmans and I couldn't lose ourselves in old times without excluding Beth or, worse, accidentally mentioning one or more of my earlier "cases," which would have blown my cover as an average, eligible joe. Mary and Beth couldn't discuss their mutual interest, the school board, without leaving Harry and me to our own devices, which would have given us more leash than Mary intended us to have.

The solution, of course, was for Beth and me to question one another politely, with Harry and Mary filling in any dead air that occurred. But Beth was uninterested and I was uncooperative, at least initially. My second glass of wine softened me. I waited for a break in the chewing and then asked Beth what she taught.

"Men to be bastards, lately," she said in a voice that while soft was not without its edge.

No one dropped a fork during the ensuing silence, but it would have been a nice touch. Beth looked as shocked as Harry and Mary. As shocked as I did, for all I knew.

"Beth's recently divorced," Harry confided, his tone more sober than his eyes as he chalked up a point against Mary the matchmaker.

"She teaches high school English," Mary said. "Owen was an English major, like me, Beth."

The hostess and I discussed a class we'd once had until Beth regrouped and rejoined us. "What do you do for a living, Owen?" she eventually asked.

I'd more or less invited the question, but I found I had no desire to answer it, not while I was seated in the Ohlman's plush, candlelit dining room, not within earshot of the tiny golden cherubs that hung from golden ribbons from the golden chandelier. For one thing, I was afraid the revelation would inspire Harry to award himself another point at Mary's expense.

Luckily I had a fallback. "I'm doing some volunteer work for a crisis phone center in Elizabeth. Adullam Line."

I told them a little about the place, keeping it general, not mentioning any real callers, least of all Jackie. Even so, I could see that Mary was concerned, as much as if she'd heard an alcoholic friend was a volunteer tour guide at a brewery.

Beth wasn't interested in Adullam Line, but she was still struggling to be polite. "How do you like Elizabeth?" she asked.

"And what about those manger scenes getting splattered with paint over there?" Harry cut in. He hadn't forgotten Mary's opinion of that topic, but she'd slipped into the kitchen to start the coffee.

"I hadn't heard about it," I admitted. "I'm not taking a paper just now. Somebody's spray painting Nativity scenes?"

"Throwing paint," Beth said. "Red paint. It was in the paper. But only one of the incidents involved paint."

"You're right," Harry said from deep inside his wine glass. "The other church had something stolen. One of the statues stolen."

"Baby Jesus," Beth said. "I remember thinking, 'What's Jesus doing in the manger already anyway? It's not Christmas Day yet.'"

"Maybe that's a clue to who stole the statue," Harry said. "A frustrated traditionalist." Then he heard himself, on some drinker's internal tape delay, and blushed, though it was hard to be sure, the wine having rosied him generally. "I didn't mean you, of course," he stammered to Beth.

"If the shoe fits," she said as Mary reentered, carrying slices of chocolate cake dolloped with whipped cream that had been drizzled with something red.

Harry made short work of his, sensing perhaps that he was close to being sent to bed without any. He held up his last forkful of the reddened topping in a salute to Beth. "Like the statue's hands," he said.

"Hands?" Mary and I asked together.

Beth answered us. "In the manger scene desecration. The red paint was thrown on the Virgin Mary's hands—"

"Back on that, are we?" Mary asked her husband pointedly.

"—and across her dress," Beth finished. "Some woman hater probably," she added, looking somewhat pointedly at Harry herself.

"Don't forget the stolen statue at the other church was Baby Jesus, a male," Harry said.

"No better way to express your hatred for a woman than to steal her baby," Beth replied.

And that did it. That echo of Jackie's story, of Russet's motive for kidnapping the beautiful Benjy, finally brought into focus the feeling I'd been having that this was all somehow familiar. The idea had sprung to life when Beth mentioned the Virgin's red hands and splattered dress, the very way the prank caller to Domestic Justice had described his wounded mother. Now I suddenly realized that both hoax calls, the kidnapping and the knifing, were perfect parallels to the desecrations.

"What's the matter, Owen?" Mary asked. "Did this husband of mine spoil your appetite? I can get you a piece of cake with plain whipped cream or no whipped cream."

I did want something, but I placed my order with Harry. "Do you still have the newspaper article about the vandalism?"

"Sure. It was in this morning's *Star Ledger*. No, wait. I used it to start the fire."

"Best move you've made all night," Mary said.

I stuck it out through coffee and then started looking around for my coat. Beth let me bear the brunt of Mary's disappointment at the early evening, then announced that she was going also. The Ohlmans saw us to the front door but not beyond it, the night having become positively frosty.

So much so that when Beth spoke to me as we neared her car her breath was as white in the glow of the garage light as her very pale face. "If you really want a copy of that newspaper article," she said, "you can have mine. It's at my apartment, which should be on your way home."

I did want the article, but it wouldn't be any job to find a copy. I'd made a mental list of likely sources while sipping the Ohlman's arabica supreme.

"Look," Beth said before I could word an excuse, "I'm sorry I wasn't better company tonight. I should have told Mary it was too soon for me. Let me make amends a little."

I said sure and followed the Audi twenty minutes east to Beth's apartment complex, where I said sure again to her suggestion that I come in and warm up a minute.

I waited in her living room, coat unbuttoned and gloves in hand, while she looked for the paper. Though bigger and nicer, the apartment reminded me of my rooms. Its decor had the same just-passing-through motif.

Beth reentered minus her coat and her shoes. She carried the *Star Ledger*, but she flipped it toward the sofa almost before she said, "Here it is."

Then she was inside my coat with me, kissing me with incredible hunger and squeezing me harder than two people with bony chests should ever squeeze one another. I say "one another" because I was squeezing her back by then and kissing her back, though it had been the farthest thing from my mind a second earlier. A second later we were in the bedroom, where we made amends, twice.

Seven

I awoke around three from a dream of splattered blood. For a moment I couldn't remember where I was. Then the smell of wood smoke in the hair of the woman sleeping beside me brought back Harry's cranky fireplace and then the whole evening. I thought of the newspaper waiting in the living room, tried to stop thinking of it, and found I couldn't.

I got up quietly, collected my pants, and slipped out into the front room. It was quite cold out there. Luckily I'd left major units of my wardrobe scattered about, including a sweater. I crawled into it and switched on a lamp next to a sofa that was as firm and spare as its owner.

Beth had left me the entire paper, and it took me some time to find Harry's article. The story was a brief bottom dweller on page twenty-one.

Nevertheless, it contained some important additional information, notably the dates of the vandalism. The paint incident had occurred first, on the previous Tuesday. The Infant Jesus had been stolen two nights later, on Thursday. The day after my maiden shift at Adullam Line. Though I'd have to check the date the Domestic Justice message was received, it seemed the hoax calls were warnings of the desecrations, not after-the-fact gloating.

More significant still were the names of the target churches, because they confirmed that this wasn't all a wild coincidence. The statue had been taken from a manger outside a church called St. John Leonardi. Jackie had given his formal first name as John. The church that owned the bloody Virgin was Holy Angels, the second word of which was very like Angela, the name of the caller's wounded mother.

I looked up from the paper to find Beth standing in the bedroom doorway. She was naked and leaning against the jam with her hips cocked outward, all of which I took to be good signs. But she was holding my shoes, which I took to be a bad sign, perhaps even a criticism of my leaving her alone.

"You know where the light's better?" she asked.

"No," I said.

"Your place," she said, dropping my shoes. Then she returned to the bedroom, shutting the door behind her and locking it.

Early that same morning—after a quick stop at Adullam Line—I visited the scenes of the crime. Bright and early, as I'd been unable to get much sleep after leaving Beth's in the wee small hours. I'd tried talking with her through her bedroom door, but hadn't gotten an answer. Hadn't heard a thing, not a snicker or a sniffle or a snore.

Elizabeth was an old city—founded in the seventeenth century no less—that had been victimized by twentieth century modes of transportation. Newark Airport pressed down on it from the north and from above, too, if you counted the racket produced by an endless stream of airliners. Next to the airport, on Newark Bay, was the giant Elizabeth Port Authority Marine Terminal, no great enhancer of the local quality of life. But the worst offender was the New Jersey Turnpike, a shaft of bad air and noise that had been driven right through the city, dividing the old waterfront from the hilly, disheartened downtown.

I found St. John Leonardi first, it being closer to the center of town and my apartment. It was a small brownstone church with a stone steeple still stained by the pollution from long dead smokestacks.

Father Ross, the pastor, was a balding man with a full beard and glasses so thick they had to be mentioned prominently on his driver's license. He also had a manner as energetic as Sister Agnes's. I used the nun's name in my introduction, without her permission, implying that I was somehow representing her and Adullam Line. That was more lying than I needed to do, Father Ross not being one of the Church's great listeners. He mistook me for a concerned parishioner and led me outside, talking away while I wondered if he'd be a terrible confessor or the one of choice.

"We put the manger scene in its usual place, you see, right next to the front steps. Thirty years, same place. Keeps it out of the wind."

That wind was blowing off the bay this morning, and the priest had come outside in only the cardigan sweater he wore over his clericals. I pulled my overcoat tighter in sympathy as we examined the straw-covered patch of frozen ground and the manger scene, a fairly small one, the kneeling Mary and Joseph no more than three feet high. The stable was just a suggestion of one, a black wooden frame heavy enough to hold a plaster angel aloft. The crib or manger was also little more than a frame and it contained only additional straw, some of which blew away as we watched, despite the protection of the steps. Mary, hands spread wide, gazed down at the emptiness. I thought of Jackie's words: "Momma's gonna be kneeling next to that crib crying, 'cause it's gonna be empty."

Father Ross could add little to the newspaper account. The Jesus figure had disappeared sometime during the night. There'd been no witnesses and no clues, not even footprints on the iron ground. None of the other figures had been tipped or even touched.

I asked the priest why he'd had the Christ Child out so early.

"You're thinking of the old days when the Babe appeared on Christmas morning and the Wise Men on the Feast of the Epiphany. Let me tell you, that Twelve Days of Christmas stuff is history. Christmas is Advent and out these days. It starts the day after Thanksgiving at the latest and by noon Christmas Day it's gone with a puff of smoke. After that it's all Super Bowl. So we have to get the word out early if we're going to do it at all."

His red, streaming face suddenly lit with a smile. "Get it? We have to get the word out early. Jesus, the Word Made Flesh. We have to get Him into the manger early. That's actually a pretty good play on words."

And the start of next Sunday's sermon, ten to one. "Very good," I said.

"I hope whoever took our Jesus needed Him, that he just didn't throw Him into the bay. Either way," he added, giving me a hopeful look, "I guess we'll have to start collecting for a new one."

"Just send me the envelope," I said.

Holy Angels was a few blocks south, on the other side of the river, beyond the green space called Williams Field. It was newer than St. John Leonardi, but not new, its 1960s angled slab of a roof and stylized I-beam bell tower more dated-seeming than the older church's gothic touches.

Holy Angels' manger scene sat on a concrete plaza between the church and the street. It was larger and more three dimensional than Father Ross's display, but that was all I could tell about it, as the whole thing was covered by gray tarps. But I knew I'd come to the right place. Just below one of the tarps, the cement showed a string of bright red spots.

No priest was available to waste his time with me in the church's classroom-size office. I had to make do with a modern substitute, a "permanent deacon," a man empowered to handle some of a priest's workload, such as funerals and baptisms and dealing with amateur sleuths. This particular deacon's name was Walt Majeski, which fit him, as he was very large, with a fifties rocker's wave of greasy black hair that went not at all with his lumberman's shirt.

I tried the same cover story on him that I'd used on Father Ross, but Majeski actually listened to it. "What's Sister Agnes's interest in this? She gonna start some new project now? Maybe a branch of the Inquisition?"

Majeski wasn't moving, and he was a man who could do not moving as well as any small building. I decided I'd have to give him more.

"We got a call the other night at Adullam Line we think might be connected to the vandalism. We wanted to get some details from you so we could test the guy if he calls back."

"What details?" Majeski asked.

"Anything the real vandal would know. Like the time of night it happened."

"I can give you a range on that. I locked up after a late wedding rehearsal. A little after eleven. At twelve-thirty, I was back to pick up the

Blessed Sacrament. I'd gotten a panic call. One of our sick parishioners was failing. Wanted to receive. I found the Blessed Virgin statue with red paint all over it. The stuff was too dry to wipe off, so it must have been thrown just after I left the first time, just after eleven."

"Any witnesses or suspects?" I asked.

"No and no," Majeski said. "I was so mad at first I couldn't think. Then I thought it might be some liberal who can't stand Christmas being about religion. Then I thought no, it can't be that. A hater like that would have trashed the whole display, not one statue. So then I thought it might be someone with something against the Virgin Mary. Maybe some fanatical Protestant obsessed with Mariolatry. But who on earth would care enough about that in this day and age to commit a crime? No one.

"Anyway, I've since heard about what happened over at Leonardi. If it's the same guy, his grudge is against the Holy Family. Look for somebody's St. Joseph to be hit next."

I asked if I could see the statue.

"Too late to see the paint. It's cleaned off by now. We didn't touch it for a day or two so the police could have a look, not that they were very interested. But we can't keep the crèche closed forever, vandals or no vandals. So the paint's gone."

There followed a loud sniff, originating from the church secretary, who had been moving back and forth behind Majeski during the whole interview.

"Got something to say, Belinda?"

"Just that if you're counting on Ray to be getting that paint off you shouldn't. He was out back smoking a cigarette when I came in this morning, and he was still out there fooling around a minute ago."

That news set Majeski in motion, and I followed. Luckily for me, he went first to the basement workshop where Ray was supposed to be, giving him the benefit of the doubt. The handyman wasn't there, and the deacon pounded off in search of him.

I stayed behind to examine the statue, which lay on its back on a workbench under lights that barely had space to hang beneath the low ceiling of ducts and pipes. The piece was much larger than its counterpart at St. John Leonardi, but otherwise very like it, a kneeling figure whose heavy base hung over one end of the bench. As the *Ledger* article had said, both the hands and the front of the dress had been splattered. I confirmed now that it had been done in multiple passes and that the blue plaster dress had received its own treatment and had not just caught the excess from the outstretched palms. The vandal had gone to some trouble to recreate the details given to Honey at Domestic Justice.

When I heard Majeski coming back through the rear of the building with an alibiing Ray in tow, I slipped out the front.

Eight

I had to go to work then myself, to the job I'd been reluctant to tell Harry and Mary about: stocking shelves at an Acme not far from the county courthouse. It wasn't the kind of work that keeps your mind anchored. That day mine was especially prone to wander, though I was careful not to glance toward the large clock on the wall above the deli counter, both because it would have made the clock run more slowly and because it might have tipped my supervisor that I was planning an escape.

When my lunch break finally came at one, I dashed out to my car, which I'd parked in the full sun in the hope of some passive solar heating. I drove to the offices of Domestic Justice. They were in a nondescript block of a building, on a side street that plunged from the main road, Elizabeth Avenue, like a luge run. The first floor of the brick cube housed a beauty college whose sign featured menacing golden scissors three feet high. The crisis line's signage was far more discreet. So much so that the words "Domestic Justice" didn't even appear on the little pink square next to the stairs leading down to the basement entrance. In their place was an alias, "Telephone Contact, Inc."

When I'd stopped briefly at dawn at Adullam Line to glance at the log book and to get Domestic Justice's address, Rhoda, the volunteer on duty, had explained the situation to me. "The location is strictly confidential, Owen. Don't give this address to anyone. They do a lot of domestic abuse counseling and they get a lot of threats. It would be hard to get people to work there if the security wasn't so good."

That security—in the form of a receptionist seated behind tollbooth-grade bulletproof glass—gave me a very hard look when I showed up asking to see Honey, but I was eventually buzzed in. Rhoda had assured me that Honey would be there if I waited until afternoon, that she only went home to sleep the morning away, that she was more of a nun than Sister Agnes, her cloister being Domestic Justice.

I found Honey in a small, damp smelling office whose door bore no name or title, only a bumper sticker: "Hatred Is Its Own Excuse." Beyond that grim assertion was a large woman seated behind a small woman's desk. She was wearing a Seton Hall sweatshirt, and her blond hair was held back from her broad, shiny face by brightly colored plastic clips placed at random or in a design that was too avant-garde for me to recognize. Contrasting with this playfulness was her expression—flat-eyed wariness—and the cigarette that clung to her lower lip as though pasted on.

"You've come from Sister Agnes?" Honey asked, repeating the information the receptionist had passed her along with my name.

"I work for her," I said.

"Shame about that eye patch they've got her wearing," she said, testing me unsubtly.

"Goes well with the peg leg and the parrot," I replied. That failed to get a hand, so I described the nun in general, flattering terms, though the simple reference to her sweat suits on which I ended would probably have sufficed.

"A shared weakness," Honey said, tugging on the *S* in Seton. "What do you want, Mr. Keane? Have a seat, by the way."

I did, noticing belatedly that the entire block wall behind her was papered in bumper stickers. The subjects covered included domestic violence, racism, air and water pollution, gun ownership, and medical testing on animals. Sitting there was like being stuck in traffic behind a gigantic Volvo.

"I'd like to ask you about a call you received the other night."

"You surely know I can't discuss our calls with you. They're confidential."

"You discussed this one with Sister Agnes. It was a prank call from a kid who told you his mother's hands had been slashed."

"Sister Agnes is a confidant of mine. Someone in the same line of business. We consult with each other often. When she gets a caller yanking her chain, she lets me know. And vice versa. As a professional courtesy."

"I'm in the same profession," I said.

Honey finally acknowledged the cigarette stuck to her lip by peeling it free and stubbing it out. "You may have passed Sister Agnes's screening. I doubt you'd pass mine."

So did I. Afraid that the crushed cigarette was a cue for me, I dug out my hole card, the *Star Ledger* article, and slid it across the little desk.

Honey had scanned it through dismissively and was in the process of sliding it back when the contents registered. She pulled the clipping toward her again and bent over it. "The call I discussed with Sister Agnes," she said looking up.

"Exactly," I said. "It was a prediction or a warning of what was going to happen at Holy Angels. At least I think it was a warning. Sister Agnes was a little vague about when your call came in."

"Monday evening, about ten. I can get you the exact time from the log."

"The statue was vandalized a little after eleven on Tuesday night."

Honey shook her hair clips and pursed her big lips down to nothing. "He didn't seem like that at all. I mean, yes, he was wasting my time. But when I called him on it, he didn't laugh or gloat. He didn't seem malicious. He seemed ..."

"Lost," I said.

She gave me a rapid reexamination and shook a fresh cigarette free of her pack. "You've spoken to him?"

I pointed to the clipping, but she had it memorized. "The stolen statue. What did he tell you? That he was going to be taken from his mother by someone? Some social workers?"

I shook my head, mentally declining the cigarette she hadn't offered me. "That wouldn't have fit the pattern." I recounted Jackie's story while Honey lit up and inhaled deeply.

"I see what you mean. Threatening boyfriend in each scenario. Made up or real?"

"I don't know."

"You couldn't know, could you? But you know why you're here, what you're after. What is it?"

"I want to know if he's called again. I checked Adullam Line's log this morning. He didn't call there last night."

"You're thinking he'll do it again? Why?"

"Because no one's caught him."

Honey liked that. "And being caught is the point of the exercise. Otherwise, why would he call twenty-four hours before he strikes? And he has to figure it will take some time for someone to figure it all out, so he has to keep at it. You're seeing all this as a cry for help."

"Yes," I said.

"These days, a kid's cry for help can be pretty damn dangerous," Honey observed. "For innocent bystanders especially."

"Is that your feeling about this kid?" I asked.

"No."

"So did he call here last night?"

"No."

"Who else might he have called?"

"Let's get something straight. Is this about protecting some statues nobody looks at twice anymore? Or is it about helping the kid?"

"Helping the kid."

"Okay. I'll do some digging. Where can I reach you?"

"I'd better reach you," I said. The Acme frowned on incoming calls.

"Give me an hour."

Nine

I ended up giving Honey several hours. A truckload of frozen turkeys had arrived for a special sale, which was an all-hands-on-deck situation at the Acme. It was going on five when I used stiff and swollen fingers to dial the direct-line number she'd given me.

"You'll be lucky to catch him this late," Honey said right off in a voice so much warmer and softer than her office persona that I barely recognized it. Even more confusing was the statement itself, which I interpreted as meaning it was too late to catch Jackie before he struck again, though it was barely dusk.

"Catch who?" I managed to ask.

"Edward Hennix. President and CEO of a corporate counseling service called Hand to Hand."

"Never heard of it."

"Must not be in your benefits package. It's a fringe some of the fatter corporations are starting to offer, confidential psychological counseling for employees and their families. Supposed to cut down on trouble—drinking, drugs, depression—in the workplace, keep the worker bees buzzing."

At the Acme, they used free coffee. "How does our caller fit in? His mother work for AT&T?"

"Probably not," Honey said. "But this Edward Hennix is an interesting character. I could tell you so much about him you'd miss him for sure. Slum kid from Newark who worked his way through Rutgers studying psychology. Was going to be the Albert Schweitzer of North Jersey but got switched onto the John D. Rockefeller track by mistake. Been piling up money ever since. Conflicted as hell about it, too, which is where our mystery caller comes in. Hennix has this big fancy call center with more capacity than his business needs right now, so he donates some time to the county, taking welfare agency calls during their off hours."

"And his center got one of the hoax calls?"

"I think so. He wouldn't say much about it, except that it was really off-the-wall."

Bingo. "Can you give me his number?"

"He asked me to give you his address. He wants to meet you. It's a trust thing. Hennix has some problems with trust."

Honey had had them herself, earlier in the day. As she read off the address, I decided I'd passed her screening after all. So had Hennix, evidently.

"Don't let his hard nose fool you. Eddie is a good man. I'll let him know you're on your way."

The good man's offices were in a very sleek building in an office park so close to Newark Airport the blue lights of the taxiways seemed to run right up to its back fence. Unlike Domestic Justice, Hennix's company didn't go in for pseudonyms on its outdoor advertising. "Hand to Hand" appeared in large backlit white letters on a low sign beside the front walk. The chrome door at the end of the walk opened itself for me when it detected my approach, just like the ones at the Acme, only faster. The door had to be fast to open for me, since I was very nearly trotting, afraid I'd miss Hennix and the vital clue.

A receptionist, working without the benefit of armored glass, called my name when I was two steps inside the door and then waved me down a hallway like a third-base coach waving a runner home. Or maybe just like a woman who was anxious to head home herself. Hennix's office was at the far end of the hallway, and I spotted him through its open door.

He was speaking on the phone and gesturing away like he had his listener across the desk, every movement of his free hand accentuated by the office lights hitting a heavy golden ring. He was more trim than thin and very dark complexioned with short hair worn like a Marine recruit's. His nose was set high and high arched, and his eyes kept track of my approach while smiling away like his wide, mobile mouth. He wore a white shirt and a blue silk tie, the shirt looking like he'd just gotten it out of the cellophane.

He wasn't nearly my age, but he'd made much better use of his post-college years. I suddenly wished I had Harry Ohlman along. He and Hennix could have compared club memberships and mutual fund balances and ex-changed secret handshakes in general while I looked on from the sidelines.

"Got to go," Hennix said when I reached his doorway. "Right. Got to go. Right. See you."

He was up out of his seat, extending his hand, before he'd hung up the phone, and he stayed up, using our handshake to pull me back in the direction I'd come. "You almost missed me. I'm pitching to a company in Linden. Express package shipper, employees all tensed up and overtimed out, all screwed down tighter than a skydiver's toupee, ready to take off like that toupee, ready to be generally unproductive and obnoxious—"

"Like the toupee again," I said, more to arrest him than top him. To stop the practice pitch certainly, but also his escape. After leading me back to the doorway of his office, Hennix had extracted a suit coat and topcoat from behind the office door and slipped them on, almost simulta-neously. Another snappy line of dialogue or two and he'd be out the door and gone. I planted myself in the doorway.

"Honey said you were an interesting study," Hennix observed, standing chest to chest with me, not moving me yet but sizing up the job.

"She likes you, too," I said.

"I can guess what she told you about me. Child of the ghetto, so guilt-ridden he can barely look at his bank statement. That bullshit's one of the occupational hazards of being a psychologist. All your peers analyze you, even the well-meaning-amateur peers like Honey. I could give you a few theories about her, Keane, including why she hangs on to a first name she hates, one that reflects an image of women hates, one that fits her about as well as—"

"A bad toupee?" I asked. "We're wasting your pitching time."

"Right. Come back tomorrow."

"Tomorrow will be too late."

"Why? Sister Agnes going to find out what you're up to and clip your wings? I guarantee I would if you worked for me and I found out you were running around playing Joe Private Eye."

A plane passed so low overhead I almost ducked. "Tomorrow will be too late because that call you got will be old news by then. I'll be able to read about the results in tomorrow's paper. The chance to help this kid will be gone."

"Help him how, Keane?" Hennix demanded, backing me into the hallway. "Do you have the slightest idea what he's up to? You ever even met a kid like him, head full of brains and no chance to use them? Have you ever been inside a housing project? Do you have any idea what that kid's up against, day in and day out, what you'd be up against if you found him?"

His tone was giving me déjà vu, and I remembered Jackie's exasperated condescension. "How do you know so much about this kid?" I asked. "You must have taken the call yourself."

"Wrong," Hennix said, drawing out the word like a game show buzzer. "I listened to the tape. We tape every call that comes in here, even wild fairy tales."

"What was this fairy tale about?"

"I'd be wasting your time telling you, because it's not going to do you any good."

"Waste my time. I'm not selling to any corporations tonight."

That reminder of the meeting he was late for tipped Hennix my way, though he headed for the front door as he spoke. "It was about a mob hit. Kid called in to say his momma's badass boyfriend was going to whack a Mafia guy over some drug deal. Plus the Mafia guy's two bodyguards.

"Honey told me about the manger scene stuff, so it was no big job deciphering this call. Three Mafiosi or wise guys equals the Three Wise Men. The Magi. No problem, except that, according to Honey, the clue to where the vandalism's going to happen is in a name, and the kid didn't give any names, not for himself or his momma or her man. Not even for the Mafia kingpin. He was just 'Mr. X.' Like out of some spy movie, which is probably where the kid got it."

We'd reached the main entrance. Once outside, Hennix paused for a moment to punch a number into a keypad next to the automatic door, disabling it, I guessed, to protect the night shift from prowlers and return visits by me. Then he marched to the nearest parking space, which held a silver Audi, as sleek as Beth Wolfe's though larger.

"Feel free to drive around Elizabeth all night trying to catch this kid in the act, Keane," he said in parting. "You won't, not in a month of trying, which means you'll be safe from him. And he'll be safe from you."

Ten

If Hennix hadn't secured the front door of his building, I might have snuck back in. Not to bother the help, but to borrow a phone book. I wasn't as discouraged by Hennix's brief recounting of the third call as he'd intended me to be, because I knew a little more about the Catholic Church than he did. Specifically, I knew a saint's name that began with an X, as in Mr. X, St. Francis Xavier, missionary hero of the Jesuits who had taught Harry and Mary and me. If I was right, Jackie had passed on the name of to-night's target church in his subtlest way yet.

I wasn't familiar with a St. Francis Xavier Church in greater Elizabeth, but finding it only required a phone book. I stopped to ask for one at a diner just south of the airport and so proud of the association that it was referenced twice in its name, Skyways Jet Service, though, from the look of the parking lot, they were serving more truck drivers than jet jockeys.

I ordered coffee, resisting the urge the place inspired to call it java, and the yellow pages. The restaurant's copy was supporting the toothpick dispenser and the after-dinner mint dish next to the cash register. I sat on a very low stool at the very low counter and looked up Churches, Roman Catholic. The book contained a decent-sized list, this very industrialized corner of America having attracted waves of European immigrants. But there was no church in Elizabeth named for St. Francis Xavier. I tried under the Fs and then under the Xs, of which there were none at all. While I was moving my finger back up the list to check again for Francis, I spotted the correct answer to Jackie's riddle, a church called St. Pius X. Mr. X himself, for anyone unfamiliar with Roman numerals, and an Italian big shot to boot.

I celebrated the discovery by ordering dinner, a big one, hamburger steak, mashed potatoes with gravy, and green beans. The waitress, concerned for my cholesterol perhaps, tried to steer me toward the turkey, but I'd played catch with too many of those that afternoon. I justified this break in the action by telling myself that it wasn't yet eight and I couldn't expect Jackie to appear much before eleven, that a place that promised jet service was sure to be fast, and that a greasy meal would help me stay warm on a long stakeout in an unheated car.

As a further precaution against the cold, I ordered a large coffee to go, but it was tepid by the time I parked in the shadow of St. Pius X. The church was another old one, sited on a hill overlooking the bay and built of brick that had once been painted white and was now going back to natural. There must have been some money in the parish at one time, because its Nativity scene was a near life-size beauty, Holy Family, shepherds, angels, and even farm animals, arranged against a flat painted to represent a stable and lit by a single floodlight. A little to one side were the Three Magi, weeks early for their traditional appearance and arranged in ascending order according to height: kneeling king, bowing king, standing king.

All three were untouched, as far as I could tell. I didn't go in for a close inspection, afraid that Jackie was somewhere nearby on a stakeout of his own. I was expecting him to be especially wary tonight. I still felt that Honey and I were right, that Jackie's calls were cries for help, that he wanted to be noticed and caught. But I understood that he was ambivalent about the process. Hence his elaborate game and the hesitancy in his voice when I'd offered to come to him. So I was determined not to scare him off.

And not to freeze to death. By eleven, that seemed like a real possibility. I was getting regular exercise, scraping my frozen breath from the inside of the windshield, but that wasn't enough to keep my blood circulating. I decided I had to do some pacing and climbed out of the car as quietly as I could. I paced away from the church, down a barely lit side street and back again. I made no noise myself in my rubber-soled, stock-boy shoes, and I heard very little, there being almost no traffic on the nearby streets or on the bay. The occasional jet that passed low overhead sounded like a freight train in the general hush.

I hadn't been on my feet very long before all the coffee I'd drunk began demanding to part company. I was taking care of that in a little alley that ran behind the church when I heard the faint sound of a blow being struck and the fainter thud of something heavy falling.

I circled the church at a run, aware as soon as I'd reached the street that something had changed. It was the lighting. The single flood that had lit the

Nativity scene was off. I'd neglected to take the Ghia's flashlight with me, and I didn't stop for it now, making do with the residue from the nearest streetlight, which reduced the colors of the scene to shades of blue and gray. Still, I was able to spot a second change. The standing king was missing his head. So was the stooping king, who now looked like he'd been bowing for a headsman's ax. The sight of that damage dropped me from a run to a very deliberate walk. I stopped altogether when I saw that the kneeling king had yet to be beheaded. Jackie hadn't finished the hit, which meant I'd either frightened him off or he was hiding somewhere in the shadows.

"Jackie, it's me," I said as conversationally as I could when I'd caught my breath a little. "Owen. We talked the other night. I came by to see whether you wanted to talk again."

Nothing. I stood there like the latest addition to the statuary, but couldn't hear the sound of movement or any breathing but my own, which gradually slowed with disappointment.

I started forward into the grouping itself, speaking a little louder now. Jackie might still be somewhere nearby, listening. "If you don't want to talk tonight, maybe you'll call—"

I caught a flash of movement to my right, from behind the tallest king. I turned my head toward it and saw him, saw a single wide eye peering at me from behind a raised bat. Then I saw the Star of Bethlehem itself, but only very briefly.

Eleven

I woke up in a bed in Elizabeth General Hospital, though all I knew at the moment of waking was that it was a hospital somewhere. Before I could puzzle out where I was exactly and how I'd gotten there, I was presented with a far more interesting mystery. I heard a chair scrape against the floor and Mary Ohlman was standing over me, her sky blue eyes youthful without all the dinner-party makeup but dark, too, with concern.

"Owen, thank God," she said.

"How?" I asked, which was short for "How did they know to call you?" I was afraid someone had found some old college love letter I'd tucked into the lining of my wallet and forgotten or, worse, that I'd absentmindedly listed Mary on a next-of-kin line of an Acme insurance form. Name: Mary Ohlman. Relationship: One True Love.

Mary understood the question and probably the concern. "The map I sent you so you could find our house for the party. It was still in the pocket of your coat. It had our phone number on it. Your wallet didn't have much in it, much they could use to contact someone, I mean. So they called me. I left Amanda with a neighbor and drove straight over here." She was still wearing the stadium coat she'd thrown on for the drive, wearing it tightly buttoned, like someone who couldn't stay.

"Thanks," I said. "Where's here?"

She gave me the name of the place, also the date and the hour. I hadn't been out all that long, not if you factored in a normal night's sleep. It was only midmorning of the day after my stakeout.

Mary had her own take on the timing. "You're lucky they found you so quickly. It got down below freezing last night."

A young doctor joined us then. He was blond and excessively tall, and his nose hair needed professional attention. He brought with him yet a third point of view regarding the time scheme.

"You had us worried. You were out for a long time for no harder than you were hit. I mean, judging by the lump and the bruising, you were hit more of a stunning, glancing blow, but it put you right under."

While he spoke, he examined my left temple. "I gave your X ray a closer look. There appears to be an indication of a prior injury to that area. An old one. Were you struck there before?"

"Yes," Mary said. "With a rifle butt."

"A rifle butt?" the doctor repeated with interest. "You were a soldier?"

"No," I said. "Just a poor judge of character."

The doctor, whose name was Steir, was a good judge of character, or else his X-ray machine had revealed other interesting information regarding my head. Perhaps a table of contents. He smiled stoically. "My advice would be to get hit somewhere else in the future. In the meantime, I'd like to run some further tests."

I shook my head and immediately regretted it. "I don't think my health insurance covers anything beyond the ice pack. Besides, I have to get out of here as soon as possible. Holiday business."

Mary reacted to that with a visible jerk, as though a current had been run through her by some unseen cardiologist. In another second, she would have been authorizing every test in the catalog. Luckily, Sister Agnes Kelly burst in just then, which meant that the Pope himself, had he been visiting, would have been demoted to looker on.

"Owen, what have you been up to? Never mind, don't tax your imagination. Honey's already told me all about it. Traipsing around looking for some boy you think is in trouble. Who turns out to be trouble. This is why I have my rule about keeping out of the line of fire. This is what can happen. You end up in the hospital or worse. If Father Andrus hadn't found you when he did, worse it would have been. All for some old pieces of plaster that will be glued back together before you are."

And on and on. Dr. Steir decided after a paragraph or two that his time could be better spent elsewhere. Mary remained, patience being her long suit, especially where I was concerned. I decided that it was in my best interests to keep the nun talking.

"How did Father Andrus happen to find me?" I asked when she appeared to be flagging.

"What? Oh that. Somebody rang the rectory bell. Some hooligan. I say hooligan because when Father Andrus opened the door there was no one there, just a blast of arctic air. He was looking around for whoever did it when he noticed the light was out in front of the Nativity scene. The rectory's right across the street from the church, you know. The bulb, he thought. Nowadays priests change light bulbs themselves, God help us, so he bundled up and went out to do it.

"When he got out there, he found that the old bulb was halfway unscrewed. He tightened it, it worked, and he saw you, lying next to the manger. Like an uncle who'd dropped in unexpectedly and decided to stay the night was how he put it. Except he said something about your having too much to drink, too. An uncle who'd drank too much and decided to stay the night. That was it. Because he thought you were drunk at first. Then he tried to rouse you, it being too cold out even for drunks, and saw the bruise on your head.

"So it seems that hooligan accidentally saved your life. Or do you think it was some passerby who only wanted someone to see that the light was out?"

Mary said, "I'm guessing that Owen thinks it was the boy who hit him. He thinks the boy rang the rectory bell so someone would come out and find him."

"He beans him, then he rescues him? Why?"

Mary delegated that one. "He didn't mean to hurt me," I said. "I scared him, showing up in the middle of things and accidentally cornering him in the scene itself. I thought he was off somewhere by then in the shadows listening to me. I didn't realize that I had him trapped. He only hit me—not hard—to get away."

"He hit you hard enough," Sister Agnes said, leaning across the bed so that her very pointed face was pointed at me, first at my lump and then at a spot between my eyes. In her own way, she was as insightful as Mary. "You're still soft on this kid, aren't you? You're still going to try and help him."

"Yes," Mary said.

"If you do, you can forget about representing Adullam Line." The nun had gone over to the other side, gone from running interference for me to double-teaming me with Mrs. Ohlman. I needed another timely entrance to save me, and I got one. A uniformed patrolman entered stage right, unzipping a well-filled nylon jacket and extracting a notebook. Not the interruption I would have picked, since the last thing I wanted to do was give a statement in front of Mary and Sister Agnes. Those two would give me no room to maneuver with respect to the truth.

But luck was with me that morning. I'd just begun to describe the crèche vandalism in general terms when the cop lowered his pencil and said, "You Catholics and your friggin' statues. Why can't you just worship the friggin' trees like the friggin' Indians?"

The next thing he knew he was being pushed into the hallway by a tiny woman in a track suit, who was demanding to know the number of his badge and precinct and the names of his lieutenant and captain and mother. Forgetting her own recent dismissal of "old pieces of plaster," she then launched into a lecture on the Catholic Church and its use of iconography that promised to last a while, starting as it did way back with the Byzantine Empire.

Mary was smiling as she listened, but the smile faded when she turned to me. "Owen, what am I going to do with you?"

In the interlude that followed, she considered her question and I indulged the fantasy of a future time when doing something about me might actually be Mary's business.

Then I shook it off. "Tell Amanda her Uncle Owen sends his love."

Twelve

Later, as I sat in the chair Mary had used, awaiting my promised release, Edward Hennix walked in. Unlike me, he was not wearing his outfit from the prior evening, but today's had come from the same haberdashery. The mouse-colored topcoat was slung over one shoulder and was therefore undistinguished, a foil only for the white shirt with the fine silver stripe that perfectly matched the silk tie, the black blazer, and the charcoal slacks. Hennix's expression was also a new one within our brief acquaintance: sheepish contrition.

"Damn, Keane," he said, "I feel like this is my fault. I underestimated you and I overestimated you at the same time, if that's possible. I mean, I never thought you'd actually track down that kid, and I humbly ask your pardon for that. But I never would have guessed you'd let him slip up behind you with a bat, either. You're an honest-to-God investigator, but you're not like the ones I read about growing up."

I'd often had the same thought, but I didn't dwell on it now. I was feeling bad enough already. The dull ache in my temple had spread to my left eye, making the afternoon's cheerful sunlight a penance. To move the discussion away from my uniqueness, I said, "How did you find out?"

Hennix waved his golden ring dismissively. "The news ran through our grapevine like lightening. We're a close-knit little group, the help-line people, the telephonic tongue waggers. Honey and Sister A and me and a few of the others working this edge of the garbage dump of humanity, we stay in touch. You lit up the board this morning, let me tell you." He'd dropped his coat on my unmade bed before settling comfortably on the spare one. "So give. How did you find him?"

It was my chance to use a dismissive gesture, but I lacked a golden ring to set if off. I described the correct reading of the Mr. X clue, wishing it were something more elaborate even before Hennix began shaking his head.

"It's always some little thing like that in detective books," he said. "They have all those words to work with, you'd think they'd have the solution hinge on some complex human interaction, instead of a bit of trivia."

"The better ones do," I said. I was pondering some complex human interaction in the here and now. Specifically, I was wondering why Hennix had come to see me. With Mary's recent example as my guide, I decided to be patient and not ask him directly. So I asked instead how his sales pitch had gone.

Hennix waved the nugget at me again. "It went okay. Bunch of people whose only real problem is incipient gout. No emotional hang-ups a good night's sleep wouldn't cure. But I don't want to be offering my services to people who really need them. That would be like selling health insurance to smokers. Too much overhead. Too much work.

"So I should have been at the top of my game with that crowd, but I never really found my rhythm. My mind kept slipping back to you and your little problem. When I should have been making empty promises to my prospective clients, I was trying to remember what you'd told me about that kid. But I couldn't remember much. Couldn't even remember what your guess was about why he's doing this."

"You didn't give me a chance to guess," I said. "You had those gouty people waiting." He had other people waiting somewhere right now, I was certain. And yet here he was in an overheated hospital room in Elizabeth, drawing admiring stares from passing nurses, several of whom seemed to be passing very regularly.

"I know I stiff-armed you, Keane, and I'm sorry. I was sorry all night. Not about being rude to you—you don't make that good a first impression—over the kid. Over not offering to help with the kid.

"I don't know how much that boss of yours or Honey told you about me, but I grew up pretty much like this kid you're hunting is growing up. Wild and scared. That may be reason one why I should have helped you. Why I feel like helping you now.

"Reason two is that I got a hand up when I needed one. A teacher here and there who told me I had brains and a mother who wouldn't let me quit. More than this kid has maybe.

"Reason three is the one you maybe heard from Honey. How I was going to be a Moses to my people once upon a time. I was going to help the neediest, instead of which I've ended up squeezing the wealthiest. So I've got this whole thing going about falling away from a call to grace. I don't know if you can identify with that."

In fact, he knew I could. He told me so with an uncharacteristically furtive glance out the window. A member of his grapevine, Sister Agnes probably, had filled him in on my own past and my own failures, supplementing that poor first impression I'd made. Once I would have been offended by that breach of confidence. Now I'd come to accept that it was how some people defined me. A failed seminarian now and forever.

"Hell," Hennix said turning back to me. "It may just be that it's Christmas time, with all the shit that goes with that. I'm speaking of the secular stuff now. The idea of being Scrooge and having a change of heart. Maybe saving a Tiny Tim.

"Which brings me back to the question of what this kid is up to. What you think he's up to, I mean. I know you believe this is all a cry for help or attention, and I think you're right about that. But why is he doing what he's doing? Why has he picked this specific pattern of vandalism?"

It was the moment for him to pause so I could make my guess, but Hennix didn't pause. He went back to his pacing, this time with a surer step.

"If you're thinking the kid might be hitting out at religion in general, at the idea of religion or the idea of God, I'd have to say I don't think so. There are statues all over town all year long he could be defacing, not to mention the buildings, the churches and temples and mosques. Same objection applies to the idea that he could have some grudge against Catholics. Why strike now? And why not hit the churches themselves?

"The targets were Nativity scenes, not churches. Not the religious beliefs the Nativity scenes stand for either, or else the churches would have been more logical targets. So what else do the scenes stand for?"

He stopped pacing and directed the question at his audience, so I answered it. "Christmas."

"Exactly. Christmas. The day every kid loves except for the kids that don't get any Christmas. The ones who watch all the lights and decorations go up and listen to all the corny songs and know that at the end of it all there's going to be squat for them, that they're being screwed over again. Christmas could come to represent the entire world a kid like that, a kid from the projects, is cut off from. The world of a normal childhood.

"So the specific act a kid like that might chose as his cry for help might be a blow against Christmas itself."

Tiny Tim as urban terrorist. It was certainly a twist.

Hennix was moving on. "Not that that gets us much of anywhere. You're still looking for a needle in a haystack. A potentially dangerous haystack for you, a white guy straight off the bus, to be wandering around in. What I'm saying is, think twice about following this kid's trail any farther. I sold you short last night. I know now you have the kid's best interests at heart, that your intentions are good. But good intentions aren't much of a shield in this world.

"If you want, I can do some poking around. In fact, that might be best. Pass the buck to me and give that cracked head of yours a rest." He retrieved his topcoat. "I'll let you know how things work out."

My cracked head was throbbing with new urgency. I was straining it, still trying to figure out why Hennix had come. Had it really been to take the Jackie problem off my hands? No. That offer seemed like an afterthought. To warn me off the case, perhaps at Sister Agnes's request? Then all his speculation about motives and targets had just been filler. That wasn't easy to believe; he'd worked so hard at putting it across.

While I was still grinding away, Hennix gave me yet another possible reason for his drop-in. He reached into the pocket of his topcoat and extracted a cassette tape.

"This message came for you late last night. Should have gone to Adullam Line, but it came to us, I guess because the Mr. X call had come to us."

He tossed the tape spinning to me. It passed through my outstretched fingers and landed in my lap.

"Don't let that get you fired up again," Hennix said from the doorway. "Think of it as a good-bye."

Thirteen

Adullam Line didn't tape its calls, but the ministry did own a tape recorder. I knew that because part of Sister Agnes's cursory training consisted of listening to tapes of sample crisis-line calls that had been compiled and published by the University of Georgia.

So when I was reluctantly sprung by Elizabeth General, I retrieved my car from the shadow of St. Pius X, stopped by the Acme to trade peeks at my damaged head for a sick day, and then drove to the old rectory where it had all begun. The phone was being staffed by a college-age volunteer who barely looked up from her fashion magazine when I introduced myself and asked after the tape player. I found the little plastic portable in a corner filing cabinet and carried it into Sister Agnes's private office, which I'd already determined to be empty. I even sat at the nun's desk. There was no point in observing the proprieties when my pink slip was already in the works.

The cassette Hennix had given me was a pristine one in an unscratched case, but it sounded old and crackly on Sister Agnes's machine. I leaned forward as the hissing began, thinking that Jackie had gotten a bad connection for his call. The static lasted so long, I began to wonder whether Hennix had forgotten to rewind the tape. Then Jackie came on.

"Tell Owen I'm sorry."

That was it. I listened to the four words again and again, but I never detected a secret meaning or anything in Jackie's voice but sincere regret. Around the fifth replay, I stopped listening and went over to asking myself the question Hennix had asked: Why had the apology call come to him and not Adullam Line? Hennix's guess had been that he'd gotten the follow-up call because he'd received the earlier Magi warning. Since I'd shown up at St. Pius X, Jackie could rightfully assume some ongoing communication between Hand to Hand and me.

It was an answer, but it didn't satisfy me. I fell into thinking of Hennix's breezy description of the loose federation of local crisis line operators, or "telephonic tongue waggers," as he'd put it. He'd also referred to the grapevine that had spread the news of my bonk on the head, and I wondered if Jackie had somehow known of this grapevine or taken it for granted. Maybe that was why each of his three calls had gone to a different line. To Jackie, they might simply be different extensions of some interconnected, invisible world of the knowing and the powerful.

As I popped the cassette out of the machine, I thought of a third explanation for Jackie's misdirected call, one that was less philosophically tangled than mine and more plausible than Hennix's. It was that Jackie had tried to reach me through Adullam Line, been told I wasn't there, and had then tried Hand to Hand.

The theory had the advantage of being easy to check, as all calls to Adullam Line were logged. I rejoined the coed who was cramming for her *Mademoiselle* final. She didn't look up as I returned the tape recorder and barely did when I reached for the log. Someone named Wilson had been on duty around the time they were X-raying my head. He'd gotten several calls in a row involving holiday stresses and strains, which he'd written up at novella length. I flipped ahead and found a very brief entry logged at midnight. "Personal message for O. Keane." But no word of the message itself.

The fashion major looked up when I cleared my throat. "It says a message came in for me last night. Any sign of it?"

She didn't answer right away. She might have been considering the make-up challenge presented by the bump on my head. Finally she mumbled, "Personal messages aren't allowed," but began searching the desktop. Beneath her magazine was a textbook in a related field, marketing, and beneath that a yellow slip. She handed it over without asking for ID.

It was the message for me all right, but it wasn't from Jackie. My midnight caller had been Beth Wolfe, the divorcee who'd given me the interesting evening and the free copy of the *Star Ledger*. The complete text of the message was her phone number. I filed it in my shirt pocket.

The receptionist at Domestic Justice remembered me but pretended not to. She called Honey or pretended to. Then she told me with a straight face that was all pretense that Honey—the secular nun who never left her bumper-stickered office—wasn't in.

I'd driven there in the first place because going back over Hennix's hospital-room lecture, during which the psychologist had worked his way down the motive list from hatred of religion to hatred of Catholics to hatred of Christmas, had gotten me thinking in terms of layers. And that had led me in turn to observe that Jackie's own work was multilayered. On the surface his calls were cries for help from a kid facing some immediate threat from an abusive male. Peel that layer back, and they were prank calls. Beneath that layer they were clever warnings of impending vandalism. And one layer further down they were cries for help again, this time from a kid facing an undefined threat. Or so I still believed.

Which meant that the calls themselves were still the vital clues. That is to say, if I was right about Jackie, if he really was as clever and complicated as I judged him to be, the original calls would have, buried deep inside them, all the information I needed to track him down.

Following that bolt from the blue, I'd sat freezing in my Volkswagen, writing down every stray detail I could remember from the call I'd received, using the back of the envelope full of paperwork the hospital had given me as my official notebook. Then I'd hurried over to Domestic Justice to interview Honey and add her memories of call number one to my list.

And been lied to for my trouble. I stood there on the wrong side of the receptionist's greenish Plexiglas trying to think of a password that would get me in. The young woman, whose head was very nearly shaved, still had one hand on the phone as though she expected me to try again.

"It's about the prank call we discussed yesterday," I said.

"She's not in," the woman repeated.

I caught sight of my reflection in the glass, of my haggard, greenish face and the discolored bump on my head, and realized how much I looked like an abusive husband who'd been taken out by a well-thrown pot and was now looking for round two. And I suddenly knew that the woman held on to the phone with a twitching hand because she was a second away from calling the police.

I retreated to the Ghia, where I considered using the direct-dial phone number Honey had given me. I decided she would have anticipated that move. The line would be busy today or unanswered. So I started out for my next stop, Hand to Hand. Started slowly, as the late afternoon traffic was thickening like old gravy. It gave me plenty of time to consider Honey's rejection. The receptionist might have been reacting to my appearance, but what was scaring Honey? Some threat from Sister Agnes? Guilt over my narrow escape?

I decided Hennix could tell me, which was an example of my intuition failing me. I moved right on to calculating the odds of finding Jackie with just two pieces of the puzzle, mine and Hennix's, without pausing to wonder whether the psychologist had been warned off by whoever had gotten to Honey.

The sun was sinking behind one of the airport terminals as I pulled into the Hand to Hand lot. I shivered my way up Hennix's front walk, shivered violently, as though my body was having a flashback to my nap in St. Pius's stable. I grabbed at the front door's chrome handle eagerly. It was ice cold, and the door it was attached to was locked.

The reception area lighting had been turned low, but I could see that the central desk was empty. The woman I'd kept late last night must have claimed her comp time this evening. The keypad Hennix had used to secure the door had a button marked "assistance." I pressed it and then went back to yanking on the door, expecting someone to buzz me in. Instead, a man who sounded like he was speaking through a cardboard tube inquired, "Can I help you?"

I gave my name, asked for the head man, and added that it was damn cold outside.

The voice said, "Mr. Hennix has left for the day."

I looked over my shoulder to the spot where Hennix's silver Audi had been parked the night before. It was parked there now, reflecting the last of a very pale sunset. I pointed this out to the man on the other end of the tube.

"Mr. Hennix has left for the day," he repeated.

I could have threatened to stay there until Hennix came out, but I was flirting with frostbite as it was. I thanked the disembodied voice for its courtesy and left.

Fourteen

The rooms I rented were always overheated because the old woman who owned the house had a susceptibility to drafts or, to borrow her own diagnosis, "hollow bones, bones the wind whistles right through." That night the place felt just right to me, which caused me to reflect that my own bones might be near to whistling. Certainly the collection of bones I called my skull felt hollow as I sat at my table-for-one in the little bay-window alcove in my front room, pouring over the list I'd scribbled on the hospital envelope, the list of stray details from Jackie's call, trying to spot some useful information.

I'd noted the names Russet and Benjy, Jackie's interest in the Mafia and smelters and science fiction films, his familiarity with two of a crisis line's more routine functions: advising on alcohol problems and unpaid bills, and his contempt for the New Jersey Nets. Not much to work with. If only I had a similar list from Honey and another from Hennix, the facts from each list might have linked themselves together in some pattern. If only.

I considered the possibilities offered by Jackie's reference to a smelter. A big black place with smokestacks near where he lived, he'd said, daring me to challenge his expertise. I could ask around the next day, see if any functioning or defunct smelter in Elizabeth matched that description. And then what? Canvas the immediate neighborhood for Knicks fans?

To save all my energy for thinking, I put my head down on my folded arms. It worked so well, I promptly fell asleep.

The phone woke me. I scrambled to reach it, so intent on the idea that it was Jackie calling back that I almost said "Adullam Line" instead of "hello."

"Owen?" a woman's voice said. "Owen Keane? It's Beth Wolfe."

We'd slept together, and we were still using last names. Guilty thoughts of that made me miss my cue. Beth said, "Are you there?" but meant, "Have you forgotten me already?"

"I'm here, Beth, sorry. I had a little accident, and it's left me groggy."

"A traffic accident?"

"No."

"Something to do with your case?"

She managed to say case very naturally, without the rhetorical quotes Harry and even Mary put around the word when they were discussing one of my mysteries.

"Yes," I said, "but it's only a bump on the head. I got a message that you'd called. I'm sorry—"

"I want to talk with you about the other night. Have you eaten anything? I made some lasagna."

Just the thought of getting back in my car started me shivering again. The vibrations must have traveled down the phone line, because Beth said, "I'll bring everything over there. You're in downtown Elizabeth, right? Just give me directions."

My instinct was to dodge it, but something in Beth's voice, a little tremor of vulnerability, made me think it over. She was facing down the risk that I'd turn out to be another bastard, lowering her guard in a way she hadn't even done when we'd been naked together in her bed. Her courage, and a growling in my stomach that had started at the mention of lasagna, changed my mind.

I gave her the route I'd used on the night of Mary's party and then fell into cleaning the place, prioritizing as follows: kitchenette first, then bathroom, then main room. My tiny bedroom I left for last. I didn't think I'd be entertaining there in my condition, but then I wouldn't have guessed, only an hour earlier, that I'd be so interested in Italian food.

I would have spent some time fixing myself up next, but I heard my landlady greeting Beth at the front door as I was tucking in my emergency sheets. Then my blind date was at my doorstep, pink from the cold and struggling with a large cardboard box.

The box got us past the awkwardness of the first few minutes, since it had to be taken into the kitchen and unloaded, the lasagna going into the oven and the salad into the refrigerator, the interior of which seemed brilliantly lit to me now that it had been emptied of old milk cartons. The perfect guest, Beth had even brought a bottle of Chianti, which we opened while the main course was warming.

We sat on my fourth-hand sofa, a vinyl number with bare metal legs and no arms that belonged in the waiting room of a rental car agency. For all its faults, it was softer than Beth's own sofa, as she observed herself. She looked softer tonight, too, and less emaciated in woolen slacks and a cable-knit sweater. Casual, but not relaxed. She drank half of her first glass of wine in a gulp, her Gothic eyes giving me their trademark peek-a-boo through her overcoated lashes.

Here it comes, I thought, the apology. But it didn't come. "Tell me how you got that egg," she said instead.

I told her at some length, recounting my whole investigation to date, the telling taking us right through the first helpings of dinner and relaxing us both.

"What about the targets?" Beth asked as she poured out the last of the wine. "Why aren't they on your list?"

We were seated by then at the little table in the little alcove, Beth examining my envelope-notebook. The window nearest her was open at her request to give her a break from the heat. The cold draft felt good to me as well, the meal and the wine having restored me amazingly. She passed me the envelope, and I wrote down the names of the three churches. But that failed to satisfy her.

"Have you given them any thought?"

"The targets?" I asked.

"Yes. You're looking for some secret message in the calls, but maybe the message is in the targets."

"Well, yeah," I said, "the attack on Christmas thing."

"I'm not talking about the symbolism of the Nativity scenes themselves. I mean the churches. Why pick those churches in particular when there's a church with a Nativity scene in every neighborhood around here? This kid has such a complex mind, the way you tell it, it's like he's playing chess with you. And you're right to think of him that way. I've got some fourth graders in my class who should be designing crossword puzzles. So maybe there's some pattern to the churches. Maybe if you put pins in a map, you'd come up with something."

"There's only three of them," I said. "They could only form a straight line or a triangle."

Beth laughed at herself, and for a second, her pale skin seemed to reflecting a light from her eyes. Then the second passed. "I guess I've watched too many detective shows on television," she said.

"Nothing wrong with that, I hope."

She pushed her plate away, running it into mine. "I'm stalling anyway. I mean, this case of yours is interesting—it's interesting that you're still trying to help this kid, bump and all—but it isn't what I came over to talk about. To apologize for."

"You've nothing to apologize to me for," I said. "I shouldn't have left you to read that paper."

"I wasn't going to apologize for asking you to go home," she said.

She hesitated, so I fired off another guess. "If it's about the dinner party, I was uncomfortable myself. Mary should have warned us."

"Owen, shut up and listen for a minute. If you keep coming up with things that I should be apologizing for, that I hadn't even thought about apologizing for, you're going to make me cry."

"What is it then?"

"Having sex with you."

"I'm usually the one who apologizes after that."

"Don't make jokes, either. I'm serious. I used you and I'm sorry. I don't want you to think that I'm that way. That I go around sleeping with strange—with men I barely know. I haven't been myself lately. It's my divorce. It has me scared all the time."

"Scared of what?"

"Of being alone," she said, her eyes glistening in spite of her best efforts.

It was like working Adullam Line without the protection of a telephone. "You're too young to be worried about that."

"Not alone for the rest of my life, Owen. Alone for Christmas. Doesn't that bother you?"

"Some," I said.

"I don't mind it so much the rest of the year. But at Christmas, when family is such a big deal, when Norman Rockwell images of family are everywhere you look, it bothers me. I had a family like that once, but they're all gone. All I had left was Gary, my husband. Now—right before Christmas—I don't have him."

She was crying now but good. I led her back to the sofa. There, despite the collective angularity, Beth's and mine and the sofa's, I tried to comfort her.

"Let's make a pact to be together at Christmas," I said, addressing the top of Beth's head, her face being pressed into my shirt, wet mascara and all. "Here or at your place. Or we could drop in on the Ohlmans. Unannounced."

"Would serve them right," she said.

Fifteen

Beth didn't stay the night. Perhaps she didn't feel up to another apology. It was just as well, both from the point of view of my throbbing head and because I would have ended up leaving her alone in bed for the second time. Around two I awoke from an uneasy sleep with visions of our dinner dancing through my head. And I remembered something Beth had said, something that got me out of bed and pacing the hardwood.

It was the idea that she dreaded Christmas because she didn't have a family. At the time she'd said it, I could focus only on her tears and pain. But when her words came back to me in the still of the night, they made me think of Jackie, made me see the whole mystery from a new angle.

Beth hadn't been interested in Nativity scene symbolism, but I still was. Edward Hennix had left me with the idea that the crèches were symbols of Christmas and targets for that reason. I hadn't questioned his conclusion at the time, but now I did. I thought of the many other symbols of Christmas dotting the landscape, and I asked myself why, if there wasn't some religious issue at work, Jackie had picked on manger scenes. Why not plastic Santas or neon reindeer or aluminum trees?

Beth's fears gave me a possible answer. Nativity scenes could also be seen as symbols of the family. An intact, ideal family: father, mother, and baby. It was an image that could bring pain to a lonely soul like Beth Wolfe. And perhaps cause someone else, a boy who, like Beth, was without a family at a time of year when families are so important, to hit out at the world.

The more I paced, the more certain I was that someone had come close to telling me this earlier in the investigation. I searched backward and remembered Walt Majeski, permanent deacon at Holy Angels, and his guess that the target of the attacks was the Holy Family. He'd been right about that, but wrong when he'd predicted that the next victim, after Mary and Jesus, would be Joseph. It had been the Magi. Why had Joseph escaped?

And how had Hennix, a trained psychologist, missed all this? How had he failed to see that Christmas was only important as the general context of the attacks, as the time of year when a person, a child, without an intact family would most resent it? Had he in fact missed it or had he been intentionally misleading me? I remembered Hennix's own nervous pacing, back and forth in my hospital room, and decided that the misdirection had been intentional. He'd wanted to send me down the wrong path. That was why his offer to take over the case had been so offhand. It hadn't been what he'd been building to. It had been a postscript, something he'd thrown in after he'd achieved his real purpose: planting a false idea in my cracked head.

But why? Because his old friend Sister Agnes had gotten to him, asked him not to encourage me? Easy to believe, but then why tell me anything? Why even come to the hospital? Why not drop the tape of Jackie's apology in the mail or—better—in the trash and forget the whole thing?

A siren started wailing somewhere in the night. I went to the alcove and opened Beth's window. The sound came in as crisp and clear as the night air. And it grew louder with every cold breath I took. I remembered the moment during Jackie's call when I'd heard a siren in stereo, through the old rectory's window and through the phone. Jackie had been very close that night, and he was close now. The answer to his mystery was close. I could almost touch it.

The sound of the ambulance began to recede. I shut the window, anxious to avoid the suggestion that my answers were also slipping away, and sat down at the table. My list of clues was still there, right where I'd left it after amending it at Beth's insistence. My pen lay beside it. I picked it up and, by the glow of my landlady's security light, added a name to my list of clues. Edward Hennix.

Then I waited for the alchemy to occur, for the addition of Hennix's name to magically transform the scribbled list into something valuable. And it happened. My eye strayed upward from the psychologist's name to the churches Beth had had me add to the list. And I noticed that Hennix ended in the same unusual letter as St. Pius X.

I grabbed up the pen again and crossed out part of each church name, leaving the *H* and the *E* of Holy Angels, the two *N*s of St. John Leonardi, and the *I* and *X* of St. Pius X. Hennix.

A coincidence? Or did I owe Beth Wolfe a very nice dinner out? She'd suggested that the target churches were themselves the message. If I was right, it was a very private message, one that only Hennix himself could be expected to decipher. More of a taunt than a message. But why even that?

Suddenly I felt so chilled I looked up to be sure I'd closed the window. But it was doubt and not physical cold affecting me. Doubt, my old traveling companion, telling me that I was overreaching, overanalyzing. I was attributing my own baroque patterns of thought to Jackie. The churches no more spelled out Hennix's name than the secret name of God. I was imagining things.

I still held the pen. I used it to scribble out letters of the church names, this time leaving only the *O, N,* and *E* of Holy Angels, the *L* and *O* of Leonardi, and the *S* and *T* and the *P* and *I* of St. Pius. Together the letters spelled "One Lost PI."

I tossed the pen away and went back to crawl between my now cold sheets.

Sixteen

I went to bed alone, but I woke up with Edward Hennix. By that I mean my first thoughts upon waking were of Hennix. And though I'd quickly dismissed my predawn hunch that he was somehow at the bottom of this— had been able to sleep because I'd consciously dismissed that hunch—it came back to me in the first few moments of the new day with the force of a conviction.

If Hennix was the key to the mystery, the key to Hennix was Sister Agnes. By Hennix's own account, he and the nun "went way back." And way back was what I wanted. Honey might also have served as a source of serious gossip, but Honey was cocooned in bulletproof glass. Sister Agnes's protection consisted solely of her moral superiority. And I thought I'd detected a crack in that, one big enough for me to slip through.

At nine sharp I was at the Catholic Life Center, checking the parking spaces along its narrow street for the nun's Plymouth station wagon. It was there and in a prime spot, only half a block from the old rectory's front door. Better still, there was an open stretch of granite curbing nearby for my Volkswagen. I took that as a sign that the karma of the universe, or at least of Elizabeth, New Jersey, was turning my way.

I had reason to doubt that augury only a minute later when I was all but knocked down on the center's icy front walk by Sister Agnes herself. She was exiting the building with her usual head-down determination and only checked herself when I called out a desperate "Good morning."

"Owen! I can't talk now, which is a lucky thing for you. What were you doing in *my* office yesterday with *my* tape recorder? And what did you mean by going back over to Domestic Justice to bother Honey? I'd sack Rhoda for giving you directions to the place, but I'm going to be shorthanded as it is. Now that ..."

"Now that I've been sacked?" I asked.

The nun's sigh froze in the air between us. "You don't have the right temperament for this work, Owen. You have to be able to leave the problem alone once you've hung up the phone. Otherwise you're not there for the next caller. Mentally or—in your case—physically. Do you have any idea how many different souls have called while you've been running around looking for that one boy?"

"The phone's been covered," I said. "It's about more than me being gone."

"Yes. It's also about you being obsessed. It's about you running around, getting yourself hurt, trying to accomplish something that will mystically undo a past failure."

Hennix had been right. Amateur psychoanalysis was an occupational hazard for crisis-line workers.

"I'm sorry, Owen, for being so blunt, but there it is. Now good-bye. It's cold out here, and I'm late. I've some donated soup to deliver to one of our kitchens."

"Canned soup?" I asked.

The nun's eyebrows rose toward her knitted beret. "Yes."

"Then it will keep. I have some questions I'd like to ask you about Edward Hennix. We can go inside if you're cold."

I was hoping she would go back inside, afraid my tough-guy act would be undercut by another shivering spell. But she held her ground. "What makes you think I know anything about Edward Hennix and that golden goose company of his?"

"He told me himself that you did. And I'm not interested in his company. I want his personal history."

"His what?" She backed me up a step as Hennix had done in his office, her technique being an unexpected leap forward. "Do you think I'd discuss

Mr. Hennix's personal business with you or anyone else? Do you think I gossip about people?"

There it was. The moral superiority and the flaw, neatly tucked into a single sentence. "I know you do," I said. "You told Hennix that I'm a seminary dropout."

I'd no sooner made the accusation than I panicked, remembering another possible source for Hennix's information. I was positing some secret connection between Hennix and Jackie, and I'd told Jackie of my onetime plan to become a priest. Suppose he was the one who had told the psychologist. But the panic passed so quickly it never had time to show on my face. Sister Agnes herself saved me by breaking her laser eye contact and placing a mittened hand on her breast.

"He didn't know the first time I spoke with him," I said, "so Honey hadn't briefed him when she'd called to tell him I was coming. She didn't know me that well then, though she probably does now. But Hennix knew all about me when he came to the hospital yesterday. You'd told him everything."

"Come inside, Owen. Please."

I'd forgotten the cold for the first time since leaving my rooms, but I followed her, anxious not to give her time to recover. She retreated no farther than the old house's glassed front porch. It was barely above freezing in there, but it felt like a greenhouse.

"I did tell Edward, Owen. And I'm sorry. He was curious about you, about what might be motivating you. And I wanted a second opinion about whether I might have made a mistake by taking you on, given what I knew of your background. My only reservation when you first came to me was that you'd find call taking hard and leave. I was afraid, based on your history, that you were a quitter." She laughed mirthlessly. "A quitter you're not."

"What did Hennix say?"

"He called you an unacceptable risk. Not because you might run away but because you might still be driven by the needs and feelings that sent you to the seminary in the first place. If so, you'd have a hard time maintaining an emotional distance."

So the psychoanalysis the nun had hit me with earlier hadn't been amateur work after all.

"I apologize most sincerely for violating your confidence, Owen."

"Apology accepted. Now tell me about Hennix."

"Owen, Owen. Two wrongs can never make a right. I can't undo an injury to you by injuring Edward."

"I'm not worried about my injuries. I'm worried about the boy who's at the center of this. Edward Hennix has done something to him and I think you know what it is."

"If Edward confessed anything to me—"

"You're not obligated to keep his secrets," I said. "You're not a priest."

"Neither are you," she shot back. "You can't repeat some ancient words and wave your hand in the air and make everything right."

"We can't refer this problem, Sister. It's been referred to us. To me. Let me try to help. I promise not to use anyone's words but my own."

"And as many of those as it takes," the nun said with resignation. "You'll need to talk with a woman named Louise Cooper. She lives here in Elizabeth; I'm not sure where. But she shouldn't be hard to find."

Seventeen

Louise Cooper wasn't hard to find. In fact, I located her before I left the Catholic Life Center for the last time. After Sister Agnes hurried off to deliver her soup, I slipped into the ground-floor offices of an outreach ministry for divorced Catholics and borrowed their phone book. No Louise Cooper was listed, but there were no fewer than four L. Coopers. One of those lived on Russet Street.

I'd never even thought of looking up the name of Jackie's alien tormentor on the index of an Elizabeth street map. I did it now, using a map I'd purchased when I'd first moved to the area. I found the map under the passenger seat of the Ghia and Russet Street on its western edge, near the old industrial part of town, only a few blocks from where I was parked.

When I arrived on Russet Street itself I was greeted by another clue I'd made scant use of, a defunct smelter, Amax Plant Number Four, according to its weathered sign. Jackie had described it as black, but in the morning light the place was actually the color of rust. It was still menacing, though, razor wire gleaming atop its prison-camp fence.

In comparison, Russet Street was narrow and ordinary, its most interesting feature a stretch of the original cobblestones showing through a modern covering of asphalt. Opposite the smelter was a row of homes so alike in shape and size I deduced that they'd been a byproduct of the plant, company houses for lucky foremen. They'd probably been identical in every detail then, but, like their street, they'd been recovered, some in aluminum siding, some in a kind of shingle stamped to look like brick, some in stucco.

The one I was after, 15 Russet Street, had acquired a thin veneer of limestone on its narrow front. Its sides were still wooden but recently painted. The very brief front walk—a square of concrete only—was bordered by the remains of mums, blasted brown by the cold.

I rang the bell before I'd begun to plan my approach to Louise Cooper, counting, as I so often did, on the inspiration of the moment. In the event, it wasn't Cooper who answered the door. It was a kid with a choir-boy face and a mouth open wide for a high note. Jackie.

Our eyes met for a long moment through the glass of the storm door. Then he was gone, leaving the front door open behind him. Seconds later he was leaving the back door behind him, closed. The sound of that reached me before I'd had a chance to move. I didn't feel up to a foot race through the backyards and alleyways of Elizabeth, so I rang the bell again.

I heard someone call "Benjy" several times. Then she appeared beyond the glass, a petite woman with closely cropped hair and Jackie's oversize eyes. She was dressed in brown insulated coveralls, or rather dressing in the coveralls. She buttoned the last button as she examined me through the glass. My forehead didn't draw any special attention, but then it wasn't the spectacle it had been the day before.

"Yes?" she said.

"My name is Owen Keane," I said. And then, forgetting Hennix in the excitement of having found the boy, I added, "I'm a friend of your son's."

"A friend of Benjy's?" Copper repeated disbelievingly.

So Benjy, the name of Jackie's darling brother, had been another clue. "He and I have never met. Not formally. But we've spoken on the phone. He called a crisis line I worked for to ask for help."

"Help with what?" Cooper demanded, now both disbelieving and displeased.

I gambled then. "I think he wants help contacting his father."

That was the way it had all come together for me, the only way it made sense. It explained why, in each of the prank calls, the bad guy had been an abusive male and why the St. Joseph statues had escaped the vandalism. The father was the source of the evil, and everyone around him its victims. If Benjy really was directing these messages, these accusations, toward Hennix, it could only be because he believed Hennix to be the evil father. But the cryptic nature of the accusations suggested that their purpose wasn't to expose Hennix. They were more like very insistent tugs on the psychologist's sleeve.

Explaining all that to Cooper through a locked storm door would have been a tough job. Luckily, I didn't have to try. She snapped the catch back and said, "You'd better come in and tell me about it."

We sat in a cozy front room that was more or less a Benjy Cooper art gallery. All around me were examples of a child's artwork in dime-store frames, the early ones in crayon, the later ones in watercolor. Many of the pictures were pastoral landscapes very unlike Russet Street.

Cooper, following my gaze, said, "Those are old drawings. I can't display his newer ones. They're all of monsters trying to tear each other's arms off."

She gestured vaguely to her coveralls. "As you can see, I'm late for work. So if you could make this quick."

I put aside the questions about her job with which I normally would have stalled, and retold the story I'd so recently told Beth Wolfe, cutting it down by minimizing my investigation and completely eliminating my stay in the hospital. I also omitted names, especially Hennix's, not wanting to lose my welcome prematurely. In the back of my mind, I was wondering how I'd convince Cooper that any part of my fantastic tale was true. But that was another challenge she took off my shoulders.

"Oh Benjamin," she said, addressing the nearest painting, which showed a pond complete with swans. And then to me, "You must think I'm one hell of a mother."

I thought it was interesting—and suggestive—that that would be her first reaction. "Your son's a complicated kid."

"Tell me about it. I never knew how complicated until this last year or so. I thought what we had here, what Benjy and I had, simple as it was, was also somehow complete. Sufficient. As sufficient for Benjy as it was for me. It isn't anymore. Maybe it never really was."

"He misses his father," I said, as something between a statement and a question.

"He misses his father," Cooper repeated wearily. "Tell me how that could happen, how Benjy could miss something he never really had, something half the kids in his school don't have, something even the television shows don't push these days. Tell me how he could miss a man he's never met, whose name he doesn't know."

"Your son doesn't know his father's name?"

"No. I've never told him. I've guarded that secret like I've guarded him. I thought I was guarding him by not telling him. I was protecting him from a man who didn't want him, from having to know that his own father didn't want him. But lately, when Benjy's been asking and asking about his father, I've wondered whether I haven't kept the secret all these years to protect myself."

"Protect you from the idea that Benjy's father didn't want to be with you?"

Another wrong guess. Beth Wolfe could have quietly kicked me for it if she'd been handy. Cooper only shook her head.

"No. When I decided to keep Benjamin, I rebuilt my life around the idea that I could raise him alone. That's what I've been protecting by denying him even his father's name: the idea I built my life on. My personal faith. Do you know how hard it's been for me to give that up?"

I thought I did, but revealing that would have gotten us too close to my own secrets. "Ms. Cooper, I think Benjamin knows who his father is."

"What makes you say that?"

"He told me his father's name, in a very roundabout way."

Cooper wasn't going to be tricked out of the secret she'd protected so long. She waited for me to say the name.

I took a deep breath. "Edward Hennix."

I knew that, for once, I'd guessed right. Cooper slumped within her quilted outerwear. "His wildness, his slyness, his sneaking out at all hours. I've watched it all coming on these last few months and never guessed that Eddie was behind it. Never guessed he'd try to force his way into Benjy's life."

"Wait a minute," I said. "I don't think Hennix contacted Benjy. I think all this has been Benjy's way of getting Hennix's attention."

"Then who—" She thought of a name before she'd finished the question, but didn't share it with me. She sat up abruptly. "I want to pay for any damage Benjamin's done, but it may take a while. If you could give me some kind of figure."

"We're not interested in any money," I said on the archdiocese's behalf.

"We're interested in Benjamin's welfare. Would you let his father come here and meet him?"

"I'm not the problem there, Mr. Keane. I've had my idea that I could go this alone seriously knocked around these last few months. If you're right that Eddie didn't contact his son, that Eddie hasn't changed his mind about wanting a son, then he's your problem. You'll never get him to even acknowledge Benjy, never mind come here."

I could only repeat the request I'd made of Sister Agnes. "Let me try."

Eighteen

I didn't attempt to contact Hennix right away. Cooper told me as I left her that she'd be gone until six and ordered me not to approach Benjy in her absence, with or without Hennix. So I passed the day at the Acme, slipping away just before five to return home and call the psychologist.

Locating him at five on a Saturday would have seemed like a hopeless task to me only a day earlier. Now I was so unconcerned I discarded my initial idea of making up some clever message based on Nativity scene imagery that only Hennix would understand. When I got through to Hand to Hand and was told that the boss wasn't in, I simply said, "I have an important message regarding Mr. Hennix's son. Please have him call Owen Keane as soon as possible." Then I read off my home number.

Three Christmas cards had come in the mail that day. I decided to pass the time by opening them. While I was ripping the second envelope, the phone rang.

I got the better part of hello out before Hennix demanded, "What do you want, Keane?"

"Thirty minutes of your time."

"You've got from now until I get mad enough to hang up this phone."

"Not over the phone. I want face to face. Then if you get mad enough, you can hit me."

"I'm that mad right now," he said. He gave me an address and broke the connection.

He hadn't given me directions, and it was well past full dark when I found his place, a gentrified warehouse right on Newark Bay, just north of the Port Newark Terminal. Hennix's apartment was a large, largely open space overlooking the moving lights of the river traffic. It had old hardwood floors that creaked eloquently as he marched away from me and the open front door.

I shut the door behind me and followed him, not getting much noise at all from the floor. A series of iron posts supported a ceiling that was almost beyond the range of the muted lighting. When I drew abreast of the third post, Hennix said, "Help yourself to some Christmas cheer."

By then he was standing at the wall of riverfront windows, his back to me, a trim figure in dark slacks and a white dress shirt with rolled up sleeves. He gestured with his own glass to a little bar that stood against one of the iron poles, looking like a kiosk in a bus terminal. I crossed to it and poured some scotch into a glass. It was better scotch than Harry Ohlman had served me, and I made a mental note to mention that if I survived to recount the evening to Harry and Mary.

Hennix didn't seem very threatening at the moment. Still, from the several little groupings of furniture scattered around the vast room, I selected a pair of leather easy chairs well away from the windows.

He must have been following my progress in those windows' dark glass. When I was settled in nicely, he said without turning, "The clock's running, Keane. What do you want from me?"

Small mysteries first, I thought. "How did Benjy find out about you?"

"I'm only guessing, but I think it was Louie's—Louise's—mother. She called me a few months back. Gave me a talking-to she'd been holding in for years. Mrs. Cooper must be a big woman. She can hold a lot. Most of it was variations on the same tune: I was doing great and her daughter was struggling to raise my son all by herself. Ruining her life doing it, too, giving up on school, doing road construction in all kinds of weather, breathing in filthy fumes from smudge pots. Tell me something, Keane. When's the last time you saw a smudge pot at a construction site in New Jersey? EPA would have a fit. Woman's still living in the fifties."

"You think she told Benjy about you?"

"Yes. And at about the same time she called me. The old lady's mouth dam must have burst. Just after I got rid of her, we started to get calls down at the center from the kid. At first it was just, 'Tell Mr. Hennix his son called.' Then he started adding little teasers. 'Tell Mr. Hennix his son's been hit by a car. Tell Mr. Hennix his son's mother's had a heart attack.' Little love notes."

"Did you answer any of them?"

Hennix finally turned to face me. "No."

We sipped our drinks. I said, "What did you say to get rid of Mrs. Cooper?"

"I told her I didn't love her daughter and her daughter didn't love me. She was just an underclassmen I happened to know when I was in graduate school. We had a few drinks one night and then we had sex. Blame it on disco.

"When Louie told me she was pregnant, I said, 'None for me, thank you very much.' Actually, I don't think I said that much. I just made myself scarce. I never thought she'd keep the kid. I sure didn't know she had. But it was her decision, not mine. The man doesn't get to decide these days."

"Lucky thing for Benjy," I said.

Hennix bristled like a kicked cat, and I wondered whether his desertion of Cooper and their child had been part of what had turned him from idealistic humanitarian to successful businessman. Then I suppressed my curiosity and concentrated on the task at hand.

"So Benjy was calling your crisis line. When the call came in about the Mafia hit, you knew who it was."

"Not right away. Not when Honey called to ask if we'd gotten anything really offbeat. The fact that she and Sister A had both gotten calls first fooled me for a little bit. Benjy'd never called anyone else, so far as I knew. I'm still not sure why those first two calls didn't come to me. I'm not sure how the kid knew I'd hear about them."

I reminded him of his description of the interconnectedness of the crisis lines, adding my own guess that someone on the outside looking in would be likely to see them just that way.

"Are things so tight for Louie that her son's a specialist on help lines?" Hennix asked.

"She's getting by. Financially. Emotionally, she's pretty beaten up. When did you realize the Mafia call was Benjy's work?"

"Between the time I talked with Honey and the time you showed up. I had this bad feeling. So I pulled the tape of the call and recognized the kid's voice from listening to his earlier efforts."

"But you still gave me the gist of the message."

"To get rid of you. Look, I've already apologized for that. I didn't think you'd be able to figure out where he was going to strike next."

"I remember your apology. It was a cover for more of that stuff about Benjy being a child of the projects. Somebody I'd never be able to track down."

"So I tried to scare you off. Why shouldn't I try to protect the kid?"

I badly wanted a swallow of scotch just then, but I didn't dare look away from Hennix's eyes. He drank. And he looked away.

"Okay. So I was protecting myself. So what? So I didn't want to have this little scene we're having now. Who would?"

He pounded over to the kiosk bar and picked up a bottle. He didn't pour another drink, however.

He doesn't want to go over there drunk, I thought, allowing myself to believe, for the first time, that he might actually go. Not that his next words were encouraging.

"You still haven't told me, Keane. Just what do you expect from me? How do you see this all playing out? Do you think it's going to be like some old Christmas movie? Do you think I'm going to walk into their lives and we're going to magically be a family? That some relationship's going to suddenly spring up between me and that kid?"

"The relationship's already there," I said, getting to my feet. "It's always been there. Denying it is screwing up that kid. Your kid. I expect you to do whatever it takes to make that right. You were going to fix the world, once upon a time. Start with him."

It was the moment to deck me, if he was still in the mood. He might even have been thinking about it, but instead he began to roll down his sleeves.

"Come over there with me," he said.

Nineteen

Amax Plant Number Four's resemblance to a prison camp had increased markedly with the coming of night, thanks to an impressive array of security lights. They kept Russet Street in perpetual dusk and all but drown out its houses' meager Christmas decorations.

Louise Cooper's house had a single string of white lights framing the front door, a detail I hadn't noticed in daylight. I might not have noticed it now, in the glare of the plant, if Hennix hadn't kept us standing so long in the cobblestoned street, studying the place.

He was still mad at me. "Hope that little elf heart of yours isn't hoping for some Christmas miracle to happen."

"Hasn't for years," I said.

"Not a bad little place," he said, but that was as far as the architectural review got.

The front door opened. Silhouetted in the frame of lights were Cooper and Benjy, the woman much smaller than she'd appeared in her work clothes, the boy positioned behind her slightly. I wondered if he was frightened now that his big moment had arrived. I was. So was Hennix.

"Damn," he said softly and walked inside.

No one invited me in. I stayed in the street until the front door shut and a little while afterwards. The door opened again just as I was starting for my car. Benjy came out, bent over sideways by a burden he carried in his right hand.

"Wait!" he called to me.

The load weighing him down so was a little pink figure with upraised hands, one of which Benjy was using as a handle. It was the Christ Child statue he'd taken from St. John Leonardi. So it hadn't been thrown in a trash can or the bay after all.

He used both hands to raise the statue up for me to take. Then we stood smiling at one another for a moment. I wanted to ask him if he'd really been trying to spell out Hennix with his church names, but I didn't. He might have said no, and then I would have spent long nights wondering who else might have been doing the spelling.

There was no time to ask questions in any case. Before I'd settled the surprising weight of the statue in my arms, Benjy was running back to the house.

I drove straight to St. John Leonardi, intending to hand over the figure to Father Ross. I found the old church lit up like the smelter. Singing was coming out to me faintly, through the heavy doors and the multicolored windows. A late Advent service or maybe a choir practice. The song was "O Come, O Come, Emanuel," appropriately enough.

I paused to listen near the church steps. The parish's little Nativity scene still huddled in its protected spot next to those steps, Mary, Joseph, and the angel, all staring down at an empty manger.

It occurred to me then that the best way to find a Christmas miracle was to go out and make your own, as Benjy had done. So I changed my mind about ringing the rectory bell. Instead, I tucked the Infant back into His bed of straw for the departing parishioners to find. Then I went home to call Beth Wolfe.

A Terence Faherty Checklist

Novels and Short Story collection

A. The Owen Keane Series

Deadstick. St. Martin's Press, 1991.
Live to Regret. St. Martin's Press,1992.
The Lost Keats. St. Martin's Press,1993.
Die Dreaming. St. Martin's Press, 1994.
Prove the Nameless, St. Martin's Press, 1996.
The Ordained. St. Martin's Press, 1997.
Orion Rising. St. Martin's Press, 1999.
The Confessions of Owen Keane. Crippen & Landru, 2005.

B. The Scott Elliott Series

Kill Me Again. Simon & Schuster, 1996.
Come Back Dead. Simon & Schuster, 1997.
Raise the Devil. St. Martin's Press, 2000.

Novellas and Short Stories

"As My Wimsey Takes Me," *First Culprit*, Chatto & Windus, 1992.
"Rise Up," *Ellery Queen's Mystery Magazine*, August 1998.
"The Triple Score," *Ellery Queen's Mystery Magazine*, January 1999; collected in *The Confessions of Owen Keane*, 2005.
"The Third Manny," *Ellery Queen's Mystery Magazine*, February 2000; collected in *The Confessions of Owen Keane*, 2005.

"Nobody's Ring," *The Shamus Game*, Signet, 2000.

"The Authentic Rose," *Ellery Queen's Mystery Magazine*, October 2000.

"God's Instrument," *Unholy Orders*, Intrigue, 2000.

"The Headless Magi," *Murder, Mayhem and Mistletoe*, Worldwide, 2001
    collected in *The Confessions of Owen Keane*, 2005.

"Main Line Lazarus," *Ellery Queen's Mystery Magazine*, February 2002;
    collected in *The Confessions of Owen Keane*, 2005.

"The Second Coming," *Ellery Queen's Mystery Magazine*, November 2002.

"The Widow of Slane," *Ellery Queen's Mystery Magazine*, March 2004.

"A Sunday in Ordinary Time," *Ellery Queen's Mystery Magazine*, August 2004;
    collected in *The Confessions of Owen Keane*, 2005.

"The First Proof," *Desperate Journeys*, Worldwide, 2005.

"Where Is He Now?" *Ellery Queen's Mystery Magazine*, February 2005.

"St. Jimmy," *The Confessions of Owen Keane*, Crippen & Landru, 2005.

"On Pilgrimage," *The Confessions of Owen Keane*, Crippen & Landru, 2005.

"Good Night, Dr. Kobel," included with the limited edition of *The Confessions of Owen Keane*, Crippen & Landru, 2005.

The Confessions of Owen Keane

The Confessions of Owen Keane by Terence Faherty is set in 12-point Garamond on 14-point leading (for the text). It is printed on sixty-pound Natures Natural acid-free paper. The cover painting is by Carol Heyer and the design by Deborah Miller. The first edition was printed in two forms: trade softcover, notchbound; and two hundred copies sewn in cloth, signed and numbered by the author. Each of the clothbound copies includes a separate pamphlet, *Goodnight, Dr. Kobel.*

The Confessions of Owen Keane was printed and bound by Thomson-Shore, Inc., Dexter, Michigan and published in April 2005 by Crippen & Landru, Inc., Norfolk, Virginia.

CRIPPEN & LANDRU, PUBLISHERS
P. O. Box 9315
Norfolk, VA 23505
E-mail: info@crippenlandru.com; toll-free 877 622-6656
Web: www.crippenlandru.com

Crippen & Landru publishes first edition short-story collections by important detective and mystery writers. The following books are currently (January 2005) in print in our regular series; see our website for full details:

The McCone Files by Marcia Muller. 1995. Trade softcover, $19.00.

Diagnosis: Impossible: The Problems of Dr. Sam Hawthorne by Edward D. Hoch. 1996. Trade softcover, $19.00

Who Killed Father Christmas? by Patricia Moyes. 1996. Signed, unnumbered cloth overrun copies, $30.00. Trade softcover, $16.00.

My Mother, The Detective: The Complete "Mom" Short Stories by James Yaffe. 1997. Trade softcover, $15.00.

In Kensington Gardens Once . . . by H.R.F. Keating. 1997. Trade softcover, $12.00.

Shoveling Smoke: Selected Mystery Stories by Margaret Maron. 1997. Trade softcover, $19.00.

The Ripper of Storyville and Other Ben Snow Tales by Edward D. Hoch. 1997. Trade softcover. $17.00.

Renowned Be Thy Grave by P.M. Carlson. 1998. Trade softcover, $16.00.

Carpenter and Quincannon: Professional Detective Services by Bill Pronzini. 1998. Trade softcover, $16.00.

Not Safe After Dark and Other Stories by Peter Robinson. 1998. Trade softcover, $17.00.

Famous Blue Raincoat by Ed Gorman. 1999. Signed, unnumbered cloth overrun copies, $30.00. Trade softcover, $17.00.

The Tragedy of Errors and Others by Ellery Queen. 1999. Trade softcover, $19.00.

McCone and Friends by Marcia Muller. 2000. Trade softcover, $16.00.

Challenge the Widow Maker by Clark Howard. 2000. Trade softcover, $16.00.

The Velvet Touch: Nick Velvet Stories by Edward D. Hoch. 2000. Trade softcover, $16.00.

Fortune's World by Michael Collins. 2000. Trade softcover, $16.00.

Long Live the Dead: Tales from Black Mask by Hugh B. Cave. 2000. Trade softcover, $16.00.

Tales Out of School by Carolyn Wheat. 2000. Trade softcover, $16.00.

Stakeout on Page Street and Other DKA Files by Joe Gores. 2000. Trade softcover, $16.00.

The Celestial Buffet by Susan Dunlap. 2001. Trade softcover, $16.00.

Kisses of Death: A Nathan Heller Casebook by Max Allan Collins. 2001. Trade softcover, $17.00.

The Old Spies Club and Other Intrigues of Rand by Edward D. Hoch. 2001. Signed, unnumbered cloth overrun copies, $32.00. Trade softcover, $17.00.

Adam and Eve on a Raft by Ron Goulart. 2001. Signed, unnumbered cloth overrun copies, $32.00. Trade softcover, $17.00.

The Sedgemoor Strangler by Peter Lovesey. 2001. Trade softcover, $17.00.

The Reluctant Detective by Michael Z. Lewin. 2001. Signed, numbered clothbound, $42.00. Trade softcover, $17.00.

Nine Sons by Wendy Hornsby. 2002. Trade softcover, $16.00.

The Curious Conspiracy and Other Crimes by Michael Gilbert. 2002. Signed, numbered clothbound, $42.00. Trade softcover, $17.00.

The 13 Culprits by Georges Simenon, translated by Peter Schulman. 2002. Trade softcover, $16.00.

The Dark Snow by Brendan DuBois. 2002. Signed, unnumbered cloth overrun copies, $32.00. Trade softcover, $17.00.

Jo Gar's Casebook by Raoul Whitfield, edited by Keith Alan Deutsch [Published with Black Mask Press]. 2002. Trade softcover, $20.00.

Come Into My Parlor: Tales from Detective Fiction Weekly by Hugh B. Cave. 2002. Signed, unnumbered cloth overrun copies, $32.00. Trade softcover, $17.00.

The Iron Angel and Other Tales of the Gypsy Sleuth by Edward D. Hoch. 2003. Signed, numbered clothbound, $42.00. Trade softcover, $17.00.

Cuddy – Plus One by Jeremiah Healy. 2003. Trade softcover, $18.00.

Problems Solved by Bill Pronzini and Barry N. Malzberg. 2003. Signed, numbered clothbound, $42.00. Trade softcover, $16.00.

A Killing Climate by Eric Wright. 2003. Signed, numbered clothbound, $42.00. Trade softcover, $17.00.

Lucky Dip by Liza Cody. 2003. Signed, numbered clothbound, $42.00. Trade softcover, $17.00.

Kill the Umpire: The Calls of Ed Gorgon by Jon L. Breen. 2003. Signed, numbered clothbound, $42.00. Trade softcover, $17.00.

Suitable for Hanging by Margaret Maron. 2004. Signed, unnumbered cloth overrun copies, $32.00 Trade softcover, $17.00.

Murders and Other Confusions: The Chronicles of Susanna, Lady Appleton, Sixteenth-Century Gentlewoman, Herbalist, and Sleuth by Kathy Lynn Emerson. 2004. Signed, numbered clothbound, $42.00. Trade softcover, $17.00.

Byline: Mickey Spillane by Mickey Spillane, edited by Max Allan Collins and Lynn F. Myers, Jr. 2004. Signed, numbered clothbound, $48.00. Trade softcover, $20.00.

The Confessions of Owen Keane by Terence Faherty. 2005. Signed, numbered clothbound, $42.00. Trade softcover, $17.00.

FORTHCOMING TITLES IN THE REGULAR SERIES

The Adventure of the Murdered Moths and Other Radio Mysteries by Ellery Queen

Murder – Ancient and Modern by Edward Marston

Murder! 'Orrible Murder! by Amy Myers

More Things Impossible: The Second Casebook of Dr. Sam Hawthorne by Edward D. Hoch

14 Slayers by Paul Cain, edited by Max Allan Collins and Lynn F. Myers, Jr. Published with Black Mask Press

Tough As Nails by Frederick Nebel, edited by Rob Preston. Published with Black Mask Press

The Mankiller of Poojeegai and Other Mysteries by Walter Satterthwait

A Pocketful of Noses: Stories of One Ganelon or Another by James Powell

You'll Die Laughing by Norbert Davis, edited by Bill Pronzini. Published with Black Mask Press

Hoch's Ladies by Edward D. Hoch

Quintet: The Cases of Chase and Delacroix, by Richard A.Lupoff

The Name Is Archer Omnibus by Ross Macdonald, edited by Tom Nolan

A Little Intelligence by Robert Silverberg and Randall Garrett (writing as "Robert Randall")

CRIPPEN & LANDRU LOST CLASSICS

Crippen & Landru is proud to publish a series of *new* short-story collections by great authors who specialized in traditional mysteries. Each book collects stories from crumbling pages of old pulp, digest, and slick magazines, and most of the stories have been "lost" since their first publication. The following books are in print:

The Newtonian Egg and Other Cases of Rolf le Roux by Peter Godfrey, introduction by Ronald Godfrey. 2002. Trade softcover, $15.00

Murder, Mystery and Malone by Craig Rice,, edited by Jeffrey A. Marks. 2002. Trade softcover, $17.00.

The Sleuth of Baghdad: The Inspector Chafik Stories, by Charles B. Child. 2002. Cloth, $27.00. Trade softcover, $17.00.

Hildegarde Withers: Uncollected Riddles by Stuart Palmer, introduction by Mrs. Stuart Palmer. 2002. Cloth, $29.00. Trade softcover, $19.00.

The Spotted Cat and Other Mysteries from the Casebook of Inspector Cockrill by Christianna Brand, edited by Tony Medawar. 2002. Cloth, $29.00. Trade softcover, $19.00.

Marksman and Other Stories by William Campbell Gault, edited by Bill Pronzini; afterword by Shelley Gault. 2003. Trade softcover, $19.00.

Karmesin: The World's Greatest Criminal — Or Most Outrageous Liar by Gerald Kersh, edited by Paul Duncan. 2003. Cloth, $27.00. Trade softcover, $17.00.

The Complete Curious Mr. Tarrant by C. Daly King, introduction by Edward D. Hoch. 2003. Cloth, $29.00. Trade softcover, $19.00.

The Pleasant Assassin and Other Cases of Dr. Basil Willing by Helen McCloy, introduction by B.A. Pike. 2003. Cloth, $27.00. Trade softcover, $17.00.

Murder — All Kinds by William L. DeAndrea, introduction by Jane Haddam. 2003. Cloth, $29.00. Trade softcover, $19.00.

The Avenging Chance and Other Mysteries from Roger Sheringham's Casebook by Anthony Berkeley, edited by Tony Medawar and Arthur Robinson. 2004. Cloth, $29.00. Trade softcover, $19.00.

Banner Deadlines: The Impossible Files of Senator Brooks U. Banner by Joseph Commings, edited by Robert Adey; memoir by Edward D. Hoch. 2004. Cloth, $29.00. Trade softcover, $19.00.

The Danger Zone and Other Stories by Erle Stanley Gardner, edited by Bill Pronzini. 2004. Cloth, $29.00. Trade softcover, $19.00.

Dr. Poggioli: Criminologist by T.S. Stribling, edited by Arthur Vidro. 2004. Cloth, $29.00. Trade softcover, $19.00.

The Couple Next Door: Collected Short Mysteries by Margaret Millar, edited by Tom Nolan. 2004. Cloth, $29.00. Trade softcover, $19.00.

Sleuth's Alchemy: Cases of Mrs. Bradley and Others by Gladys Mitchell, edited by Nicholas Fuller. 2005. Cloth, $29.00. Trade softcover, $19.00.

FORTHCOMING LOST CLASSICS

Who Was Guilty? Two Dime Novels by Philip S. Warne/Howard W. Macy, edited by Marlena E. Bremseth

Slot-Machine Kelly by Michael Collins, introduction by Robert J. Randisi

The Evidence of the Sword by Rafael Sabatini, edited by Jesse Knight

Francis Quarles: Detective by Julian Symons, edited by John Cooper; afterword by Kathleen Symons

The Grandfather Rastin Mysteries by Lloyd Biggle, Jr., introduction by Kenneth Biggle

Masquerade: Nine Crime Stories by Max Brand, edited by William F. Nolan, Jr.

The Battles of Jericho by Hugh Pentecost, introduction by S.T. Karnick

The Casebook of Sidney Zoom Erle Stanley Gardner, edited by Bill Pronzini

Dead Yesterday and Other Mysteries by Mignon G. Eberhart, edited by Rick Cypert and Kirby McCauley

The Minerva Club, The Department of Patterns and Other Stories by Victor Canning, edited by John Higgins

The Casebook of Jonas P. Jonas and Others by Elizabeth Ferrars, edited by John Cooper

The Casebook of Gregory Hood by Anthony Boucher and Denis Green, edited by Joe R. Christopher

SUBSCRIPTIONS

Crippen & Landru offers discounts to individuals and institutions who place Subscriptions for its forthcoming publications, either the Regular Series or the Lost Classics or (preferably) both. Collectors can thereby guarantee receiving limited editions, and readers won't miss any favorite stories. Standing Order Subscribers receive a specially commissioned story in a deluxe edition as a gift at the end of the year. Please write or e-mail for more details.